# THE TENANTS

M. A. HUNTER

First published in Great Britain in 2025 by Boldwood Books Ltd.

Copyright © M. A. Hunter, 2025

Cover Design by Lisa Horton

Cover Images: Shutterstock and [Magdalena Russock] / Trevillion Images

The moral right of M. A. Hunter to be identified as the author of this work has been asserted in accordance with the Copyright, Designs and Patents Act 1988.

All rights reserved. No part of this book may be reproduced in any form or by any electronic or mechanical means, including information storage and retrieval systems, without written permission from the author, except for the use of brief quotations in a book review. This book is a work of fiction and, except in the case of historical fact, any resemblance to actual persons, living or dead, is purely coincidental.

Every effort has been made to obtain the necessary permissions with reference to copyright material, both illustrative and quoted. We apologise for any omissions in this respect and will be pleased to make the appropriate acknowledgements in any future edition.

A CIP catalogue record for this book is available from the British Library.

Paperback ISBN 978-1-83561-742-7

Large Print ISBN 978-1-83561-741-0

Hardback ISBN 978-1-83561-740-3

Ebook ISBN 978-1-83561-743-4

Kindle ISBN 978-1-83561-744-1

Audio CD ISBN 978-1-83561-735-9

MP3 CD ISBN 978-1-83561-736-6

Digital audio download ISBN 978-1-83561-737-3

This book is printed on certified sustainable paper. Boldwood Books is dedicated to putting sustainability at the heart of our business. For more information please visit https://www.boldwoodbooks.com/about-us/sustainability/

Boldwood Books Ltd, 23 Bowerdean Street, London, SW6 3TN

www.boldwoodbooks.com

*For Hannah, Emily, and Ethan.*

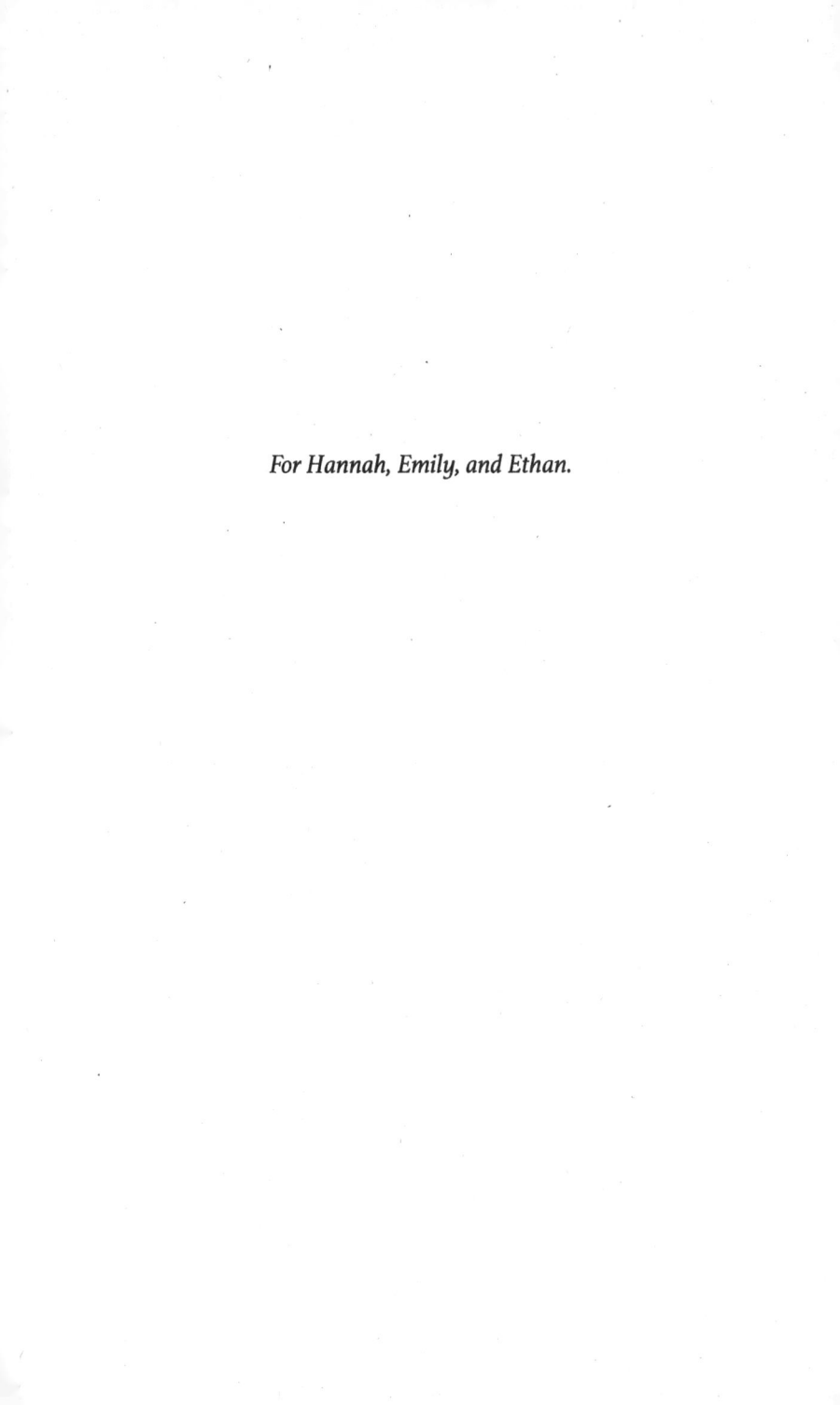

# 1

## SUNDAY, 10.37 P.M.

My calf muscles are starting to cramp and I can't remain sitting here for much longer without standing and stretching. But I'm not going anywhere until I know Jenny is safe. I can hear her singing along to the radio in the kitchen, and I catch myself smiling at her dulcet tones. I'm not sure she's even aware of the fact that she's singing some of the wrong words to the song, but I'm the last person who should correct her. My rare singalongs are reserved for the shower, and even then only when it's a classic song I just can't resist duetting on.

Chad is due home any minute, and once he's back, I'll take my leave and not encroach on their evening any further. I saw him heading out for his regular nightly run earlier, clad in bicycle shorts and headband. The neon skin-tight shirt he was wearing made my eyes water, but as hideous as it looked, at least he should avoid being knocked down by a tired motorist. The roads that connect like a mound of spaghetti on a fork are generally safe – there have been no fatal motor accidents in all the time I've lived here – but with the summer sun long since set, it's better to be safe than sorry.

Chad jokingly suggested I could tag along with him; at least I assume he was joking, given everything. I politely declined as I always do. I'm a firm believer that people should only run when they're being chased, and I'd far rather work out my frustrations on the exercise bike in my flat upstairs. I can cycle for as long or as little as I want without having to worry about reserving enough energy to make it home in one piece. Pete donated it to me during the first lockdown and it really did prove a lifesaver. I dread to think how out of shape I might be now without it. At least my overprotective and judgemental brother was good for one thing.

I've already missed two calls from him, and when I say missed, it would be more truthful to say ignored. I know why he's phoning and I'm just not ready to have that conversation with him. Deep down, I know he's only saying these things because he's worried, but nobody asked him to adopt a paternal role after Dad died. I've told him countless times that I'm okay and that he shouldn't worry. He just needs to let me get on with things. And maybe if he focused more on his own life, his wife wouldn't have left him.

I silently chastise myself. I know that isn't fair; he isn't the main reason she left. And frankly, it was probably only a matter of time before she upgraded. He was always punching above his weight with someone like that.

Maybe that's my way to switch his focus from me; I could suggest he start dating again. At forty, he's still young enough to meet someone new and settle down, if that's what he wants. Personally, I prefer being on my own. Whenever people ask why I live alone I am quick to tell them that it is my choice to be single. I don't want someone else to be dependent on me. Besides, I have enough on my plate tending to my tenants like Jenny here.

## The Tenants 3

She hasn't attended the last two monthly residents' meetings, and I want to understand the underlying cause of that. The meetings aren't mandatory, but they're supposed to be fun and educational so that we're all on the same page. In my experience, there is nothing worse than frustrations building between neighbours. These people are my family, and the meetings are an opportunity for everyone to air any grievances in a safe space so we can continue in harmony. And I can understand how work or other social commitments could clash with the monthly meeting, but that is why I don't always stick to the same day and time each month.

In an ideal world, each of my eight tenants would be in attendance, though there always seems to be at least two participants absent. That's why I started producing the summary newsletter, covering the key points of agreement for anyone who had missed the meeting. I know it's a bit anally retentive, but I've witnessed what can happen when these frustrations are allowed to build over time. Chad promised he would keep Jenny updated, but she's made no effort to come and explain why she missed last week's meeting or to offer an apology. And that is why I've stopped by this evening.

The sound of the door slamming tells me Chad is home. I hear him enter the kitchen and Jenny immediately warns him to keep away from her until he's had a shower. There's a joviality to his response, and my shoulders relax a fraction. The kettle reaches its crescendo a moment later and I hear the cupboard door being opened and closed and then the clink of two mugs being placed on the counter.

Everything is fine, I tell myself. Jenny's absence probably has absolutely nothing to do with their relationship being in trouble, which was my initial assumption. Chad and Jenny are both fine, and there's probably some other reason she couldn't make last week's meeting. Pete is always warning me that I overthink these things, but without proper communication it is so easy to jump to the wrong conclusions. I'll make sure Jenny knows her presence was missed, and hopefully that should be enough to ensure she is at the next meeting.

I really want as many tenants as possible at the meeting because we need to agree our approach for Halloween. Although it's still two months away, the last thing I want is a repeat of last year's egg throwing by disgruntled trick or treaters. James's idea just to switch off all the lights and pretend nobody was home failed miserably, and I had to hire a professional window-cleaning company to sort the damage. The last thing I want is for doorbells to be ringing all night, but maybe if we put out a bucket of sweets and a sign encouraging trick or treaters to take one item each then we'll avoid armag-egg-don as Bill called it.

I quietly chuckle at the memory. James claimed it was Bill keeping a sidelight on in his flat that alerted our visitors to the fact that there were people home, but he has no proof it was Bill's fault. And as my oldest resident, Bill has a special place in my heart, and I won't hear anyone badmouthing him.

'For fuck's sake!'

I start at Jenny's sudden outburst.

'Chad!'

My brow furrows at the sudden aggression in her tone. I can only assume that Chad must have left the kitchen to go and shower as instructed, though I haven't heard the water running yet.

'What have I done now?' he asks, his tone playful, presumably in an effort to undercut the tension.

'There's no fucking milk! What was the last thing I said to you before you went out this morning?'

'Oh, shit, I'm sorry, I totally forgot.'

'Well, that's just great, isn't it? One thing I asked you to do for me, but no, you were too busy going to watch the football with your fucking mates.'

'I said I'm sorry,' he says, all playfulness evaporated. 'I'll go and get some now. Jeez, just relax.'

'Um, no, you won't, because nowhere will be open this late on a Sunday,' she parries back, her anger obvious to anyone listening.

'What about the petrol station out on the main road?' he fires back with more than a hint of desperation. 'I'll run over there.'

'It's closed for refurbishment.' I hear her sigh. 'Just forget about it. I won't have this much-needed cup of tea, and in the morning I'll have to forego my smoothie, won't I?'

'Listen, I'm sorry, I forgot. It must have slipped my mind—'

'And how many times have I heard that recently?' she interrupts. 'It's like if it doesn't involve your job or football then it doesn't matter to you.'

'Hey, that's not fair,' he says, his voice an octave higher; defensive.

'Isn't it? There was a time when I was your number one priority, but ever since you returned to the office, I'm little more than an afterthought.'

Her voice is shrill, but there's hurt in it as well. I can't see her from where I'm sitting, but I imagine there are tears in her eyes as she's speaking.

There's a pause before Chad speaks again.

'Listen, I'm sorry I forgot the milk. You're right that I should have set myself some kind of reminder. I'm sorry that you can't have your tea now, but maybe I can go and ask one of our neighbours if we can borrow—'

'It's after ten, and most of the other tenants in this hellhole are probably already in bed.'

My eyes widen at the dig. Is that what she really thinks of our home? Maybe there is more to her absence from the meetings than I previously thought.

'I will go out first thing and find some milk,' Chad says now, his tone dismissive, 'so at least you can have your smoothie. Okay?'

'Just go and have your fucking shower,' she says, defeated.

I know enough to understand this little outburst is about more than milk. Part of me wants to go and hug Jenny and tell her everything will be okay, but I'm still wounded from her dig about the block of flats. I go out of my way to make sure everyone is as settled as they can be, and if it wasn't for the plasterboard between us now, I'd be tempted to give her a real piece of my mind.

Instead, I stand from the small stool where I've been perched for too long, and stretch the cramp from my legs, before shuffling along the narrow space, careful to step over the creaky floorboard, and ducking beneath the cobweb that hangs between the large hot water pipes and the wooden frame keeping the plasterboard in place. I really should bring a duster and vacuum cleaner down to the passageway and give it a proper clean, but there never seems to be a moment when everyone is out at the same time, and I dare not let them know I'm back here.

I follow the beam of my torch to the end of the passageway, before placing my foot on the first rung of the ladder and make my way up the thirty steps until I crawl back in through the trapdoor beside the water tank in my airing cupboard.

I hate it when my residents argue over such small and simple things to fix. That Jenny has noticed Chad's lack of care tells me so much about the instability of their relationship. My gut tells me it won't take much to fix things, and I will start by giving Chad a bottle of milk from my fridge first thing, so he doesn't have to go out. I'll also try and catch up with Jenny properly at some point. If she's really not happy here, then I need to better understand exactly what is upsetting her. Dad always used to tell me there are solutions to virtually every problem, it's just about taking the time to explore the root cause.

I scribble 'milk for Chad' at the top of my To-Do list and consult the other tasks for the morning. I need to speak to Danielle about leaving her bike in the communal hallway as James is not happy at having to squeeze past muddy tyres. I also need to check whether Bill wants me to water his plants when he heads off to visit his daughter next weekend. Usually he asks, but if I can take one thing off his plate then I should make the effort.

My phone's display shows another missed call from Pete, but I don't have the energy or patience to call him back. I switch off the lights and head to bed. Tomorrow is going to be a busy day. I will fix things between Chad and Jenny whether they want my help or not.

# 2

## MONDAY, 7.45 A.M.

I groan at the incessant beeping of the alarm, and it takes two attempts to collect my phone from the wireless pad on the bedside table. I stab my finger at the snooze button on the display, and eventually silence returns to my bedroom. I don't remember setting the alarm for this ungodly hour, but I must have done at some point otherwise I wouldn't be awake now. It takes sixty seconds of silence before I deduce that it's Monday and the prospect of another day of weekend is nothing but wishful thinking.

The thick blanket of fog in my mind keeps my head pressed into the pillow, secure beneath the thick duvet. Daylight is peeking through the gap in the curtains, but all I can see is a blur of light grey as condensation on the window provides a translucent glow. I've been meaning to fix the curtain pole, but like most other things in my life, it sits at the bottom of my list of priorities.

I try to recall what's in my calendar for today, but I can't visualise it. It's Monday, which means my food delivery is coming between twelve and one, so for breakfast I'll have to make do with whatever is in the cupboards. I have a meeting with a prospective new client some time before that but I can't remember if that's at ten or eleven. Is that why I set the alarm? I wouldn't have thought I'd be worried about sleeping beyond nine.

The client, Lauren, emailed to request the appointment, saying I'd been recommended by a mutual acquaintance, and I sure could do with a paying job to tide me over for the next few weeks.

There's a small shift in the shape of the duvet as George leaps up onto the bed and marches towards my pillow, before he presses his soft face against my cheek, purring as he does.

'Morning, handsome,' I say quietly, reaching my hand up and around his neck, so I can play with his ears; our morning routine.

Although there is a strict no pets policy for the other residents, George is totally domesticated and, like me, prefers the safety of what he knows.

'I don't suppose you've put the kettle on for me, have you?' I ask rhetorically, and he purrs with dissatisfaction. 'I will feed you once I'm dressed. It's still early.'

It would be so easy just to stay buried in the soft and warm bedding, stroking the cat, but now that my mind is awake, I know there's no way I'll drift back off to sleep. Pushing away the duvet, I swing my legs over the side of the bed, wincing as the soles of my feet make contact with the ice-cold laminate flooring. I half open my eyes, surprised to find my rug over the other side of the room. A flash of me falling into bed and the rug skittering away last night instantly slams to the front of my head. Stretching out my leg as far as it can reach, I catch the corner of the rug with my toe and wiggle until it slides closer to the bed.

I stare at it, unhappy that it looks wrong, but for the life of me I can't figure out why. So, I stand, and cross to the bathroom, the freezing ceramic floor tiles even more of a shock to the system than the wood. I stay very still, my eyes closed, focusing my mind on a sensation of warmth that I'm not feeling, and when the urge to race back to bed has passed, I study the rug once more. It's now positioned in the corner between the bedside cabinet and drawers beneath the bed, which is where it should be, and yet...

And then it hits me, and I can't understand how I didn't see it sooner. The black and white zigzag pattern is going in the wrong direction. Crouching down, I pull on the rug, twisting it one hundred and eighty degrees, and then slide it back into its nook. The fog in my mind shrinks a fraction. My stumble into bed last night must have been far grander than my memory is able to recall right now. But, satisfied that everything is now back in its right place, I reach into the shower cubicle, and switch it on, running my hand beneath the cold stream until it begins to warm. I nudge the switch for the extractor fan with my elbow as I exit the room, heading through to the open-plan living room and kitchen, filling the kettle at the tap, so I can make tea as soon as I'm washed.

I rinse out my favourite mug, drop in a tea bag and open the fridge to retrieve the milk. And in that moment I hear Jenny's voice in the back of my mind: *There's no fucking milk!*

That was why I set the alarm. I remember now thinking that I needed to make sure I was up early enough to leave the bottle by Chad's and Jenny's door.

Hurrying back to the bathroom, I switch off the water, throw on my bathrobe, and grab the unopened bottle from the door of the fridge. I hurry out of the door, only remembering to collect my keys from the peg just before it closes. I hope I'm not too late. The convenience store ten minutes up the road doesn't open until eight, so hopefully Chad hasn't left yet.

I'm breathless as I make it down to the first floor, forgetting how much longer it takes to traverse the winding staircase. I take a moment to compose myself and then march purposefully towards Flat 7, just as Chad is opening the door.

'Oh, hey,' he says, catching me off-guard. 'Were you looking for me? I'm just heading out.'

He's wearing tracksuit bottoms and a hoodie, his usual blond curls tucked beneath a granite-coloured beanie hat. Handsome in the traditional sense, he always seems to have boundless energy, and it's a wonder Jenny manages to keep up with him; especially given the age gap between them. The tenancy agreement is in Jenny's name, but Chad has lived with her since day one. They pay their rent on time, and there have been no complaints about them from any of the other residents, so who am I to judge?

'Off for another of your runs, are you?' I say, inwardly cringing at how uncomfortable I find making small talk.

'No, just nipping to the shop. I'll go for a proper run later tonight if I can finally tempt you to come with me?'

I've never been good at reading social cues, and there's a part of my brain telling me he's trying to flirt, but I don't know if I'm just misreading the situation. I dismiss the thought as quickly as it appears.

'Thanks, but no, I prefer to exercise indoors.'

He frowns at this.

'Oh, yeah? Have you joined a gym then? I thought with your... well, you know, your condition, you'd avoid that sort of thing.'

*My condition.*

My choice to stay inside where it's safe and I'm not constantly searching for means of escape is not what I would call a condition.

'I meant I exercise in my flat,' I correct.

He gently taps the top of his head as if chastising himself.

'Of course you do. Sorry, I've put my foot in it again. I apologise.'

I wave my hand dismissively so he doesn't think I'm offended.

'Forget about it. You said you were going to buy milk?'

He closes the door behind him and gives me a curious stare, and that's when I realise he didn't mention buying milk. I'm about to correct myself, feeling the walls closing in, when he smiles.

'Yep, that's right. Why, do you need me to pick you up some as well?'

I pull my hand out from behind my back and show him the plastic bottle.

'I was actually coming to ask whether you and Jenny need a spare pint. I had an extra one delivered in error and it'll take more effort to phone the company and have it collected and refunded. I'm not going to use it, so, please, be my guest.'

I offer the bottle out, and he looks from me to it and then back again.

'Are you sure?'

'Yes, please, it will only go to waste if I keep hold of it.'

He accepts the gift with a warm smile.

'That's very kind of you, and saves me a trek this morning. Do you want some money for it?'

I quickly shake my head; Jenny and Chad no longer arguing is worth the cost of a pint of milk in my eyes.

'If anything you're doing me a favour by taking it off my hands.'

He slips his key into the lock, before turning back and looking at me again.

'I don't know how you do it, but you're like some kind of guardian angel, do you realise that?'

'I don't follow, sorry.'

He slips off the beanie hat and his hair flops forwards, complimenting his golden tanned skin.

'You just seem to have this... I don't know what you'd call it, like a sixth sense or something. You always seem to know exactly what we need whenever we need it. It's uncanny. If I didn't know better, I'd think you had us all under surveillance.'

I laugh as casually as I can, and am relieved when he joins in.

'Maybe I do,' I say, with a wink.

'Well, Jenny has checked the flat from top to bottom and she hasn't found any hidden cameras,' he says, laughing uproariously, but I can't tell if he's joking or not.

The door opens seconds later and I see Jenny peering out through the gap. She quickly pulls the kimono across her chest when her eyes meet mine.

'Oh, hey, babe, we were just talking about you,' Chad says, leaning through and kissing her cheek for no obviously discernible reason.

She doesn't reciprocate, her gaze practically burning a hole through to my soul.

'Talking about *me*? What were you saying?'

Chad opens his mouth to speak, but seems to think twice and quickly changes tack.

'Oh, nothing really. We were just joking about how Eve is like some kind of guardian angel or fairy godmother or something. Look, she just happened to have a spare pint of milk she was coming to offer us.'

He holds out the bottle, but she makes no effort to take it from him, her fingers whitening as she grips tighter to the edge of the door, keeping most of her body behind it.

'I thought you were jogging to the shop to buy milk,' she says, eyes still firmly on me, now taking in my appearance in the pink bathrobe.

'Well, I don't need to now, thanks to Eve. Here you go, you can go and make your smoothie now.'

She remains behind the door, and I wonder if there's a hint of jealousy in her glare. Both Chad and I are in our early thirties, fifteen years her junior, but how can I make it clear to her that I have zero romantic interest in Chad?

My pre-lease research into Jenny revealed that she was recently divorced from an estate agent who'd lost their life savings through gambling. She told me almost as much the day we first met, and I sensed a kinship between us that I hoped would one day develop into friendship, but the last couple of months something has definitely felt off.

The skin pinches around her hazel eyes, and her roots are showing, but she's still very attractive, and I can't see any reason Chad would look elsewhere. That I'm down here speaking to him dressed in next to nothing probably isn't helping matters, so I straighten my robe, ready to take my leave.

'I'd better get back to my shower,' I tell them turning and making my way back along the corridor, until I feel the weight of a hand on my shoulder.

Turning back, I'm expecting to see Chad behind me, apologising for Jenny's cold front, but he's nowhere in sight.

'I know what you're up to,' she practically spits through gritted teeth.

'I don't know what you mean,' I say defiantly. 'I promise you I have no interest in Chad.'

I say it firmly, meaning every word, but it's as if she hasn't heard a single syllable.

She waves a finger in my face, but it's what she says next that chills my bones.

'I'm not someone to be fucked with, Eve. I'm on to you.'

# 3

## MONDAY, 12.27 P.M.

I drain the dregs of the coffee, before returning my mug to the tiled coaster on the corner of the desk. The meeting was only supposed to be an hour but we're now pushing ninety minutes, and if it doesn't end soon, we'll both have to dial back in to the video call server.

Lauren is staring straight at me, only she isn't looking at me, rather her attention is focused on the latest mocked-up poster I'm sharing on the screen. Her eyes are such a bright blue that it's almost like I'm staring into a summer sky. They drastically contrast with the red-streaked, cropped hair that I didn't expect when she dialled in. Her elfin-like features don't command a presence, and I'm sensing that may be the reason her brother and business partner, Tim, insisted on joining her in the room. I'd never have known they were related if she hadn't said; they're chalk and cheese. For her softly spoken, and carefully chosen words, his voice seems to grate every nerve. Raspy, like a forty-a-day habit has taken a toll, and with a shirt and tie that instantly feels too formal. In fact, his tie is so tight I can barely make out the tiny knot squashed beneath the collar of the blue striped shirt.

By contrast, Lauren – though she has insisted I call her Lo – is in a pair of denim dungarees, only one strap fastened, revealing a white and navy horizontally striped t-shirt beneath. I'm in a loose-fitting throw that covers a multitude of sins, but gives me the freedom to tuck my arms beneath it for comfort.

'What we're looking for is your commitment to deliver the brief,' Tim says, and I must admit his tendency to state the obvious is also starting to rankle.

I stop sharing the screen and open the concise outline that Lauren emailed over last week, quickly skim reading it to refresh my memory.

'You're looking to diversify into supplying cakes for corporate events,' I say succinctly.

'Not just cakes,' he clarifies unnecessarily. 'The whole shebang: rolls, pies, vol-au-vents, fries, in addition to wraps, fresh cream cakes, and beverages. We want to offer an end-to-end service for our prospective clients.'

'But at the moment it's just the three bakery shops that you operate?'

'That's right,' Lauren says, smiling proudly. 'We were competing for a lease for a fourth, but the landlord went in another direction.' Her brow furrows as she says this, and instinct tells me this corporate diversification wasn't her idea.

'And what you want from me is a series of still adverts that you can place in a number of publications,' I say.

'Yes,' Lauren says.

'It needs to be big and bold,' Tim adds, a glint of something in his eye. 'I want the advertisements to pop off the page.'

'Do you have a core market you're targeting?'

'We don't want to pigeonhole ourselves, so it needs to appeal across multiple industries.'

I think he's missing my point, so I try again.

'But the publications you're planning to advertise in are targeted at who exactly?'

'We have contacts at a number of outlets who have guaranteed prominent space in industry-leading magazines.'

I take a breath to keep my impatience in check.

'Yes, but are these magazines likely to be read by senior executives in these industries, or by the people on the ground more likely to be entrusted to organise these corporate events you're trying to break into?'

'Well, the former, obviously,' Tim says, an edge to his voice.

'Hey, listen, far be it for me to question your marketing strategy, but in my limited experience, this is a tough market to crack, and a few full-page spreads in some glossy magazines won't be enough.'

'Um, my degree in Business and Marketing begs to differ,' Tim boasts. 'Do you have a background in marketing as well, Eve?'

'No, but I have a diploma and lived experience. I'm not criticising, I just don't want to waste your time and money. I think if we work together, and fine tune that target market, I can pull together a bespoke package for you that will—'

'With all due respect,' Tim interrupts, showing none, 'my sister and I have been quite clear with our expectations of you. If you're not capable of delivering that, then you should just say.'

*What an arsehole*, I think but don't say, off camera squeezing the stress ball I keep beside the desk for such occasions.

'I'd like to remind you that you approached *me* about this project, because I came highly recommended. I can absolutely deliver what you've requested in your outline, but I don't want to be held accountable when it fails to deliver on your expectations because you asked for the wrong thing.'

I want to immediately apologise, such is my inherent need to people please, and I don't have to remind myself how beneficial the extra income would be right now.

'You're right: you were recommended to us,' Tim fires back, without missing a beat, 'but we were also warned about you too.'

'Tim, no,' Lauren says, a hand shooting up to her mouth.

'We were told we'd never get to meet you in person,' he continues, staring into the camera, his gaze almost penetrating my soul. 'They said something about a fear of open spaces?'

This is the part of the conversation with prospective clients that I always dread. I'm not ashamed of my agoraphobia, and to me it is less of a fear of open spaces or simply being outside. It is a fear of being in a situation where my escape might be difficult or where I won't be able to access help. And I know what the root cause is – God knows, my therapist reminds me when we meet each week – but that doesn't make it any easier to deal with.

When meeting new clients, I always hope they won't ask to meet in person, so I can avoid having to explain my situation, and the internal struggle I have when I imagine others judging me. But they don't know what it's like. They don't know what it was like *that* day...

I feel tears prick at the edges of my vision, but I won't cave in front of Lauren and her obnoxious brother.

'I work from home,' I say trying to remember the script I always use, 'but that doesn't detract from the quality of my work. You've seen the resumé I sent over, along with the overwhelming feedback from previous clients, all of whom have found it a mutually beneficial working relationship.'

'You don't need to explain yourself,' Lauren says, leaning forward in solidarity.

'I was merely asking to help me understand better,' Tim counters. 'You have to admit it is an unusual situation.'

'Is it?' I snap. 'It was only a couple of years ago that we were all working from home and the world didn't implode, did it? I have my own space and an environment that benefits my creativity. The work I've shared is testament to that.'

'I guess I'm just old-fashioned,' he says. 'I like to look a person in the eye when I'm making a deal with them.'

I resist the urge to roll my eyes, and remain silent, sensing it would serve his purpose better if I was to react.

'So, is it just public places like supermarkets you can't go? Or is it more localised than that?'

'You really don't have to answer that,' Lauren chips in again, momentarily muting their end and saying something to her brother.

She's right: I'm not obliged to answer that question, and doing so risks alienating them both, so I don't tell them that I haven't stepped outside the confines of this apartment building in nearly five years. I don't tell them that even thinking about stepping foot outside sends my mind into physical shutdown.

'Sorry about that,' Lauren says as she unmutes their microphone. 'Tim didn't mean to be so rude.'

'It's all right, I have a thick skin,' I lie.

Tim claps his hands together.

'Well, how about this then? If Mohammed won't come to the mountain, what if we come and meet you instead? That way, we can talk through your ideas, and get a sense of where you operate and how you craft your work.'

Lauren immediately mutes the microphone again, but this time also switches off the camera, leaving just my floating head on the screen. I should just fall on my sword and inform them that I don't think this is going to work out. I have no intention of having strangers walking about my flat, assessing my potential performance based on how clean the floor is. If the references I've already provided aren't sufficient then I don't need the headache. I'll just have to tighten my belt for a few weeks.

The screen flashes and Lauren's face returns.

'I am so sorry about Tim,' she says, her blue eyes twinkling. 'Please don't reject our request because my brother doesn't know how to keep his foot out of his own mouth. I promise, from this moment on, you'll only have to deal with me. And I don't want to come and inspect your home. Bea said you're the best around, and I trust her opinion.'

There's no sign of Tim, so I can only presume she told him off and asked him to leave the room.

*Good riddance!*

'It is a shame that you can't come and see one of the bakeries to get a sense of our branding and customer focus. All my staff are trained to put the customer first, offering recommendations and happy to chat for as long or as often as the customer wants. We have so many regulars that they're almost like an extended family.'

'So, why the corporate sideline, if you don't mind me asking?'

'We all have overheads to pay, am I right? It's Tim's idea to diversify the risk or something. The plan is for him to oversee that arm of the business, with supplies purchased from me and a couple of other close third parties giving that homemade feel to these events and making profit for both arms of the business. Although it delays expansion to a fourth shop for another year, he reckons the new arm will be turning a profit by then, allowing us to expand both arms simultaneously.' She shrugs. 'He's the commercially focused one; I just like to bake, and come up with new twists on classics.' She pauses, her gaze averted. 'If it's okay with you, I would like to deliver a few samples of our customer favourites, so you can taste what they do. Would that be okay?'

Is this her way of trying to get a look at where I work more subtly than her brother? I can't think of a polite way to decline, and even if she does come over, it doesn't mean I have to invite her inside.

'That would be lovely, thank you.'

'Good. And listen, if you really think that Tim's strategy is flawed, would you be able to work up why and how you would approach it instead? It will bruise his ego, but he'll prefer that to throwing away money.'

I reach for the black diary on the unit beside the laptop and make a show of flicking through the pages.

'I have another project that I should finish later today,' I say, not looking at the camera in case she can see through the lie, 'so I can probably have a rough plan to you by the end of the week, and then you can discuss with Tim and let me know some time next week.'

'Perfect! And listen, I really am sorry about Tim. He's overprotective because I was let down by a former business partner and he doesn't want me being ripped off again. I think his heart is in the right place.'

'You don't need to apologise for an overprotective brother; I have one of my own, so I understand how frustrating they can be.'

She smiles again, and I find myself mirroring the action.

'I have a really good feeling about this,' Lauren says, and I can't help but nod, as she ends the call and the intercom buzzer sounds.

# 4

## MONDAY, 12.40 P.M.

I practically trip over George as I swing off the desk chair, reaching for the intercom handset. George skuttles off, unimpressed by my acrobatics to avoid treading on him. You'd never know he has a bed and scratching post beneath the window ledge in the living room for the amount of time he spends lying in any small sunspot he can find.

There's a woman I don't recognise in the grainy black-and-white image of the portal on the wall beside the door.

'Vector Design, Eve speaking,' I say into the handset like I'm accepting an unsolicited phone call.

'Tesco delivery,' comes the curt reply.

'Can you leave it inside the door and I'll be down in two secs,' I say, pressing the door release button, and returning the handset.

A quick glance in the large round mirror beside the intercom to check I don't look like I've just stumbled out of bed, and then I grab my keys and leave my flat, checking that George isn't going to make a bolt for freedom. I catch sight of him lying in a fresh sunspot beside his bed, and close the door behind me, hurrying down two flights of stairs to the ground floor.

The door at the end of the communal corridor is still closed, and there's no sign of the delivery driver. I assumed she'd have propped open the door with something whilst she went and fetched my shopping, but she must have misunderstood, as I find her stacking plastic boxes just outside the door.

I open the door, and press my knee into the side of it.

'Where's Keith today?' I ask casually, as she lifts the final box onto the tower, and then proceeds to dig inside, searching for her tablet.

'Holiday,' she says, stabbing at the screen with a gloved finger.

I don't remember Keith mentioning a holiday the last time we spoke, but maybe he didn't mention it to avoid causing me additional worry.

'We made two substitutions,' the driver informs me. 'There were no extra-large bottles of the hair conditioner you ordered, so they selected two slightly smaller bottles. Is that okay?'

One of the disadvantages of ordering my groceries online is that such decisions are taken out of my hands. I imagine any normal person, upon finding their favourite brand of conditioner is sold out, might then head to an alternative shop to search for it.

'They were on a buy one, get one half price offer, so the additional cost is only 55p. I can take them back and apply the refund if you prefer.'

'No, it's fine. The contents of the bottles are the same, and I can always pour them into the existing bottle I have upstairs,' I reply, stopping myself when I realise I'm oversharing.

'So you're accepting the substitution?'

'Yes,' I say, smiling, even though she has yet to make eye

contact with me, let alone show any kind of pleasantries. 'I'm Eve, by the way,' I say, ducking my head slightly and forcing the eye contact.

'Great,' she says, forcing an insincere, thin smile.

'And you are?'

She taps the small badge pinned to the lapel of her fleece. She doesn't look old enough to be a Joan. I always imagine a Joan to be in her late sixties, with greying hair, but this woman can't be much older than me, her highlighted hair tied back in a messy bun.

'The other substitution is one of the three bottles of wine you ordered,' Joan continues, studying the tablet like it holds the meaning of life. 'They've picked an identically priced Chardonnay in place of one of the bottles of Sauvignon Blanc you ordered.'

'That's fine,' I say, quickly, conscious that keeping the door open this long is allowing all the heat to come in. Keith usually goes through the minutiae once he's brought the boxes inside for me, but Joan hasn't taken the hint.

'Sign here,' she says, twisting the tablet to face me.

Keith usually gives me a stylus pen to sign with, but Joan hasn't offered one.

'Do you have a stylus?' I ask.

'Just use your finger.'

I scrawl my signature but it's thick and blotchy and looks nothing like my usual. It doesn't seem to bother Joan, who taps the screen again and turns to head back to her vehicle.

'Are you going to bring the boxes inside?' I call after her. 'Please?'

'Company policy is just to bring them to the door,' she calls back over her shoulder, opening the truck door and hurling the tablet in on the passenger seat.

'I appreciate that might be the case, but Keith usually lifts them just inside the door for me, and then I extract my bags.'

'Not my job, sorry.'

'But do you think you could make an exception on my account?'

She eyes the tall stack of boxes, and then the two-metre distance to where I'm standing, the door still propped open by my knee. She looks unimpressed.

'Sorry, company rules,' she says.

This is the last thing I need. Even if I attempt to explain why what would be an easy task for her is impossible for me, I'm not sure anything will penetrate her lack of empathy.

'Please,' I try again, staring into her eyes, hoping for even just a smidge of compassion. 'I realise it probably sounds like a strange request, but I need you to bring the boxes just inside the door. I'm not asking you to carry them up to my flat, nor empty them; just to bring them inside the frame of the door.'

She frowns, but her feet remain planted. I'd offer to pay her for her trouble, but I don't think she'd even cave for that.

'I promise that Keith does this for me *every* time.'

The first time Keith stopped by during the first lockdown in 2020, I remember him insisting that he couldn't carry the boxes inside, but when I explained my situation to him, he agreed on the understanding that I wear a mask when opening the door and stay a safe distance back. And I've stuck to the same day of the week and timeslot ever since to avoid this exact situation arising.

'As I explained, it's against company policy, and if I breach that and something occurs, then I'll be liable.'

'Nothing is going to happen to you. All I'm asking is for you to move the stack a couple of metres closer. Please? Otherwise, I'm not going to be able to take delivery of my shopping.'

'You've already signed for it, so you have to take delivery of it.'

'But I physically *can't*,' I say, feeling my own frustration brewing, desperately trying to think of any way I can convince her to ignore the rule book.

'If I was to do as you asked, and ignore the rules that have been put in place for our safety as much as your own, and I... I don't know... let's say I slip and injure my back, I'd then have to report the incident at work and they'd know I breached policy and might not give me sick pay.'

I find it very hard to believe that any company would behave in such a way, but I have no grounds to argue.

'Or, for all I know, you might be a psychopath who intends to hold me hostage if I step inside. Either way, I could be sacked for gross misconduct.'

'Would it make you feel more comfortable if I move to the end of the hallway? I mean you no ill will, but you don't understand why I can't accept the boxes out there.'

'Listen, lady, I'm sorry about whatever you're going through, but I have other deliveries I need to make, and you're now holding me up. If you refuse to remove your bags of shopping from the crates, then I'll be forced to take your order back to the shop with me, but because you've already signed to accept delivery, you'll have to raise a claim with the customer service team.'

*This is ridiculous!*

'I'm agoraphobic,' I finally say, but her expression doesn't change.

'Of course you are. Are you going to collect your groceries or am I taking them back with me? Can you hurry up and make a decision?'

'I really am agoraphobic. I can't step outside.'

Joan reaches into her pocket and pulls out a phone before putting it to her ear, though I've no idea who she's calling. It's probably wishful thinking to hope she's phoning her supervisor to request permission to bring in the shopping.

I stare at the tower of five blue crates, willing them to move closer, but they remain stationary, the cold wind doing little to sate my rising body temperature. I shuffle my feet a fraction forward, trying to remember all the guidance Dr Winslow has provided over the last year.

*Remember, there is nothing outside that can hurt you.*

But that wasn't true on Halloween 2019 when *he* attacked me. Snatches of memory try to break through my carefully constructed wall, and I snap my eyes shut, willing them to stay away, and trying to focus on memories of a time when I wasn't so terrified.

I can just about hear Joan's voice over the sound of the blood rushing through my ears, but I can't make out what she's saying or who she's speaking to.

My shoulder crashes into the door, as my knees almost buckle, and I suddenly need to get out of the sleeveless throw as my blood boils, but my arms are suddenly weightless, and no amount of flapping is getting the poncho from around my neck. My eyes open as I crash to the mat, and the world splinters into a hundred different colours, and the tower of crates seems to be spinning towards me as the weight of the world comes crashing down around me.

And it's then I suddenly realise I can't breathe. It's as if my body has forgotten or is refusing to perform the one action I've been doing since the second I arrived in this world. It feels as though someone has put a bag over my face, and even though I'm opening and closing my mouth, no air is entering. I try swallowing to clear any blockage, but there's nothing. *I'm going to suffocate* is the last thing I think before the world fades to black.

# 5

## MONDAY, 1.15 P.M.

My cheek is pressed into something straw-like, and the darkness reveals nothing of my location. I can hear what sounds like rain tapping against a hard surface, and as I try to adjust my position, I sense that I am lying down; the ground is firm against my shoulder and arm.

*Where am I?*

I search my memory for any indication of what led to this moment, but there is nothing I can register.

*Am I dead?*

I'm not sure how to begin answering that question. But now that I'm trying to engage my senses, I can feel something close to my head. I try to concentrate on the sensation of fingers running through the hair above my ear. For the briefest of moments I'm reminded of my mother stroking my head, trying to pacify my upset.

*Did I fall, and she's trying to make me feel better?*

And yet I know instinctively that isn't the case because she's dead. So, someone else then? A friend? A stranger?

'Easy, Eve,' a man's voice says. 'You're okay. I'm here with you.

I think you might have bumped your head, but you're going to be okay.'

*I bumped my head? So I've been in some kind of accident? Is that why I can't remember what happened?*

I can smell Bill's Old Spice, and it isn't an unpleasant familiarity. It is his fingers that are brushing against my temple as he comforts me. And if Bill is here, then it probably means I am still safe within our home. And the relief is palpable.

And then my memory engages and I remember the disagreement with Joan, and how close I came to stepping outside.

My eyes snap open to check exactly where I am, and I'm relieved to see the cobweb-ridden lightshade above my head in the hallway. I catch sight of Bill's tired face smiling down at me.

'There, there,' he coos gently, and I realise my face is pressed into the large doormat by the front door, and I comprehend just how close I am to the horror of the outside world. Rain is splashing against the tiled platform less than a metre away from where I am lying.

I throw my hands out, desperate to push myself into a sitting position, and to put distance between me and the dangers of the air beyond the door. But my initial attempts are met by the resistance of tired muscles, and I fall flat on my face again.

'Easy, let me help you,' Bill's warm tones comfort. 'On three.'

I feel him squeeze his hands beneath my armpits as he counts down, and then he's lifting me up and into his embrace. We're still seated, but now my back is pressed against his chest, and there is distance between me and the now closed front door.

'What happened?' I venture croakily.

'I'm not sure. I found you like this,' he says.

I spot a mound of plastic shopping bags just inside the doorway, but there's no sign of Joan.

'There was a delivery van just leaving when I got back,' Bill continues. 'I assume this is your shopping?'

I think of all the frozen items currently defrosting before us, and whether any of it can still be saved.

'How long have I been like this?'

'Well, assuming you passed out while the delivery truck was here, then we're only talking minutes, rather than hours.'

At least that's something.

'How are you feeling?' Bill asks next.

*Embarrassed; ashamed*, I don't tell him. This is exactly why I don't even bother thinking about leaving. It doesn't seem to matter how many times I tell Dr Winslow that I genuinely can't leave, she doesn't seem to understand that this is more than just whimsy. My mind won't allow me to leave, and it fights against me whenever I dare to think about the possibility.

I realise how irrational I sound, but I have no other way to describe what happens when I get this close to leaving. Even now, with the door closed, and knowing deep down that I'm once again safe, my heart is racing, and a cool sweat is seeping down my back. I don't want to live like this, but I'm powerless. This is what neither Pete nor Dr Winslow realise: accepting that I will never leave this building is the only thing that brings me any peace.

'I should get that shopping away,' I say, trying to prop myself up without Bill's support. But I feel his hand press against my shoulder and slide me back against his chest.

'There's no hurry,' he says. 'The groceries won't spoil for a while yet. Besides, it's nice that I get to take care of you for once.'

I pat his hand, grateful that he was the one who discovered me in such a vulnerable state, and not one of the others. I'm not sure Jenny would have been so sympathetic and kind.

'You never seem to stop caring about the rest of us,' Bill

continues. 'And I know you won't rest for long, so for the next ten minutes you are under my care, and I am in charge of all decisions and actions. If you did bump your head on the way down, then it's probably best to get you checked over.'

'I can't go to the hospital...' I begin to say, but he cuts me off.

'I wasn't going to suggest we go anywhere. We don't need to when we have a qualified GP on the premises who is more than capable of giving you the once-over.'

'Oh, I'm not sure about that. Jenny and I aren't...'

My words trail off. I don't want to give him any indication that one of our neighbours might be questioning my behaviour. I instantly hear Jenny's words from last night in my head: *most of the other tenants in this hellhole are probably already in bed.*

'I mean, Jenny is probably at work,' I say quickly, hoping he didn't pick up on what I was going to reveal.

'No, no, she's locuming this week,' he counters.

Is she? That's something I usually know, but I can't remember the last time I checked the second calendar in my flat. I quickly try to calculate the dates in my head. Has it really been four weeks since she was last locuming? That would certainly explain why she wasn't dressed when she caught Chad and me in the corridor earlier.

I inwardly cringe. *Caught* makes it sound like we were up to no good, and buys into her paranoia. I've done nothing wrong to make her question my behaviour or attitude, but clearly that exchange is playing on my mind, and I'm going to have to act fast to smooth things over with her. I can't allow her negative thoughts to impact my interactions with the rest of my tenants.

'I don't want to disturb Jenny if she's in Zoom consultations with patients,' I say instead, smiling, in an effort to put his mind at ease. 'I'm sure I'll be fine.'

'Nonsense,' he says, now standing. 'What if you've got

concussion from bumping your head? The last thing any of us can afford is something befalling you.'

It's sweet that he's so worried, but now that the door is closed, and my shopping is inside, the anxious energy is starting to dissipate.

'I've not forgotten about what you did for me when... well, when I lost my Elsie.'

My mind instantly returns to the night when I found Bill passed out in his living room, an empty bottle of pills on the table where he was slumped and an open bottle of whisky still gripped in his hand. I remember his pulse, so weak that it took several attempts to find it.

'I'll never know what brought you down to my flat that night,' Bill continues, his voice more solemn now, 'but I've thanked God every day since.'

Even I'm not sure exactly what gave me the urge to check on Bill that night. We'd briefly spoken that morning when I'd caught him on his way to church. He was dressed in a suit and tie, which wasn't unusual, and although he'd sounded chipper, despite Elsie's passing four weeks before, there must have been something in what he said, or how he said it that played on my subconscious.

I remember feeling ill at ease for the rest of the day, but being unable to figure out why. It was like I'd forgotten something and for the life of me I couldn't figure out what. It stopped me falling asleep, and as the clock turned eleven, I had to get up and check on everyone. I stalked the passageway, listening for any sound of discontent in each flat, but I was met with virtual silence in all bar Bill's. At first, I assumed he was asleep, and then I heard the faintest sound of music playing from inside. And given the time it struck me as unusual for Bill to be awake so late.

And as I climbed back up the ladder and in through the trapdoor, my mind wouldn't rest with the urge to check on him. He didn't answer after three minutes of urgent knocking, and so I used my skeleton key to enter his flat.

'I like to think Elsie spoke to you that night,' he continues quietly now. 'I believe she's still watching out for me, even all these years later. And I think she wanted me to hang on that night, so she sent you as a guardian angel to bring me back from the brink. And if it wasn't for your actions that night, Eve, I never would have met my grandson. I don't think you realise just how big a role you play in all of our lives.'

Personally, I don't believe in ghosts, not that I'll ever admit as much to Bill – to each their own in my book – but the weirdest thing is that when I entered Bill's flat, the record player wasn't even plugged in. There was a record on the platter, 'I Love You More and More Every Day' by Al Martino. Bill later told me that this was the song he and Elsie had first danced to at their wedding in 1965, and when I asked him to play it to me, a chill ran the length of my spine. It was that voice I'd heard through the wall that night, and I have no explanation how that was possible.

'Are you able to stand?' Bill asks, and I give him a firm nod, though I need to rely on him to help me straighten, as my legs are still shaky. 'Well, the least I can do is help you bring some of these groceries up to your flat.'

'Oh no, there's really no—'

He leans in closer.

'I won't take no for an answer. I'll just make sure you're settled and then I will get out of your hair.'

He tests the weight of the shopping bags, and hands me two, lifting the remaining three himself with one hand, and giving me his arm to cling to as we slowly make our way up the stairs to my flat.

'Thank you, kind sir,' I say when we reach the door. 'I'll be fine from here.'

There's a look of disappointment on his face, and I sense maybe he was hoping I'd invite him in for a cup of tea, and usually I wouldn't think twice, but for the life of me, I can't remember whether I closed the trapdoor in the airing cupboard last night. And I can't afford to take the risk that he sees.

# 6

## MONDAY, 4 P.M.

Dr Winslow's face fills my screen as my laptop joins the video call. I'm five minutes late – fashionably late if this was a party – and part of me is surprised that she has waited. She fails to cover the look of surprise on her face when mine joins hers on screen.

'Good afternoon, Eve,' she says, staring into my soul.

'Hi,' I say, not wanting to make a big deal of the fact that I have failed to dial in to the last two scheduled sessions.

'And how are you, Eve?'

'Peachy,' I reply flatly; my go-to response when I'm deliberately being sarcastic, indicating that everything is far from good, but without formally stating that I'm unhappy.

'Care to elaborate?' Dr Winslow asks.

Psychological therapy was Pete's idea. When he became aware of my refusal to leave this building, he automatically assumed it was something that could and should be fixed.

'It isn't normal to spend the rest of your life behind closed doors,' he would tell me over and over, to which I would simply reply, 'Define *normal*.'

The world isn't the one I remember. And it never will be. The face masks and sanitation stations might be gone, but the Covid virus remains out there, ready to spread with an uncovered sneeze or cough. And it's just one of a billion strains of virus or disease that I could come into contact with by stepping outside.

'But you could just as easily catch something by coming into contact with any one of your tenants,' Pete will argue.

And he's right, I could catch a cold or Covid, or any other virus because my tenants still leave and continue with their lives, coming into contact with the unwashed masses. But, and this is key, the chances are dramatically reduced. And it isn't just the plethora of illnesses that pose a threat beyond the front door.

I still haven't elaborated for Dr Winslow as my mind processes what I should say. The dozen or so appointments I've attended in the last year haven't been of any tangible benefit to me. I know all about the meditation exercises Dr Winslow encourages. And I've even tried a few without success. And I know about the support group that meets locally – less than a mile from my front door, Dr Winslow reminds me each time – but clearly the impact of agoraphobia on them is less severe than mine, because at least they can make it to the back room of a social club. I don't think anyone understands just how impossible that is for me.

'How are you getting on with the breathing exercises I emailed over?' Dr Winslow asks next, when I fail to engage. 'Did you print them off and stick them up like I suggested?'

I reach into the drawer beside the desk and withdraw the printed sheet, and hold it up to the screen.

'Good. Good. And has that helped to remind you to practise every day?'

'It hasn't,' I admit, but in fairness, I've left it in the drawer rather than sticking it up. I did attempt two days' worth of breathing exercises, but my outlook remained the same. Maybe these exercises would be beneficial to someone who *wants* to leave their home, but I'm quite content here. Apart from this morning's incident with Joan's refusal to bring in my shopping, I've had no desire to go beyond the door. And had my regular delivery driver Keith been there, it wouldn't have been an issue.

'I see,' Dr Winslow says, breaking the growing awkward silence. 'You've missed our last couple of sessions, but you've joined today, which is great, but is there a reason why? Is there something specific you want to talk about?'

The truth is I'm fed up of Pete's incessant calls. Even though he pays for these sessions, Dr Winslow isn't allowed to reveal the content of our discussions. But I imagine she's quick to tell him when I don't attend, and this is what has triggered the increase in calls in the last week.

'Have you made any attempts to leave the building since we last spoke?'

I don't answer at first. A little voice in the back of my head is telling me there may be some truth in what she's said: did I decide to dial in for more than just Pete's sake? I didn't need to connect to the call. And I could have returned one of Pete's calls or sent him a message instead. There is no reason I had to join the call, other than my subconscious wanting me to.

'There was...' I begin, my words trailing off as I contemplate whether I really want to give Dr Winslow any encouragement.

'Go on,' she says.

I sigh audibly, unable to think of a way to avert the course I've started us on.

'There was an incident this morning.'

'What kind of incident?' she asks, her brow instantly furrowing.

'The bitch of a woman delivering my groceries refused to bring them inside and threatened to take them back.'

'And what happened?'

'I passed out apparently,' I say, not wanting to make it any more dramatic than I need to.

'How far did you get out?'

'I didn't. I collapsed in the doorway.'

'But you wanted to go out? That's a positive sign.'

'No, I didn't. I wanted her to bring the bags inside, but she refused. I didn't know what to do. I didn't want to go outside, and then before I knew it, the walls were closing in, and I woke up being nursed by one of my tenants.'

'Calm down, Eve, it's okay, you don't need to shout.'

I pause, not even conscious that I had raised my voice.

'What's really going on here?' Dr Winslow continues.

'I told you, the woman made things unnecessarily difficult for me.'

'And that angered you?'

'Wouldn't it you?'

She doesn't immediately respond, and I can see her eyes trying to read my face through the screen.

'What do you think is really making you so angry right now?'

Aside from your pointless questions, I don't retort.

'Could it be the loss of control?' she suggests. 'After all, that's part of the reason you keep yourself hidden away inside, isn't it? When you boil it down, your refusal to go outside is a means of you snatching back some kind of control in your life. Wouldn't you say?'

I don't answer, doing my best not to react.

'So, when things feel like they're spiralling out of your control, you become frustrated and try to wrestle it back.'

I glance behind me towards the fridge door. I promised myself I wouldn't have a drink before the session, but she's pressing more than usual.

'And what happened to your shopping?' Dr Winslow asks, switching the topic.

'It was inside with me.'

'Did you bring it inside?'

'No, it must have been the delivery driver,' although having said this, for all I know Bill could have brought it in for me.

'Have there been any occasions recently when you've wanted to go out?'

'Honestly, no. Why would I want to leave? I have everything here that I need. I don't understand why I'm the one who's considered weird for not wanting to go outside. If you knew how dangerous it is out there...'

'It's a pretty lonely place when we isolate ourselves though. Do you ever feel lonely?'

'Nope.'

'And what about romance? Are you in a relationship with anyone at the moment?'

'No.'

'Would you like to be?'

'No. It isn't a crime to be single by choice.'

She holds her hands up, palms out in a passive gesture.

'I'm not saying it is, and after two divorces, I totally understand that outlook.' She takes a breath. 'There is a place for desiring intimacy though. It is possible to enjoy the single life whilst also longing for sensuality. They don't have to be mutually exclusive.'

My cheeks flush, and I want her to stop this line of questioning.

There's also a place for sex toys and imagination, I don't say.

'And how is the drinking?'

My cheeks blaze in an instant, and I adjust the laptop's position, suddenly conscious of the open-plan kitchen in the background.

'You've previously mentioned you enjoy a drink most nights, but there are dangers associated with drinking alcohol in isolation, especially when there are underlying mental health concerns.'

This is Pete, I'm convinced of it. What has he been saying to her? Probably telling her I'm an alcoholic because I enjoy the odd glass or two of wine.

'It's been a couple of weeks since I had anything to drink,' I say firmly, 'so there's nothing for you to worry about.'

'I didn't say I was worried, but it's interesting that that's what you drew from my question.'

Fancy psychologist tricks again. I remember now that this is why I stopped attending these sessions. She's trying to get into my head, putting in words that weren't there.

'Are you ready to talk about the incident that triggered your reluctance to leave your home?'

'It wasn't just one thing.'

'Wasn't it? I really wish you'd talk about that night, Eve. I only have the account your brother gave me. I really believe that if we could tackle that incident head on, we'd make progress in helping you overcome your fear.'

I hear the sound of the rain howling, the feeling of the overcoat pulled tightly around my waist, but the street was so dark that night due to the power cut across the city. And then the feeling of being watched, being hunted...

I kill the camera on the laptop, and push myself away from the screen.

'Hello? Eve, are you still with me?'

I don't reply, crossing into the kitchen and opening the bottle of Sauvignon Blanc in the door of the fridge, taking a long swig before returning to the desk, the bottle now on the floor beside my feet.

'Sorry, someone was at the door,' I say, switching my camera back on. 'What were you saying?'

'I was asking you to trust me, Eve. I appreciate it's difficult, and not helped by the fact we're talking via a computer screen, but I think we would make greater progress if we discussed the mugging and assault you suffered.'

Flashes of me running along that dark road fill my head; the sensation of being grabbed around the waist; the branches of the bush scratching at my face as he forced me through.

'I don't want to make you relive something so painful, but I was going to suggest we could try to review it together using hypnotherapy to provide a safe environment to do so. I've had some good success helping other clients to overcome traumatic experiences, and if you'd let me—'

'They never found him,' I say, cutting her off. 'He's still out there. Somewhere. And for all I know he's waiting for me. I don't want to relive those memories because it isn't going to help catch him, or stop him doing it again. *I* am the only one who can prevent that happening, and in the five years since I closed that door, I haven't been attacked once. And nor have I felt so hopelessly terrified. So, why the fuck would I ever want to leave?'

She doesn't answer, and maybe this is finally the breakthrough she needs to stop pushing. If I can convince her that she is wasting her time, then maybe she'll reveal as much to Pete and he'll stop funding this charade.

'It wasn't your fault, Eve,' Dr Winslow eventually says. 'You do realise that, don't you? I've come across too many victims of such crimes who blame themselves for the depraved behaviour of the perpetrator. What happened to you, it wasn't your fault.'

I know it wasn't my fault, and it annoys me that she'd assume that's what I think.

'There is progress being made with agoraphobics using virtual reality, and I'd like you to consider joining a study that's being funded by a colleague of mine. Essentially, he will send over a VR headset that you wear like a pair of swimming goggles. This then creates the visual stimuli of being outdoors while consciously you're aware that you're safely within your flat. The idea is to train the mind out of the feelings of panic or anxiety that might arise. For the first few uses of the tool, I would be on the call with you, asking you to describe what you're seeing and how it's making you feel, allowing me to coach you in techniques to overcome those feelings. I think you'd be a great addition to the trial. I don't need a decision today, but will you consider it? I will email over some more details about what's involved, and then when we speak next week, you can let me know one way or another. Is that okay?'

'I'll take a look,' I say to pacify her, quickly ending the call, saying that I have another meeting to attend.

Closing the laptop, I reach down for the bottle and carry it to the sofa.

# 7

## MONDAY, 8.25 P.M.

My eyes snap open, and it takes several seconds to realise why the ceiling looks so odd, and why it feels as though someone is squeezing my spine. And then I sit up and find my eyes level with the end of the sofa. Did I pass out again?

The last thing I remember is the awkward call with Dr Winslow, and my eyes now fall on the upturned, empty bottle of Sauvignon Blanc on the coffee table to my right.

The flat is in virtual darkness, with only a thin trail of yellow light creeping through the curtains from the streetlight beyond the window. It's late, but I assume it's still Monday, though just how late it is isn't immediately obvious. How long have I been asleep?

My phone isn't anywhere in sight, but I run my hands across the coffee table and sofa just in case. But finding nothing phone-shaped, other than the television remote, I force myself onto my haunches, and eventually up and into a standing position. A sharp blade cuts through my thoughts as the blood rushes from my head, forcing me to squint and wince as it feels as though a grenade has detonated inside my skull. My mouth feels so dry that it's hard to even swallow what little saliva remains. Drinking on an empty stomach is never a good idea, and it doesn't look as though I had the forethought to open a packet of crisps, let alone to cook myself a wholesome meal.

I shudder forward a step, reaching out for the back of the sofa to steady my slow progression through the living room and into the adjacent kitchen area. And then I feel along the granite countertop until I'm standing beside the large sink and drainer. Running the cold tap, I push my head beneath the stream of water, sucking in as much as my mouth can hold, quickly swallowing and returning for more. But being at this odd angle only ignites the pain behind my eyes, and I have to stop as a bright light comes close to forcing me back into unconsciousness. Reaching up, I open the cabinet above the sink and fiddle about until my fingers brush against a plastic ice cream tub and I pull it out. Snapping off the lid, my fingertips peruse the collection of silver packets until I locate the paracetamol, and pop out two tablets, swallowing them dry. I stand there for a moment, willing the pain to instantly dissipate, but the ache remains, puncturing my every thought. Eventually I pop out a third pill and swallow that down with another shot of water from the tap. All I know is I'm not going to be able to function until my head clears.

*And how is the drinking?*

Dr Winslow's words fire loud in my mind, but shame won't allow me to acknowledge her motivation for asking the question. It's her fault. Had she not started asking me questions about the night when I prayed for death and was left wanting then I wouldn't have felt the need to quieten the voices in my head. I wouldn't have opened the bottle but for her, I tell myself, even though I realise this is probably a lie.

Collecting a mug from the drainer, I fill this from the tap, and slowly carry it through to my bedroom, taking tentative sips until

I am sitting on the edge of the mattress. It smells musty in the room, and I should open a window and tidy up the pile of clean laundry on the chair beside it, but I don't have the energy to start. And then I hear the rumble of voices, and realise this sound must have been what disturbed me.

I can't make out what I'm hearing at first, and close my eyes to focus, trying to pick out any specific words that will help me identify who's speaking and why I can hear it. Sliding off the bed, I crawl on all fours towards the sound, and it's only when the door to the airing cupboard comes into view that I realise the sound is vibrating through the open trapdoor.

I was sure I closed it after Bill helped me carry the bags of groceries up here, and yet I can see the floor is raised through the gap in the door. I shuffle closer, swinging the door open wider so I can better hear the speech, but it's still muffled that I can't make out more than the occasional word. But what is obvious are Danielle's and James's voices. They're arguing again, and the moment I hear the word 'bike' I know what I need to do.

Closing the hatch in the floor, and replacing the rolled carpet, I crawl towards the front door, willing my mind to kick into gear, and inwardly pleading for the pain to yield for long enough that I can deal with the loudest of my tenants before they disturb everyone else.

I make it to the front door, and use the coat stand as a support, dragging myself up it, like a fireman's pole in reverse. It takes all my effort and nearly brings the pole crashing down on me. Finally I'm up, and collect my keys from the hook on the wall, and pull open the door, immediately hit by a welcome blast of cool air that hits like a slap to the face. I tightly grip the handrail as I follow the stairs down to the first floor, and then to the ground, James's and Danielle's voices growing louder and more clear with each step.

'Good, you're here now. Tell her she needs to shift this bloody bike!' James roars the moment he sees me.

Danielle is standing just inside her doorway, the bike in the corridor leading down to the main door where I passed out earlier. James has managed to get past the bike, but there are patches of mud against the grey trousers covering his knees. He's brandishing his briefcase like a shield across his chest, maybe in an effort to protect his shirt and pink tie from the bike.

Despite the throbbing in my head, I know two things: I don't want this disagreement to continue in the hallway where everybody in the building will have front-row seats; and whilst the bike is obstructing access to the front door, James's outburst is over the top.

'Well? Are you going to tell her to shift it?' James says while I try to work out the quickest route to resolution, which isn't easy in my state.

'Where the hell am I supposed to shift it to?' Danielle snaps back. 'Look inside my flat and tell me where I should keep it?'

'Leave it outside where it belongs.'

'And have some toerag steal it? No, thank you. The bike is worth over a thousand pounds, and I need it to get to work. I don't know about you but I can't afford to throw away a thousand pounds without blinking.'

'Oh, so you think it's fair to disrupt the rest of our lives instead then?'

'Disrupting what? All you have to do is walk sideways.'

'Look at my suit trousers. Are you going to pay for them to be dry cleaned?'

'Dry cleaned? That suit is from a supermarket, it doesn't need dry cleaning. I'll put your trousers in my washing machine if that'll please you.'

I step between them, holding out my arms, my fingers splayed, hoping to break the argument.

'I think you both need to calm down. I acknowledge that James is unhappy with Danielle's bike being left in the corridor, but I also understand why Danielle doesn't feel she can leave it outside.'

'It's a bloody fire hazard as well,' James chimes in.

'And how the hell is a bike going to start a fire? It's not rocket-propelled,' Danielle snaps back before I can get a word in edgeways.

'It won't *cause* a fire, but if there was a fire in one of the flats, your bloody bike is blocking the quickest route to the exit. Eve, legally she can't be allowed to obstruct a fire exit, can she?'

I'm not as clued up on regulations as I probably should be, but there is a ring of truth to what James is saying.

'So, if you allow her to keep blocking the corridor, I have every right to report you, and maybe even sue you for breach of contract.'

'Let's just both calm down, please,' I say, raising my voice. 'Shouting isn't going to resolve anything.'

'Well, this is the fourth time I'm complaining about her obstructing the corridor, Eve, and you've done bugger all about it previously, so if shouting is what it takes, then you leave me no other choice.'

I spot Bill's door open a fraction, but he must think twice about coming out, as it quickly closes again.

'Either you do something about this bike once and for all, or you'll leave me no choice but to seek alternative accommodation.'

I despise ultimatums, but the thought of having to let out the flat to prospective new tenants, and all the due diligence that goes hand in hand with it, fills me with anxious dread. And I can't afford to leave the flat unlet for the substantial period it will take for me to vet prospective new tenants.

'I will sort it, James, you don't need to make idle threats,' I say, fixing him with a hard stare.

'Well, you'd better fix this, or I will do it myself.'

He turns on his heel and marches along to Flat 4 before disappearing inside.

'Do you want to come in for a drink?' Danielle asks me, stepping back and heading further inside her flat. I follow through, closing the door behind me, and it is even more obvious now that there is no room for a bike inside this narrow hallway.

Danielle hands me a glass of something cold and white as I emerge into the open-plan living room and kitchen. It's probably the last thing I need, but I want her onside.

'You're going to tell me to leave the bike outside, aren't you?' she asks, pouring herself some wine.

'James is right about it obstructing the fire exit,' I concede, sitting down on the sofa, my legs still unsteady.

'But even the best bike lock in the world won't put off some of the scumbags around here. I'd have to detach my wheels and saddle and bring them inside each night just to be safe. It'll take time and space I don't have, just to please one irritant. I've had no complaints from anyone else, have you?'

In fairness, James is the only person who has raised concerns about the bike being in the way, which is why I've not taken any action until now.

'What if I had a small shed or lock-up space installed just outside the building? Somewhere safe and undercover where you can leave your bike each night, without fear of anyone getting inside it.'

'Really? You'd do that for me?'

'If that would give you more confidence about not leaving the bike in the hallway, then yes, I'm happy to. It means we won't be breaching fire regulations, and will settle things between you and James.'

'Oh my God, yes, that would be brilliant. I'm happy to go with you and pick one out if that would help.' She pauses. 'Oh, sorry, I forgot about...'

'Don't worry about it. I'll do some research online and see what the options are, and share with you before I pick one. How does that sound?'

The smile breaking across her face answers my question.

'You really are the best landlady, do you know that? Always providing above and beyond.'

I don't like to blow my own trumpet, but I can't say it isn't nice to hear positive reinforcement for the care I take of my neighbours.

'And as for that James, I swear to God he's only moaning about the bike because I said I didn't fancy him.'

My ears prick up at this last point, and Danielle must notice my expression change.

'Didn't you know? Oh, yeah, he asked me out not long after I moved in last year, and I politely declined, telling him I'd just got out of an abusive relationship and wasn't looking for anything romantic. But then he followed me to work one day, and it really freaked me out.'

'How do you know he was following you? Maybe he was just going the same way to work.'

She looks momentarily hurt that I have dared question her observation.

'Because of the way he was moving; skulking. When I had to cross a road, he would slow down. I think he thought I didn't know he was there. He hung back and was on the other side of the road, but he kept pace with me. If there hadn't been other people on the street, I don't know what he might have done.'

This sounds nothing like the James I know, but I can't see why Danielle would lie.

'And then our paths crossed one night when I was out with a couple of girlfriends and he was an embarrassment. Clearly drunk and slurring his words, he tried to force his tongue down my throat before moving on to my mates. It makes my blood boil how some men treat women. Do you know what I mean?'

Only too well, I don't say.

# 8

## MONDAY, 9.33 P.M.

The microwave pings to announce dinner is ready, but it's now after nine and my appetite has all but given up. Opening the door, I extract the plate of congealed pasta and yellow cheese sauce, surrounded by a plume of light grey steam. I've not eaten anything substantial all day; breakfast was a handful of cookies; lunch a large packet of crisps; and now dinner a frozen ready meal. I need to do better. There was a time when I enjoyed cooking, but I've lost the urge to be creative, as often more extravagant cooking requires more effort to clean up afterwards. I can practically hear Pete's admonishment if he could see the state of my flat. I really need to devote some time to getting things in order, as it wouldn't surprise me if he arrived unannounced to check up on me.

I do my best to force half the pasta dish down, but even salt does little to elevate the bland offering, and I eventually give up, washing it down with some of the Chardonnay Joan brought this morning.

The James that Danielle described has left me questioning just how well I know him. My interactions with him have always been professional: he's courteous, always pays his rent on time, doesn't worry about trivial matters, and in fact his only murmur of complaint relates to Danielle's bike. He attends the monthly meetings, is happy to muck in when the garden area needs a spruce, but otherwise keeps himself to himself. Or at least that's what I thought until Danielle described the lecherous way she's caught him watching her periodically.

'There have been too many times when he just happens to be in the corridor at the same time as me,' she said. 'Or he just happens to be returning home just as I'm going out, or going out just as I'm returning. I found him wandering about outside my office one evening, and he claimed it was pure coincidence, that he had been visiting a client nearby, but I'd seen him hanging around for several minutes, like he was waiting for the chance encounter.'

Danielle is twenty-six, very attractive, with long red hair, and a smile that brightens any room. Aside from the bike complaint, she's given me no trouble in the last ten months since she moved in. She has so much energy that I feel better about myself whenever I'm around her. I think there are people like that who just manage to bring the best out of others; or the worst in people like James, apparently. I've no reason not to believe Danielle, and I'd like to think that she wasn't just telling me these sordid stories about James to stir up trouble. But it's now made me more wary of him. I don't like the thought of any of my tenants making life less bearable for any of the other residents. I just want everyone to get on and move forward in the same direction. Is that really so much to ask?

I do my best to keep things mellow between everyone, and I thought I had a good handle on who each person is and what pushes their buttons, but Danielle's revelations this evening now have me questioning not only my opinion of James, but that of everyone else.

Of course, Danielle could just be painting James to be more trouble than I think in the event that I have to ask one of them to leave. I can see why she would do that to secure her own future, but I don't want to think that she could be so conniving.

My first step is to order a bike shed that Danielle (and any of the other residents) can use for storing valuables outside. With the bike out of the corridor, James will have no legitimate reason for complaint, and that will allow me to keep a closer eye on his relationship with Danielle. If he continues to find fault, then that would suggest Danielle is right and there's more going on behind those eyes than I've realised. But if things settle again, then maybe I'm just overthinking this, and things can return to normal. It isn't a big wish, but hopefully one I can make come true.

Mind made up, I'm going to go and speak to James now. He will have seen how Danielle invited me in for a glass of wine, and I don't want him to think I'm picking sides in this argument. Ultimately, if I had to choose a victor, his argument is more valid than hers, even though he is making it into more of a problem than it probably is. But I don't want either to think I'm taking sides; I want to remain impartial in my judgement. But I don't want him going to sleep thinking that he needs to find a new home. If I tell him I'm going to order the bike shed and that Danielle has agreed to store her bike in there, then it should buy me a couple of days to find a shed and have it installed.

I stop as I'm about to open the door, hearing Danielle's words in my head: *He followed me to work one day... he hung back and was on the other side of the road, but he kept pace with me. If there hadn't been other people on the street, I don't know what he might have done...*

In an instant I'm transported back to that Halloween night; the sound of quickening footsteps on the wet pavement behind me, and then the tug as arms grabbed my waist and forced me towards the bush.

I grip the frame of the door, willing the flashback out of my head. I'm seeing connections where they don't exist. I have to remember that Danielle has a vested interest in having me question James's motives and behaviours. Five years ago, I didn't know James, and he didn't live in the area. He didn't move south until the first lockdown lifted, a good nine or so months after the mugging and assault.

In all of our interactions, he's never once expressed any kind of sexual interest in me – I'm just not his type. I don't have the glow of someone like Danielle, and where she dresses to accentuate her assets, my wardrobe generally consists of jogging bottoms and loose-fitting tops. I dress for comfort, but that's nothing new. Logically, the man who assaulted me is as likely to be anyone as it is James. There is nothing for me to be afraid of.

And yet I remain rooted to the spot. What if Danielle is right and I've totally underestimated James? What if he's just been waiting all this time to have a second crack at me?

I almost laugh at the ridiculousness of the questions in my head. It's the alcohol talking. And it's not like I have to go into his flat. I'll just knock on his door, and tell him about the shed from the safety of the hallway. I could grab Danielle on the way so the two of us explain what's going to happen so I can start to mend things between them. But then I remember Danielle mentioned she was going to a friend's birthday dinner and wouldn't be back until morning.

I could wait until then to speak to James, but I saw how angry he was earlier, and if that continues to simmer in his subconscious there's a chance the morning will be too late.

I reach for my keys on the hook, and carefully place two of them between my curled knuckles, so I can scratch in the (highly unlikely) event he tries anything. With a deep breath, I head out of my flat and down the first flight of stairs, but stop at the sound of voices as I'm about to descend the next.

Someone is giggling – a woman, I think – and then there's a crash as though someone has crumpled into the wall.

'Shh, you'll wake my neighbours,' I hear James say in a too-loud whisper.

And then suddenly two figures pass by at the foot of the stairs, but I only catch sight of the woman's long black hair and they're gone, and a door slams closed.

I wasn't aware that he'd started dating anybody new; I certainly haven't caught wind of a new romance in the snatches of conversation I've overheard. At least he sounded happy, but my revelation about the bike shed will now have to wait until morning, and I don't like how relieved that makes me feel.

But once back upstairs, my curiosity won't allow my mind to settle, and so I raise the trapdoor in the airing cupboard, and head down the telescopic ladder until I am on the cobweb-covered wooden panels that stretch into the darkness. I ignore these for now, instead, shifting my weight onto the second ladder and continuing my descent. The wooden walkways stretch in both directions, but I continue to my left and then turn left again, squeezing between the breezeblocks, and trying desperately to keep the cobwebs out of my hair.

I can hear them just beyond the wall in front of my face. My nose is only inches from where I can hear them tearing at each other's clothes; the woman squealing with excitement at whatever James is doing to her. I don't want to listen to them having sex, and yet I don't immediately head away. Deep down, I want to hear the sounds of pleasure James makes, just so I can rule him out as the man who attacked me.

And then there's a thud, and particles of plasterboard shimmer down on me like gold dust in the dim light of my phone. I have to pinch my nose to stop myself sneezing and revealing my presence.

But now I'm conscious of just how quiet it's gone inside. What was that thud? My gut tells me something heavy was thrown against the wall, but was that just passion giving way, or have things taken a turn for the worse?

I press my ear against the cool breezeblock, straining to hear anything beyond, and my imagination is making huge leaps, when I hear a small chuckle, and the woman's voice, a hint of an accent that I can't place.

'When my friend said you liked it rough, I didn't think she meant it.'

At least she's still alive, which sates the fearmongering in the back of my head.

'You've no idea,' James's muffled voice comes next. 'Is that okay?'

She laughs gaily again.

'I'm more worried about whether you can handle *me*. On your knees.'

I've heard enough, and immediately step to my right, but my hand knocks against one of the upright beams, and I clutch at air as my phone spills to the floor. I crouch down to pick it up, certain they must have heard the commotion. I remain statuesque, waiting for one of them to speak. Plasterboard particles continue to settle around me as I will time to pass. I don't want to hurry away if they're listening for any sound.

And then the woman screams out with pleasure, and I take it as my cue to bolt.

# 9

## MONDAY, 11.46 P.M.

I stifle a yawn as I make my way to the ladder, satisfied that all is well on the ground floor. Bill is watching what sounded like an old war movie – at least I assume that's what the rat-a-tat-tat machine-gun like noise was. I couldn't hear anything from Caz's flat, but the passageway borders her kitchen, rather than bedroom or living room, so I can't be sure she was even home, although to be fair, Caz isn't much of a party animal; she generally keeps herself to herself, and I really wish I could bring her out of her shell a bit more. Our interactions have been largely limited to the monthly tenants' meeting, but she usually stays pretty quiet. I can't tell if she's intimidated by some of the others, or just introverted by nature. I make a mental note to try and engage with her more.

I couldn't hear anything coming from Danielle's flat either, but I'd imagine she's probably fast asleep following another intense day at the hospital. I hope she's not too embittered by James's verbal assault earlier. I can't stand it when my tenants don't get along. I'm sure the bike lock-up outside will smooth things out for James, and subsequently with Danielle too. I'll let him know about it first thing to buy myself a couple of days to pick and purchase something. I reach Flat 4, and feel dirty when I hear the sound of groaning coming from inside. I never realised just how adventurous James is, and it doesn't quite fit with Danielle's description of him earlier. The James she painted was someone capable of stalking, but I've never seen that side of him. But, given his ultimatum, it wouldn't surprise me if Danielle felt the need to embellish slightly to keep me onside.

I can't bear to listen to James and his guest any longer, and creep quietly along the passageway, until I'm at the foot of the ladder and slowly begin to climb. There isn't anything concerning coming from Mike's and Fi's flats, but that doesn't surprise me, given the time. Mike is a teacher and Fi works at a solicitor's firm, somewhere in the city, so they'd be mad to burn the candle at both ends. I can actually hear the sound of Mike's snoring vibrating through the wall.

I stifle another yawn as I tiptoe towards India's flat, but this time I do hear the rumble of voices from within. I can't quite make out what's being said, so I press my ear against the ice-cold brickwork, now able to make out the faint sound of India's voice.

'And I don't understand why he'd believe he'd ever have a chance with me,' she says. 'He's just so... gangly. No man should be that tall and that skinny, and those large, square glasses do not help him. He looks like that American serial killer, you know the one they did a Netflix show about?'

'Jeffrey Dahmer?' I hear a second woman's voice say.

'Yeah, that's the one. Do you know what I mean? Mike could be Dahmer's twin, almost.' She laughs at this. 'Why he chose that style of glasses is beyond me! I know you can't shine a turd, but you can make it look more presentable. Some designer glasses that better suit the shape of his face, and a bit of time at the gym so it doesn't look like the skin is hanging off his body would be steps in the right direction.'

'You could always suggest that to him,' says the second voice.

'No, no, no. I can't stand being in the same room with him. He's so creepy looking, and I think he thinks he's flirting with me whenever I'm around, and I don't want to encourage him.' She pauses, but I don't hear the other woman speak. 'Can I let you in on a secret? It's really bad, and you can't tell anyone else.' Another pause. 'I told him that Fi is single and interested in him.'

Their shrill laughter sends a shiver down my spine.

'I know that's really evil, but I thought if she became the new object of his affections, he'd stop bothering me. Does that make me an evil person?'

'Maybe, but poor Fi. You'd have been better off telling him Eve fancies him; if anyone deserves Mike's weird infatuation it's her.'

I frown at the mention of my name, and realise exactly who India is talking to.

'I don't understand what your problem is with Eve. Sure, she's a bit too involved in what we're all up to, but I've had worse landlords than her.'

'I'm sure she's trying to steal Chad from me. I caught the two of them outside my flat this morning. She wasn't even dressed, just wearing a bathrobe, and I swear she would have flashed him if I hadn't stepped out when I did.'

I think back to Jenny's warning this morning: *I'm not someone to be fucked with, Eve. I'm on to you.*

'Oh, come on, you're twice the woman she is, and I can't imagine Chad would ever look at her twice.'

'I hear him slipping out sometimes. He says he's going for a run, but what if he's actually sneaking up to her flat?'

'I'm sure that isn't the case, Jenny. You're a knockout, and

Chad would be a fool to be carrying on with anyone else; especially someone like Eve.'

These comments hurt more than I want to admit. Although I have no interest in Chad, I expected more respect from two women who I've been nothing but supportive to.

I feel a tingling in my nose and it's all I can do to hurry along the platform to the gap between the flats, and grab my nose to try and minimise the sound of my sneeze. I remain perfectly still, trying to gauge whether either of them could have heard the sound. I think I was far enough away, but I don't want to give them reason to question what's going on behind the walls, so I head back up the ladder to my own floor. I've learned two things tonight: firstly, I need to help Mike find a love interest outside this building; and secondly, I need to avoid being seen alone with Chad, otherwise Jenny might act on her suspicions.

## 10

### TUESDAY, 9.11 A.M.

My ringing phone starts me awake, but I don't immediately reach for it, trying to get my bearings as fog swamps my mind. There is daylight streaming through the curtains, which means I need to get up, but it really doesn't feel like it's been that long since my head hit the pillow. The clock on my bedside table says it's after nine, and it was on three when I last checked it, so I must have got some sleep, even though I still feel exhausted.

The phone stops ringing, much to my relief, and I'm tempted just to roll over and go back to sleep. One of the problems with being self-employed is that I don't get paid when I pull a sickie. But maybe I could stay here until lunchtime, and then get up. I don't rest and unwind nearly enough, and maybe this brain fog is my body's way of telling me I need a break to recover.

George raises his weary head from the duvet as the phone rings again, and I grizzle as I realise that fate is telling me today is not for rest. I snatch my phone from the charging dock, and almost cancel the call when I see Pete's name on the screen. He's phoned five times already, and the fact that he's still ringing means he's unlikely to stop if I don't answer. There's also a chance he'll turn up unannounced if I decline his call.

'Morning,' I say, with a fake cheeriness.

'Finally,' he sighs. 'Why are you still in bed so late?'

'Who said I'm in bed? I've just come out of the shower.'

'Oh. Well, that's good.'

'I've got a million and one things to get done today, was your call for any particular reason?'

'You've forgotten what day it is, haven't you?'

My eyelids snap open, as panic strikes the side of my head. It's Tuesday, I think, but what is the significance of that?

'Um, no, of course I haven't,' I murmur, pushing the duvet back and hurrying through to the kitchen, studying the calendar on the wall.

'Happy birthday,' I say when I see the date.

'Thank you. Your card and gift haven't turned up yet.'

'Oh, haven't they?' I bite at my fingernails. 'Damned postal service! I ordered both weeks ago, and they were supposed to be delivered today. Maybe they'll turn up in a few hours. Sorry.'

I grind my teeth, waiting to hear whether he's bought the lie.

'Can't be helped,' he says, but that neither confirms nor denies whether he believes me.

'Have you got any nice plans for the day?'

'No, nothing special. I was hoping my little sister would phone me up and invite me out for dinner somewhere...'

It's my turn to sigh.

'You know I can't do that.'

'No, I know you *choose* not to do it. Can't you make an exception for your big brother? Please? It is my birthday.'

Some things never change.

'It really isn't a choice, and you know that. God knows I've told you often enough.'

'What does Dr Winslow have to say about it?'

Legally, I know Winslow isn't allowed to disclose the details of our sessions to Pete, even though he pays for them, but the two of them used to go to school together, and so I'm not certain she doesn't let the occasional titbit slip out.

'My sessions with Dr Winslow are private.'

'I know, but I'm curious to know whether she thinks your refusal to leave is healthy or not.'

I roll my eyes, willing myself not to rise to the bait. There is condensation on the inside of the windows, so I cross and open the main one, the sun painfully bright, but the cool air a welcome relief.

'Are you still there?' he asks, when I don't respond.

'That depends, are you going to keep criticising me? If you are then I'm hanging up.'

'No, don't do that. Listen, I'm sorry, but you know it's just because I'm worried about you, sis. Regardless of what you and Dr Winslow may say, it isn't healthy to isolate yourself in the way that you are.'

'I have George,' I say, running my hand between his ears as he purrs with satisfaction.

'You need to socialise and meet *people*.'

'I am sociable with the people I live with.'

'They're your tenants, it doesn't count.'

'Of course it does. We talk about all sorts.'

'That's as may be, but you're forgetting two important distinctions. Firstly, they have to pay you rent, so any kindness they show you is sort of a requirement of keeping their landlord onside. And secondly, it's not like you're going out to socialise with them. It's not like you're getting away from the same dreary walls and routine.'

'I like routine.'

The line crackles as he sighs into it again.

'How about I pick up some takeaway for us both and come round tonight?'

My eyes slowly pan around the room. The line of empty bottles beside the sink, the waste containers of food beside them because the dustbin is overflowing. The dust clinging to virtually every surface. I inwardly groan. The last thing I need is Pete coming over and judging me, but he's going to think I'm hiding something if I make up an excuse.

'That sounds good,' I force myself to say.

'Great! Chinese or Indian?'

'It's your birthday, you choose. You know what I like from both.'

'Okay, okay. What time should I come around. Is seven okay?'

'Sure, I'll see you then.'

The call ends and my eyes fall on the detritus of the flat once more. I'm really in no mood to be cleaning up, but I know the longer I leave it, the worse it will be. I should be starting work on the bakery campaign for Lauren and her overly protective brother Tim, but cleaning will weigh on my mind until I get it done.

I collect yesterday's t-shirt from the floor and give it a cursory sniff, my nose wrinkling at the whiff. It's been weeks since I emptied the laundry basket, and I've no doubt that will be the first place Pete checks. I carry the t-shirt over to the yellow plastic bin and lift the lid, but no amount of squashing it in will make it fit, so I carry the bin back into the kitchen, and turn it upside down. Weeks of worn clothes tumble to the floor as I shake the bin. There is a spectrum of colours by my feet, but I don't have time to waste separating the items, so I shovel up as many garments as I can hold and squash them into the drum. I load the remaining items, and then toss in a laundry pod and set the machine to start. It sputters and coughs before the drum begins to spin. At thirty degrees, the colours shouldn't run.

Returning the laundry bin to the corner of my bedroom, I make the bed, plumping the pillows and duvet. I should probably strip and change the bedding too, but I need to wait until the washing machine has finished its current load. Heading to the bathroom, I stop when I see the hatch in the airing cupboard is still raised. I used to double-check it was closed every night before I went to bed, but like so many things, it's another standard I've allowed to slip. I'm about to lower the hatch when I hear a woman's scream. I freeze, straining to hear anything more, uncertain I didn't imagine it in this state of hangover. But then I hear a second yelp echo through the hole in the floor.

Throwing on my robe, I hurry out of the flat, taking the stairs down two at a time. I hear Danielle before I see her. She is standing by James's door, and is thumping a balled fist against it.

'I know you're in there,' she screams. 'Open up.'

Caz is poking her head out from behind the door of Flat 3, but nods gratefully when she sees me at the foot of the stairs, before closing it again.

'I know you took it!' Danielle shouts at James's door.

'Danielle, please calm down,' I say in my most reassuring voice.

There's venom in her eyes when she turns, but it quickly dissipates when she realises it's me.

'Oh, good, I'm glad you're here. Maybe you can tell this thief to open up and give it back.'

I step closer, deliberately keeping my voice low, and hoping Danielle follows suit.

'Why don't you take a deep breath, and then tell me what's happened.'

'What's happened is this arsehole has stolen my bike, and now I'm going to be late for work.'

I hadn't noticed the lack of bike in the corridor until she mentioned it.

'You think James has taken your bike?'

'No, I *know* that arsehole has taken it.'

'Wait, back up, you saw him move your bike?'

'No, because he's too sneaky, but I've just come out of my flat and the bike is gone.'

'You didn't move it somewhere else last night?'

'No! Why would I? You said you were going to buy a bike shed for outside but I could continue to use the corridor until it arrives.'

I take a step backwards, staring at the space where the bike has spent most nights propped up. There is a muddy tyre tread print on the pale carpet, but nothing a soapy clean won't get out.

'Did you hear anyone moving about in the corridor during the night?'

'No, but I didn't get home until gone twelve.'

'Wait, I thought you were staying away last night.'

'I was going to, but then a friend asked if I'd cover her shift this morning so I came home instead.'

'And the bike was here when you got home?'

'Yes.'

I stare at James's door. It's not an unreasonable assumption to leap to, given he's the only person who's gone out of their way to complain about the bike. I look at my watch and it's well after nine. James has usually gone to work by this time, but I cross to the door and knock on it.

'James, it's Eve, can you open the door, please?' Seconds pass, but I don't hear any movement from inside, so I try again. 'James, it's Eve,' I say, louder this time. 'Please open the door.'

*The Tenants*

'Can't you just go in?' Danielle badgers from my shoulder. 'You have spare keys for all the flats, don't you?'

'Yes,' I say turning and sighing, 'but I can't just enter without forewarning.'

'But he's either not home, or he's pretending he's not there, and I need my bike to get to work. All you need to do is unlock the door, so I can get my bike and be on my way. You can have a word with him to sort out this mess when he returns.'

I knock at the door again, this time pressing my ear against it, but can't hear anything over the sound of my own heartbeat.

'James, if you don't open the door, I'm going to be forced to use my own key to gain entry.'

There's still no sound from inside, so I reach into the pocket of my robe and extract the keyring, finding the one numbered with four and insert it into the lock. I count to three before turning the key and pushing the door open. I'm hit with a burst of warm air from within. There's no sign of Danielle's mountain bike in the narrow corridor, so I step further inside, announcing my arrival in case James is still fast asleep in bed.

The door to the small bathroom is ajar, but a quick glance confirms the bike isn't in there so I continue to the living room, slowly opening the door, but Danielle pushes past me before I can stop her. And then she lets out a bloodcurdling scream.

## 11

### TUESDAY, 9.19 A.M.

I find Danielle still screaming just inside the doorway to the living room, but I'm not expecting to see James hanging from the ceiling rose in the centre of the room. His face is so puffed up that he's almost unrecognisable, but he's wearing the same shirt and trousers I saw him in yesterday.

My instinct is to try to help him, so I hurry over to the body and try to lift his legs onto my shoulders in the hope that there's still life in him. But I instantly feel the dead weight bearing down on my back, and realise my efforts are futile.

'Phone an ambulance,' I call out to Danielle, who is just standing there, her mouth agape but sound no longer emerging. The blood has drained from her face as she continues to stare up at James.

'Danielle, please,' I say again, stooping to extract myself from James's legs.

'Is he...?' she gasps, and I force myself to look back up at him.

'I think so,' I confirm, neglecting to mention how cold and stiff his legs felt in my hands.

I left my phone upstairs in my flat, so when Danielle extracts hers from her pocket, her fingers trembling, I take it from her and place the call.

This isn't the first dead body I've seen, but previous experience isn't making this any easier. I think back to late last night when I heard him and his guest desperately tearing each other's clothes from their bodies. He didn't sound depressed, nor as if he was contemplating ending it all. It just doesn't make sense.

I tell Danielle we should probably wait outside until the police and paramedics arrive, but I have to lead her out and back to her flat. Bill and Caz are peering out of their respective doorways, alerted by Danielle's scream. I tell them everything is fine and to go back inside their flats. I hate lying to them, but I need to buy myself some time to process what I've just seen. I make strong tea for us both and sit her down at the small square table in her living room. She is frozen, barely blinking, almost like she's in a trance.

'Drink the tea,' I instruct, placing the cup before her. 'I added sugar because it's supposed to be good for shock.'

She finally notices the cup, but makes no effort to pick it up.

'I can't believe it,' she whispers. 'Is this a dream?'

'I wish it was,' I say, perching on the edge of the sofa.

'Do you think he did it because... because of me?'

I frown at the question, internally dismissing it.

'What makes you say that?'

'Because he was annoyed about my bike being in the hallway. You saw how angry he was yesterday. What if I'm the reason...?' Her words trail off as her voice cracks with emotion.

'There could be a million and one reasons why James felt that was his only way out, but I'm certain it had nothing to do with your bike.'

'What about the fact that I rejected him when he asked me out? Could that have tipped him over the edge?'

I don't want to mention what I heard and saw last night, so I simply shake my head instead.

'I'd be very surprised if it was anything to do with that. I don't think you can blame yourself for what happened.'

Her eyes snap up to mine.

'Do *you* blame yourself?'

The question throws me.

'No, why would I?'

'I know how proud you are of meeting all of our needs, so I'd understand if this made you feel like you'd failed James.'

The statement is like a kick to the stomach. It hadn't even crossed my mind that there might have been more I could have done to support him, but now it's all I can think about.

Were his complaints about Danielle's bike really a cry for help? Should I have spent less time trying to find a solution to the disagreement and more time asking James what the real root cause of his unhappiness was? Would it really have taken a lot of effort for me to knock on his door and have an honest conversation? If I'd twigged how unhappy he was, I could have put him in touch with Dr Winslow. Danielle is right: I could have done more.

And now the guilt of that insight is overwhelming.

'Did he have any family we should contact?' Danielle asks next.

'Um, I'm not sure. I can't remember. I'll check my notes and see what I can find out.'

'Your notes?'

I realise now what I've just said and my mind spins with questions about how to dig myself out of this hole.

'I meant the tenancy agreement he signed when he moved in,' I say quickly. 'There are next of kin details on there I think, um, so I'll have a look and see what I can find.'

I don't look at her for what feels like an age, clenching my jaw and hoping she doesn't ask any more questions about the copious notes I keep on each of them. I'm relieved when an uneasy silence falls across the room, and the knot in my stomach unwinds a fraction.

Within ten minutes, there are two police officers at the door, swiftly followed by two paramedics. I let them into the building and use my skeleton keys to open James's door. They ask me so many questions that my head spins, but I do my best to answer them.

His name is James. No, he didn't seem unhappy. I last saw him yesterday. No, I don't know what time it happened.

One of the officers, a woman with short, spiky, bleached blonde hair asks me if we can talk privately, and I suggest we go up to my flat, but it's only when I'm opening the door that I remember how messy it is inside.

'Cleaner's day off,' I muse as I show her in and ask if she wants a cup of tea or coffee.

She doesn't immediately answer, doing little to hide the fact her eyes are scanning every nook and cranny.

'No, I'm fine, thank you. But please make yourself one if you wish.'

I can feel the adrenaline wearing off and ideally I'd have something a lot stronger than coffee, but fill the kettle, reminding myself that the sooner I answer her questions, the sooner I can get on with my day.

'You're the landlady here, is that right?' she asks, leaning against the counter and noticing the empty bottles in the sink.

'Yes, that's right. I inherited the building from my father when he passed.'

'Oh, I'm sorry to hear that. How long ago did that happen?'

'It's fine. It was six or so years ago, so it doesn't hurt like it once did.'

'Forgive my bluntness, Eve, but how old are you?'

'Thirty-one. What does that have to do with anything?'

'Oh, nothing, sorry, it just seems like a big responsibility. And it's a bit unusual for a landlord or -lady to live on the premises.'

'Is it? Well, I like being needed, so being at the beck and call of my residents is something I enjoy.'

'Do they make a lot of demands then?'

'Nothing too unreasonable, no.'

'And do most of your tenants get along okay?'

'Generally speaking, yes. We have a monthly gathering where grievances can be aired.'

'So there are some issues between the tenants?'

I don't know what she's getting at.

'We're all adults living under one very large roof, and we're all from different walks of life, so yes, inevitably there can be occasional friction, but no more than in the average household.'

'Tell me about James.'

'What do you want to know?'

'What was he like?'

I consider the question.

'He was a good tenant. Always paid his rent on time. I think he worked for an IT company, but I'm really not sure.'

'Did any of his neighbours have any *grievances* – as you described them – with James?'

I don't know whether I should mention what Danielle told me in confidence last night, about James making a pass at her, and her belief that he was going out of his way to be around her. I have no evidence that it is true, and I saw the other officer taking Danielle away to speak to, so it's probably more her place to say than mine.

*The Tenants* 73

'No, not that I can immediately recall.'

'And did James have any issues with other tenants?'

I should probably mention the bike situation, but I don't want to cause Danielle trouble over something so trivial, especially when we'd managed to resolve it last night. God knows, she was already feeling guilty enough without the police harassing her.

'Nothing springs to mind,' I say, worried she'll pick up on the deceit in my tone.

'What about friends or significant others? Was there anybody special in James's life?'

I picture the woman with the long black hair disappearing towards his room, but I have no idea who she is or how long they've been seeing one another.

'Not that I'm aware of, but I don't keep tabs on my tenants twenty-four-seven.'

I really hope she can't see the sweat pooling at my hairline.

'You were the one who phoned to report the death, right?'

I nod.

'Can you talk me through what led to that call?'

'Um, I'd entered James's flat to speak to him about something, and that's when we found the body.'

'We?'

'Um, yeah, sorry one of the tenants, Danielle, was with me.'

'Do you make a habit of entering your tenants' homes unannounced?'

'No, it wasn't like that. I knocked several times, but there was no answer.'

Her brow furrows.

'So, why did you enter the property?'

I'm unintentionally tying myself up in knots. I should have mentioned the argument about Danielle's bike, but if I now correct myself it is going to seem suspicious. What is it they say about becoming tangled in a web of lies?

'Danielle believed that James might have taken her bicycle, and so that's why I was trying to speak to him. As I said, I knocked several times and then assumed he'd already left for work, and so I used my key to enter his flat to search for the bike. And that's when we found him.'

'Wait, you allowed this Danielle to enter his flat as well?'

I know what she's getting at, and if I could go back and redo things this morning I would, but it is what it is.

'She was running late for work and desperate to find her bike, and—'

'Did she find it?'

The interruption temporarily throws me. In all the hubbub since finding James, I haven't thought about where Danielle's bike is. It definitely wasn't inside James's flat, so does that mean someone else has taken it?

'Um, no, the bike wasn't inside the flat.'

'Why did she think it would be?'

'James had complained about her storing her bike indoors in the corridor and so she thought he might have hidden it out of spite.'

I see her jot a note on her pad.

'So there was trouble between them?'

'No, I wouldn't say trouble, and it was all resolved last night anyway, so I'm sure it had nothing to do with why he decided to... well, do what he did.'

'Resolved how?'

'I'm arranging for a storage unit to be delivered so that Danielle can secure her bike outside the property.'

'And James knew this?'

## The Tenants

I think back to last night. I'd intended to tell him until I saw him with that woman.

'Yes, he did,' I lie, wanting to dig Danielle out of the hole I've created around her.

'When did this all get resolved?'

'Last night, around six or seven o'clock, I think. I can't be sure exactly when as I didn't look at the time, but it was after they'd both returned from work.'

'So why did Danielle believe he might have hidden her bike in his flat?'

I close my eyes as I realise I've made matters worse.

'I don't know. I heard Danielle banging on his door this morning and trying to get him to open up. That's why I went down to try and resolve whatever was going on, and that's why I allowed Danielle into his flat to look for the bike.'

'Are you in the habit of letting yourself into your tenants' properties when they're not at home?'

'No, of course I'm not, and I resent the implication.'

'I didn't mean to offend, I just can't follow the logic. If this disagreement between them wasn't serious, as you've said, and you claim it was resolved last night, why would James take her bike?'

'He didn't. It wasn't in his flat. I think Danielle just leapt to the wrong conclusion.'

'And when you spoke to them both last night between six and seven, that was the last time you saw James?'

I've painted myself into a corner now. If I mention seeing him later in the evening, she's going to ask why I was heading to his flat, but I've lied and said he already knew about the bike shed. If I correct my story now, it's going to call my actions further into question.

'Yes, it was.'

'And how did he seem when you spoke to him?'

'He was fine. Happy, I guess.'

'Happy?'

'Maybe that's the wrong word. He seemed satisfied that the bike would no longer be in the corridor.'

She closes her notepad.

'Okay, thank you, Eve, I appreciate what you've witnessed this morning will have been a shock. Have you got anyone you can phone and speak to so it doesn't continue to play on your mind?'

'I'll be fine,' I say. 'My brother is stopping by later today.'

'Good. Good. If you think of anything else, please do give us a call.'

I show her to the door, and slide down it once it's closed. Danielle was right: I should have done more to make sure James was okay. I'm going to have to double my efforts with the other tenants.

## 12

### TUESDAY, 11.30 A.M.

It takes an hour or so to find the motivation to get dressed and attack the detritus of my home. I start small, making my bed and emptying the overflowing laundry basket into the washing machine. I open the windows in my bedroom and living room in an effort to vanquish the staleness, and then chase it out with squirts of air freshener. And then I attack the kitchen, filling a black sack with junk food containers and empty bottles. I allow my mind to think about James and how well he hid his apparent depression. Like most, I was under the impression he had his life pretty well sorted, but it's impossible to know what goes on behind closed doors. Looking down at the bag in my hand, it seems James isn't the only person hiding things.

James moved south following some work troubles from what I managed to uncover when he applied to move in. My first impression of him wasn't great, but during the interview he broke down in tears and pleaded with me, and that vulnerability, that desperation, moved me. He accepted culpability for his past, citing stress at work and a reckless affair, and I could hear how bad he felt about it. Was that a sign? Should I have foreseen that this is where things would end? My notes don't mention anything about family, and I can't immediately recall whether he mentioned any siblings in passing. There will be a funeral to arrange, and at some point I'm going to have to get the flat listed again. Am I obliged to mention to future tenants that someone died in the flat? I'll hire professional cleaners to come and scour the place, and in fact maybe I'll get someone in to redecorate it. I worry that mentioning what's happened might put off some future prospects.

I really don't need the added stress of searching for a new tenant, that was the situation I was trying to avoid by agreeing to buy a bike shed for Danielle to use.

I inwardly curse. I should have knocked on his door last night. I avoided it because he was with that woman, but maybe if I'd knocked on the door and interrupted them, and told him about the bike shed, then maybe he wouldn't have...

The 'what if' game is a pointless one. I didn't speak to him and now it's too late. Ultimately, it might have made no difference anyway. I doubt it was a spur-of-the-moment decision, so it might have made no difference. I just wish I'd done more so I didn't feel so guilty.

George rubs himself against my legs as I tie the handles of the sack. If Pete witnessed the state of my flat it would only serve to strengthen his opinion that I'm unwell, but the alcohol and ready meals are the coping strategy I use to balance my time. What he doesn't understand is how much effort it takes to run my business *and* take care of my tenants. It's more than a fulltime job.

'I'm not like James,' I say out loud.

And it's true. I'm not depressed. I'm terrified of the world beyond the front door. But given what happened the last time I was out there and alone, I've good reason to be scared. It's almost like he's forgotten that I was attacked, even though he accompanied me when I made multiple statements to the police in the vain hope they'd catch the monster responsible. What kind of person can do something so vicious and vulgar and still sleep at night? It's beyond comprehension. My conscience wouldn't let me rest.

I start at a banging on my door and check the time on my phone. Pete said he wouldn't arrive until after seven, but it would be typical of him to turn up early and try to catch me out. Well, not today, buddy.

Smugly, I cross to the door, and open it, startled when I see Bill staring back at me.

'Oh, is that for me?' he asks, staring down at the black sack I'm still holding.

'Um, yes,' I say, trying to compose myself. 'Um, if you could take it out for me that would be grand.'

Bill takes the sack from me, but places it on the floor just outside of the door.

'I'll take it down in a minute, but can I speak to you about something first?'

His face looks pasty, but I can't tell if that's the exertion of climbing two flights of stairs, or if his health is worsening. He was diagnosed with Type 2 diabetes last year, and although his daughter does come to visit occasionally, it isn't nearly often enough.

'Come in,' I say, stepping back. 'Can I make you a cup of tea?'

'Oh, no, I won't keep you long,' he says, entering, and then hovering in the kitchen.

I fill the kettle regardless, and then usher him towards the sofa, now noticing the sweat beading at the edges of his nest of silver hair.

'Oh, thank you,' he says, his face hanging low. 'I take it you've heard about James?'

I nod.

'Yes, Danielle and I were the ones who found him.'

Bill's eyes widen, and he reaches out and gives my hand a gentle squeeze.

'How are you holding up?'

I shrug because I don't know how else to answer the question.

'Lots of police about downstairs. They're knocking on everyone's doors, asking whether James was depressed or not.'

If I didn't know how bad things were for him, I doubt any of the other residents would know, but I don't say this to Bill.

'It's just such a shock,' I say instead. 'I only spoke to him yesterday, and I can't believe he's gone.'

He gives a gentle squeeze again.

'Death's pretty sneaky like that. One day you think you have a future and then poof, it's all gone. I wish I'd known it was Elsie's last day. I certainly wouldn't have gone out to the bookies. I'd have stayed home and spent every second with her. It's my biggest regret.'

'I'm sorry, Bill.'

'No need to feel sorry for me. Elsie and I shared forty-two years of love and happiness, so I feel very lucky. And, if she hadn't gone first, I never would have met you.'

He smiles warmly, but I think I'm the lucky one to have Bill here, especially after losing Dad.

'Did you...' I begin, but I'm not sure what I hope he says. 'Did you have any idea that James was so unhappy?'

He shakes his head, but his face droops again.

'I had very little to do with him, to be honest. I knew the bike in the corridor bothered him, he made no secret of that, but apart from the occasional hello when passing, I didn't know much about him. Kept himself to himself most of the time.'

Mention of the bike stirs something in my mind.

'You don't happen to know what happened to Danielle's bike, do you?'

'I don't follow. Has something happened to it?'

'It's missing apparently. It was in the corridor last night, but was gone when Danielle was trying to leave for work. That's why... that's why we went to James's flat. She thought he might have hidden it inside to teach her a lesson or something.'

'I don't know what all the fuss was about. I know it didn't block my way to the front door, but on the odd occasion I've come up to see you, it's never been a problem. There's plenty of space to squeeze through.'

I think back to the muddy stains on James's trousers, but could he have deliberately been trying to get Danielle into trouble?

'What did you want to speak to me about?' I ask Bill, bringing my mind back to the present.

'Given what's happened, and the prospect that the police will probably hang about until they've spoken to everyone, I wondered whether it would be an idea to call an emergency tenants' meeting. I imagine some are at work at the moment and don't even know what's happened. It would make sense for you to share the news with everyone to stop any rumours spreading.'

It's a valid point, and not something I'd thought about, but Bill's right, in times of crisis, communities need a leader; someone to take control and provide reassurance.

'It would also give you the chance to see everyone's reactions to the news,' he continues.

'What do you mean?'

He studies my face as if trying to read it.

'In case one of the residents was involved,' he adds when I don't respond.

'Involved how?'

He shrugs.

'I overheard two of the police officers talking. The man in uniform was talking to an Asian lady in a suit and trousers. A detective, I think.'

I hate that there's still a generation that feel the need to mention a person's ethnicity when it happens to be anything other than Caucasian.

'Anyway,' he continues, 'I caught them saying something about marks on his wrists, like they'd been tied at some point. They're not convinced James hung himself voluntarily.'

I frown at this statement, sensing Bill is letting his imagination run away with him.

'The officer who interviewed me didn't mention anything like that.'

'They wouldn't though, would they? In case you were the one who did it.'

'Wait, Bill, I had nothing—'

'Well, I know that,' he interrupts. 'Of course I do. But that doesn't mean someone else we live with isn't involved.'

I shake my head at how ridiculous he sounds.

'But who and why?'

'Beats me. But if you call a meeting tonight and break the news to everyone, I can keep an eye on others' reactions, and maybe the killer will let something slip.'

I try to keep the smile from my face. I know Bill is a fan of TV crime dramas, but I never took him for an amateur sleuth.

He stands, and straightens the legs of his trousers.

'Just think about it. Yes?'

I tell him I will let everyone know we need to meet, and show

Bill to the door, watching as he collects my rubbish sack, ready to take it to the bins outside.

'Just ask yourself this,' he says as he reaches the top of the stairs. 'Who had most to gain from James dying?'

He doesn't elaborate, heading down the stairs while I close the door. There's only one person with anything close to resembling a gain from James's untimely passing and that's Danielle. But she's a nurse, and I can't imagine she's capable of it. But then, maybe it's impossible to really know what people are willing to do.

## 13

### TUESDAY, 1.20 P.M.

I've been sitting at my laptop for over an hour, but the screen remains blank. I should have started sketching ideas for Lauren's new venture by now, but I can't stop thinking about what Bill said.

*I overheard two of the police officers talking... They're not convinced James hung himself voluntarily.*

I don't remember seeing anything to make me doubt that James tied the rope around his own neck, but my memories of what I saw are splintered at best. I remember the shock of walking into the room when Danielle started screaming, and I remember seeing the figure dangling from the ceiling rose, but then I looked away – I had to. I didn't want to see James hanging there; I was desperate to get away.

Were there marks on his wrists? I didn't look. At no point did I consider that he wasn't there of his own volition. It just makes no sense. If I wanted to kill someone, I'd use a knife, or drug them in some way. I wouldn't go to the effort of trying to lift them into a homemade noose. And why would James allow that to happen? Why didn't he fight back? Why didn't he scream out?

'Stop thinking about James,' I say aloud, hoping the affirmation will kick my creative instinct into gear. 'Focus on the marketing campaign.'

I write the name of the bakery on the blank page on the screen, and then draw some arrows, trying to focus on what Lauren said about the proposed business model. Minutes pass, and despite my best efforts, I can't maintain my concentration, and close the lid of my laptop. I know Lauren and Tim are expecting to see initial ideas by the end of the week, but with my mind not engaged, anything I do today will be rubbish. I'll just have to start again in the morning when I've come to terms with what has happened.

I head into my bedroom and lie down, the cool touch of the duvet cradling me while I focus on my breathing, trying to kick-start my body into relaxing. I can hear birds cheeping in the tall oak tree out on the main road, and the occasional passing car. I think about all the sights and sounds I'll never experience again because of the agoraphobia. The smell of almonds roasting in sugar at Christmas. Dad would always buy us a bag as a reward for helping him pick out Mum's Christmas present. I miss the crunch on my teeth and the sweetness on my tongue. I tried to make my own version last Christmas but the sugar burned and I couldn't get the pan cleaned afterwards so it ended up in the bin.

I'll never hear the excited chatter of children playing in the school yard when I walk past. I'll never see the sun setting over the sea. I'll never smell the first mown grass of spring when everything feels fresh and full of potential. I'll never feel the cold snap of winter on my cheeks. All these experiences have been stolen from me by the man who attacked me that night. He'll never know just how much he took from me. And the worst part is he's still out there somewhere. He could live on this road for all I know. How many times might he have walked past my window and I didn't realise? Has he ever stopped and looked up and lingered on the memory of his crime? Does it bring him remorse, or does he savour the thrill of knowing he got away with it?

This is no good. I wanted to stop thinking about James, but I didn't want to wallow in the mess of my own life either. I need to know for certain whether I missed something with James, or whether Bill is right and someone else is responsible. My eyes fall on the airing cupboard door, and I know what I need to do now. Swinging my legs from the bed, I slip on trainers, and cross to the door, swinging it open, before lifting the trapdoor. A cloud of dust shimmers up out of the darkness, and I reach for the torch hanging from the pin in the wall, and switch it on.

The telescopic ladder stares back up at me. I still remember the first time I discovered the hole in my floor. The child in me imagined it was a passageway to a magical world where everything was just brighter and easier and happier. There was a wooden ladder here before, but it used to creak and whine whenever I used it, so I replaced it. The old one is still down there somewhere. Not going out made it difficult to dispose of without raising questions.

Dad was already dead when I moved in, but I can only assume he was the one who put the wooden ladder there. He never lived here like me, but this flat was used for storage, so never let before. I can't say for certain, but he must have known about the passageway, and it's not something I dare tell anyone else about. I'm sure it wouldn't bother most of the tenants to know there are hidden walkways behind the walls, but some – and I'm thinking Jenny here – would have a problem with it. I still don't know why she was so off with me yesterday morning. I had planned to try and clear the air but with everything else it slipped my mind. I make a mental note to try and speak to her after this evening's tenants' meeting.

Taking a deep breath of clean air, I slowly descend the ladder until I reach the wooden board. It's so dusty down here with fibre insulation lining a lot of the walls, in addition to eroding plasterboard. If I stay down here too long I'll spend the rest of the night coughing. I continue down to the ground floor, and tiptoe towards the wall where I heard James and his guest in the throes of passion last night. Delicately placing my ear to the cold brickwork, I strain to hear the conversation on the other side of the wall.

At first it's just a gentle mumble of incoherent voices. I hadn't thought, but with James hanging himself in the living room, most of the conversation will probably be centred there, and away from the kitchen. But I remain where I am, still listening.

I can't believe it's barely twelve hours since I last heard James alive and well. A memory stirs.

*When my friend said you liked it rough, I didn't think she meant it.*

There was thudding to suggest their sex was maybe masochistic in some way. Bill said they found markings on James's wrists, but nobody has asked whether there could be another cause for them. If he was role-playing with that woman in some way, that might explain those markings. I neglected to mention the woman when I made my statement to the officer in my flat, but maybe if I tell them, they'll realise that there is no foul play at work here. But how do I now amend my statement without dropping myself in it?

'Bring me up to speed,' a woman's voice says, startling me.

'Right, ma'am. Victim was discovered a little after nine this morning by two neighbours. One is the landlady Eve Pennington, who lives in Flat 9, on the top floor. The other was Danielle Jacobs, who lives in Flat 2, and was apparently searching for a missing bicycle. She believed the victim may have brought it into his flat and so she demanded the landlady open the flat for her to search.'

'What's your reading of the two women?'

'The woman from Flat 2 admits to not getting along with the victim. They'd had one or two comings together in the last six months because she would leave her bike in the corridor and he didn't like it. She's a nurse at the ICU at the General Hospital and won't be back until this evening.'

'Anything to the disputes between them?'

'Nothing significant according to the landlady.'

'You believe her?'

'I think *she* believes it.'

'Tell me about the landlady.'

My ears prick up.

'Council records confirm she owns the building and as I said she lives on the top floor.'

'Have you been in her flat?'

'Yes. Saw a few empty bottles of wine standing in the sink. Couldn't say how long they'd been there, but smelt alcohol on her breath, tinged with mouthwash.'

I feel the heat rise to my cheeks. I was hoping she hadn't noticed the bottles, but I didn't expect her to be so judgemental.

'She'd been drinking this morning?'

'Can't say for sure.'

'What did she tell you about the victim?'

'Said he was a good tenant. Always paid his rent on time.'

'And what did she say about the alleged dispute between the victim and the bike owner?'

'She said it was all resolved last night after he kicked off again.'

'Resolved how?'

'Landlady says she was ordering a bike shed to be placed outside the building.'

'And the victim knew about this?'

'Yep, according to the landlady he did.'

I grind my teeth together. I knew I shouldn't have lied.

'Is she still around?'

'The landlady? Yeah, should be. I haven't seen her go out anywhere.'

'Good. I think I'll go and have a chat with her. Can you show me the way?'

My eyes widen in panic, but I don't hesitate, before tearing off back along the wooden platform and to the first ladder.

## 14

### TUESDAY, 1.35 P.M.

I'm crawling through the hatch when I hear knocking at my door. Breathless, I scurry through, the carpet scraping against my kneecaps, as I spin and lower the trapdoor back into place, and push the airing cupboard door closed. There's a second round of knocking at the door, and I hurry across and open it to see a woman in a dress suit and rain mac staring back at me. She's fractionally taller than I am, pretty, with a dash of makeup to accentuate her cheekbones, and jet-black hair cut into a neck-length bob.

'Eve Pennington?' she says, with a hint of a northern accent.

'Yes,' I reply, desperately trying to slow my breathing.

'I'm Detective Sergeant Kim Atwal, and I'd like to ask you some questions about James DeVere. May I come in?'

I step back and allow her to enter my flat, still unsure whether I should come clean about what I witnessed last night. I'd rather be honest, especially if it helps them with their investigation, but I don't know how to explain why I'm changing my story.

I follow her through to the living room, and encourage her to sit on the sofa, while I perch on the edge of my desk chair. My pulse is racing so fast that she must be able to see how uncomfortable I am.

She's staring back at me in silence, and then she points at my face.

'What were you doing before I came up here?'

The question throws me and I instantly assume she must have heard me scrabbling up the ladder, or maybe she somehow sensed I was listening behind the wall, and that's why she raced up the stairs to try and catch me out.

'There's dust and a cobweb in your hair,' she adds, and my hand shoots up to where she's indicating and I run my hand through my hair. It's slick against my skin where I'm now sweating profusely.

She must know where I've been...

'Let me help,' she says, standing and pulling at something above my head.

When I look I see the long stretch of white, cotton-like web she's extracted.

'Were you cleaning or something?'

'Yes,' I quickly say, leaping on the suggested explanation. 'My brother is visiting later, so I had to get things tidied.'

I don't know why I felt compelled to add the extra detail, and instantly regret it. She'll see that I'm trying too hard.

'Older or younger brother?'

'Older.'

'And I imagine he's quite protective of you?'

'Aren't they all?'

She smiles at this.

'Do you have any other siblings?'

'No, just Pete.'

'Well, I have four older brothers, and as much as I love them, it's like having four fathers, always keeping an eye on what I'm up to. Always worrying about the kinds of people I have to deal with on a day-to-day basis.'

I feel the tension in my shoulders starting to ease, and I almost want to laugh about how paranoid I was feeling when I first let her in.

'The place looks tidy to me, so you've obviously done a good job,' she adds with a warm smile.

'Thank you.'

'May I call you Eve?'

I nod.

'Thank you, Eve. I understand you own the building?'

'I inherited it when my father passed.'

'Oh, I'm sorry to hear that. Have you always lived here?'

'Oh, no, I grew up in a small village in the north of the county, and then went away to university for three years, and moved in maybe five or six years ago.'

I don't know why I'm sharing all this superfluous detail. There's something about this woman that I like, and I want her to like me too. I need to be careful about what I say.

'And as landlady you collect rent from each of the tenants?'

'Correct.'

'I also understand that you were the one who found James DeVere this morning.'

I shudder as an image of his swinging body flashes through my mind.

'Well, Danielle was the one who first saw him, but yes, I was with her.'

She pulls out a small notepad and flicks through the pages.

'That would be Danielle Jacobs?'

'Yes.'

'And how was it the two of you happened to be inside James DeVere's flat?'

I know for a fact that she already knows the answer to this because I overheard the other officer telling her as much. Is she trying to catch me out? I take a moment to compose my thoughts.

'Eve, can you tell me why you and Danielle Jacobs were inside James DeVere's flat?'

'It's difficult,' I say. 'I don't want to inadvertently get anyone else into trouble.'

'This isn't about blame, Eve, and in the long run it's always better just to tell the truth.'

I take a deep breath.

'Okay. I heard shouting coming from downstairs and headed down to investigate. I observed Danielle knocking at James's door and shouting about him having taken her bike.' I swallow hard. 'There has been some animosity between the two of them – nothing violent, just a difference of opinion. James made a couple of complaints to me about Danielle leaving her bike in the corridor and how it blocked his way. It came to a head last night, and I told Danielle I would order a secure container to be placed outside the building where she could lock up her bike instead.'

'Sounds sensible. And were they both happy with that solution?'

This is it; the moment I have to change my story.

'Danielle certainly was, and it was my intention to do some research and order the unit today. I was planning to tell James about it this morning, when...'

She purses her lips.

'So, James didn't know you'd found a solution to his complaint?'

I shake my head and see her scribble a note into her pad.

'No, he didn't. So, when Danielle said she thought he'd taken her bike and hidden it inside his flat, naturally, it wasn't an unreasonable assumption to leap to. I didn't think James would do something like that, and the reason I unlocked his flat was to disprove the theory.'

She considers this.

'And was the bike inside the flat?'

'No.'

'What do you think happened to the bike?'

I open my mouth to respond, but I haven't thought about where Danielle's bike disappeared to.

'I honestly don't know.'

'Could one of the other residents have moved it?'

I frown at the question.

'I mean, it's possible, but I can't think who would have. James was the only person who ever complained about the bike being in the corridor, so I wouldn't know where to begin with trying to figure out who else might have done it.'

'How well do you know your tenants?'

'Fairly well. I do due diligence on everyone before I offer them a tenancy agreement, and I take this seriously because I also live here and need to be sure we'll get along. And I make an effort to check in on each of them periodically to make sure they're happy. But, as I say, I can't think of anyone else who would have taken Danielle's bike last night.'

She scribbles a further note into her pad.

'Let's move on. There is evidence that James may not have been alone in his flat last night. Are you aware if he had a girlfriend or partner?'

Danielle's words stir in the back of my mind: *Clearly drunk and slurring his words, he tried to force his tongue down my throat before moving on to my mates.*

'I don't think he had a girlfriend, but...' I picture the glimpse of James and the woman with long black hair who were sneaking into his flat last night. 'I did see him with a woman last night.'

Detective Atwal's eyes widen.

'Go on.'

'I barely saw her, but she had long black hair. Dark like yours, but it came down below her shoulders. She was wearing a black mini dress.'

'Tall? Short?'

'It's difficult to say as I was at the top of the stairs. I think she was about James's height, maybe a fraction shorter.'

'Build?'

'Thinner than me, certainly.'

'Have you seen this woman before?'

'No.'

'And has James mentioned that he's been seeing anyone?'

'Not to me.'

'And what time did you see them?'

'Between nine and ten, but closer to ten, I think. Sorry, I didn't check my watch.'

She makes a note of it.

'There's something else,' I say quietly. 'I heard... I don't know how to describe it.'

'Go on.'

I sigh with discomfort.

'I think I heard them having sex, but it was quite violent. There was crashing and banging. I wondered whether maybe... maybe it was a bit of S&M?'

Her brow furrows.

'What makes you say that?'

*When my friend said you liked it rough, I didn't think she meant it.*

'It just sounded *rough*.'

'How did you hear this banging and crashing about from your flat?'

'Well, the reason I was out of my flat and saw them was because I was coming down to speak to James about the bike shed. He'd earlier threatened to move out if I didn't do something about the bike blocking the corridor, and I wanted to alleviate that fear. So, I was outside his door, about to knock when I heard them crashing about.'

'And how do you know it was consensual?'

'I heard them both giggling about it.'

'Did you knock on the door?'

'No. I wish I had as then James wouldn't have...'

I hear Bill's words in my head: *I overheard two of the police officers talking... They're not convinced James hung himself voluntarily.*

'I still can't quite believe he's gone. I had no sense that he wasn't happy with how his life was going.'

'Were the two of you close?'

'Not particularly, but I like to think of my tenants as extended family. Does that sound trite?'

'Not at all.'

'But you're satisfied that he did... you know... it was his intention to die?'

She gives me a curious look, and I need to tread carefully here.

'We're exploring all avenues, Eve. Do you have information that might steer us in another direction?'

'No, it's just... I'm sorry, one of my tenants said he overheard some of you talking and mentioned markings on James's wrists and that you might suspect he was murdered.'

'And what do you think about that?'

'I'd like to know if someone was murdered in my building, but I just wondered whether the markings on his wrists could be related to a sex act with the woman with long black hair.'

'What makes you say that?'

'Listen, I'm not into anything kinky, but I'm aware that some people enjoy being dominant or dominated, and that can include binding and asphyxiation. I've read *Fifty Shades*, and so I just wondered whether what happened could have been an accident. Like maybe James asked to be tied up, but something went wrong, and then the woman fled in panic.'

She's staring at me so intently that I feel obliged to look away.

'You seem quite clued up, is there something else you wish to share, Eve?'

'No.'

'Are you sure? Can you confirm your whereabouts around 1 a.m. this morning?'

'Is that when it happened?'

'There or thereabouts. What were you doing at that time?'

'I was probably asleep up here.'

'And is there anyone who can verify that? A boyfriend or husband perhaps?'

'No, I was alone last night.'

She glances over her shoulder at the kitchen.

'You were alone all night?'

'Yes, apart from when I saw James and Danielle arguing, and when I spotted James with that other woman.'

'My colleague who took a statement from you earlier said she saw several empty wine bottles up here, and could smell alcohol on your breath first thing.'

'So what?'

She tilts her head to one side.

'The way she described, it sounded like you might have had a bit of a party up here.'

'No, I was alone.'

I can feel my cheeks burning.

'So, James wasn't up here drinking with you?'

'No, absolutely not.'

'And you weren't the mystery woman who tied him up and fled his flat in a panic?'

'No!' I snap. 'I told you there was another woman with him.'

'A woman with long black hair that nobody else saw.'

'There was nobody else around when I saw her... I'm not making this up.'

'I didn't say that you were, Eve, I just wanted to clarify your statement.'

She slaps her knees and stands.

'I'll go now, but if you think of anything else – no matter how small – please do contact me.'

She passes me a business card.

'My mobile number is on the back. Feel free to call at any time. Day or night.'

I show her to the door, now wishing I hadn't bothered mentioning what I saw last night. She clearly doubts my version of events, and I would have been better keeping quiet. I resent that she thinks I could somehow be involved in what happened. And the worst part is it's not the first time I've been accused of being involved in someone's death, but this time I know I had nothing to do with it.

## 15

### TUESDAY, 5.20 P.M.

I should be working, but my attempts this afternoon have been in vain. I can't concentrate with the constant parade of police and scientists coming and going from the building. I've been sitting, staring out of the window for what feels like hours. They've erected some kind of small canopy around the communal entrance and there is a band of crime scene tape flapping in the wind blocking access from the road. Any hope I had that they'd keep the incident quiet is long gone.

What I don't know is whether this level of attention and people is standard when someone has taken their own life. It seems excessive to have so many faceless people dressed head to toe in bright overalls if James did die by suicide. But then, their faces are covered by masks, so I could just be seeing the same two or three people coming in and out.

I haven't dared sneak through the trapdoor to listen in on Detective Atwal's conversation again, out of fear of being heard. I use the passageway to ensure my tenants are as content as they can be; it's for their benefit, but I doubt any of them would understand that if they found out. I only want what's best for all of them. And it grates that I have failed with James. The more I replay our conversations through my mind, the more I see red flags that I should have noticed.

James's complaints about the bike in the corridor usually followed his return from work. Post-work he was always more stressed, but that I realise was probably an indication of the kind of pressure he's been feeling from his job. I should have asked him if everything was okay.

And there's been something bugging me about the snippet of conversation I overheard between him and the mystery lady with long black hair.

*When my friend said you liked it rough, I didn't think she meant it.*

When I spoke to Detective Atwal I was focusing on the possible masochism inference in what she said as an explanation for the markings on his wrists. But what I failed to mention is that the woman referenced her friend. I've never had a friendship where I'd feel comfortable discussing my inner fantasies and turn-ons, let alone one where I've shared secrets *and* a lover with a friend. The woman stated that she not only knew that James had slept with her friend, but she also knew what his turn-ons were and she'd still chosen to meet with him.

He'd never brought her back here before, which makes me think her presence in his life is only recent, and possibly someone he met that night. And I know it's a huge conclusion to jump to, but it begs the question of whether he'd hired her for the night. There's a logic in that somewhere: if I knew it was going to be my last night alive, I'd want to do something I enjoy for the last time. Of course, I have no evidence that the woman with the long black hair is a prostitute, but based on what Danielle told me about James's efforts to hook up with her, it doesn't feel beyond the realms of possibility. I should probably mention it to Detective Atwal, but I didn't appreciate her suggestion that I was somehow involved. And if I suddenly mention more about what I heard last night, she might assume I'm just trying to throw someone else under the bus to move the spotlight from me.

I blink twice when I see a woman with red-streaked, cropped hair standing just beyond the police tape. She's bundled in a light blue overcoat, carrying a pink and blue cake box. I rack my brain, trying to recall whether I've forgotten arranging a meeting with Lauren, but we weren't supposed to meet again until Friday, and that is via video call. There is no reason for her to be on the pavement outside the crime scene, and I dread to think what impression this is creating of me and my business prospects.

My phone starts ringing a moment later and I see her name on the screen. It's tempting not to answer and to hope she heads home, but if she tells her brother Tim what she's seen he'll probably convince her to cut all ties. I have no choice but to try and get her inside and offer some kind of explanation. I answer the call.

'Hi, Lauren, what can I do for you?' I say, moving away from the window in case she happens to look up and see me watching her.

'Oh, hi, Eve, I'm sorry to call out of the blue. I'm just outside your building because I thought I could drop those samples for you to try. Sorry, I should have phoned ahead and checked if it was convenient.'

*Yes, you should*, I don't say, swallowing my frustration instead.

'That's very kind of you,' I say. 'I'll be right down.'

I grab my coat and my keys and leave the flat, dodging several faceless figures in white overalls until I make it to the ground floor. There is a figure standing just inside the front door, leading to the small canopy. They give me a curious look.

'I'm Eve Pennington from Flat 9. Um, a client has arrived with a package for me, can you let her in?'

The figure lowers their mask and talks into a phone and a moment later I see Lauren being escorted to the canopy. Her eyes are an even brighter blue than appeared on my laptop screen, and she's shorter than I was expecting, but it's the fear on her face that has me wanting to quickly invite her inside. I can't send her off without clarifying why there's such a police presence at my place of business.

'Can she come in?'

The man at the door talks into his phone again, before nodding, advising that they've finished processing the communal areas so Lauren won't need to put on overalls. I hadn't even realised that might be a requirement.

'What's in the box?' the man asks as she steps through the canopy.

'Just some cakes. Do you need to look inside?'

He considers her response before shaking his head and allowing her to pass. 'Let's go up to my flat and then I'll explain everything,' I tell her, leading the way to the steps, pausing briefly as I pass the corridor to James's flat, my eyes meeting with Detective Atwal's. I don't wait to see if she has any further questions for me, and head up the stairs.

Once inside, I offer Lauren a cup of tea, but before I can offer to take her coat, she pulls a bottle of wine from the large black leather bag on her shoulder.

'I thought we could share a glass...' she says, her voice trailing off, as doubt crosses her face.

'Do you know what? After the day I've had, I think that's a very good idea.'

I usher her to the sofa, offering to take her coat. She places the colourful cake box on the small coffee table, and hands over her coat and the bottle. I hang the coat on the back of the stool I was perched on by the window, collecting two clean glasses from the cupboard beside the fridge and half-fill them with wine.

'Cheers,' I say, as I hand a glass to Lauren and she clinks it against mine.

'To the start of a good partnership,' she says, taking a sip.

The wine is bitter on my tongue, but my brain seems to enjoy the slap to the tastebuds. I didn't recognise the label on the bottle, but I can tell it's more expensive than what I usually consume. I sit down beside her and take a second sip.

'I hope you don't mind me just turning up like this?' she says, still perched on the sofa. 'I was worried that Tim's behaviour yesterday might have left a negative impression. I want you to know that we're both really keen to work with you. He's just...'

Her words trail off and I can see she's struggling to find her words, but as I'm watching her, there's something else bothering me: I never told her where I lived.

'Tim always says I'm too trusting – I've had troubles before – so he subconsciously projects this mean guy act when dealing with new people; but deep down he's a real softie.'

That's certainly not the way I would have described him, but I'm willing to accept she knows him better. I take another sip of wine.

'I'm curious, how did you know where I live?'

She frowns at the question.

'I'm pretty sure you told us when we first met, didn't you?'

Did I? I'm not in the habit of giving out my home address, but I can barely remember anything of our first conversation last week.

She must see the doubt and confusion in my face.

'Oh, no, I remember what it was,' she says quickly. 'When my friend recommended we speak to you about this project, she mentioned the address. She said you were local to the area, and when I asked her where your office was based, she read out your address from your invoice.' She leans forward and takes a drink of her wine, before sitting back on the sofa. 'It really is a lovely home. Have you lived here long?'

I'm wary of giving away too much detail.

'Several years,' I say.

'I thought I'd got the wrong place when I saw all the police swarming around downstairs. It's lucky Tim didn't come with me, as I'm sure he would have overreacted.'

'What you saw downstairs... one of my neighbours died by suicide today.'

Her hands shoot to her mouth.

'Goodness. How sad. I'm sorry for your loss.'

I don't tell her how guilty I'm feeling for not spotting the warning signs.

'You really didn't have to come all this way,' I say, trying to lift the mood, 'but I appreciate the gesture.'

'Think nothing of it,' she says, removing the scarf from around her neck. 'It was an excuse to get away from the shop for an hour. I used to go to school not far from here, so it's been a bit of a trip down memory lane.'

'Oh, really? Which school?'

'St Anne's, just off The Avenue. Do you know it?'

'Sure. I know where you mean.'

'Which school did you attend?'

'Oh, I went to a school near Salisbury, so you probably wouldn't have heard of it.'

I don't want to mention the name of the school in case she's aware of the rumours that haunted my time there.

'What sweet treats did you bring?' I say, nodding at the box.

'It's a sampler I was thinking we could use when meeting

prospective new clients. There's a bite-sized piece of the various offerings we can supply. Enough for them to get a sense of what we can provide without swallowing our profit line. Don't feel like you have to try them in front of me. I'd rather your opinion not be swayed by me being in the room.'

There's that shyness again that I saw on the video call yesterday. It's almost like she's shrinking into herself.

'Do you know what, I haven't eaten properly all day, and it's probably a good idea to line my stomach with something.'

She puts her glass on the table and lifts the box, opening the lid and sliding it between us. Each of the nine treats is delicately housed in a paper case.

'There's a coffee éclair, a mini scone with apricot jam and clotted cream, two macarons – the purple one is fruits of the forest, and the amber one is pumpkin and wild honey – um, what else is in there? Some baclava – you're not allergic to nuts, are you?'

'No allergies that I'm aware of, apart from going outside, of course.' I add a light-hearted chuckle, which she reciprocates.

'There's a lemon and lime cheesecake, a baked vanilla cheesecake, and a toffee and pecan blondie.'

'These look amazing, Lauren. I promise you I'm not just saying that.'

Her cheeks redden slightly.

'Thank you. As much as I *love* baking, I love seeing people enjoy my creations just as much, so please do try something.'

I'm not sure where to start, but reach for what I assume is the lemon and lime cheesecake, based on the swirls of yellow and green on the top. It melts in my mouth, tickling my tastebuds as I swallow.

'Holy fucking shit, that's good,' I say, covering my mouth at the unplanned outburst.

Lauren laughs.

'That's the sort of quote I'd love to include in the campaign, but probably best not to,' she says laughing uproariously.

I reach for the amber-coloured macaron next, and the hard shell crumbles as soon as it touches my wet lips, and the sweetness of the honey feels like a warm hug on a cold and damp day.

'You are a magician,' I say as I swallow it down. 'How on earth did you learn to bake like this?'

'Honestly, I didn't have many friends when I was growing up and so I ploughed my attention into my passion. I used to watch *a lot* of cookery shows, and then I started to experiment with flavours and textures, and it all grew from there. Do you bake much?'

'Ha! I can't remember the last time I cracked an egg, let alone tried to bake a cake. I probably shouldn't admit this to you, but I mostly heat up food, rather than actually cook. Don't hate me.'

'Don't be silly. There's no judgement here. I can't draw to save my life, but you have a real flair for creating visual imagery out of nothing. I was so impressed with your initial conceptual designs, and I can't wait to see what's to come.'

I reach for my glass.

'In all honesty, I've not started yet. The police have been coming and going all day, not giving a minute's peace.'

'Oh, no, I'm so sorry. And now you've got me invading your space as well. I knew I should have phoned before just turning up like this. I'm sorry.'

'No, don't be silly. You're a welcome distraction, and if you come bearing gifts like this you can visit whenever you want.'

She reaches for my glass, and says she'll top us both up, and I do nothing to stop her. Right now, all I want to do is chase away the images of James hanging from that rope.

## 16

TUESDAY, 6.55 P.M.

Lauren is tipsy as she stands, gripping the edge of the sofa for support.

'Oh, I can't believe how late it is,' she says, shaking her wrist, and then adjusting her watch with her free hand.

'Don't worry about it. Are you going to be okay getting home?'

'Yeah, I promised Tim I would call in and give him an update, so I'll walk to his and then he can drive me home.'

I watch her, envious of how the wine has already formed a soft cushion around her brain. The two small glasses we've consumed aren't even close to taking the edge off my anxiety.

'What are you going to tell him?'

She turns and tries to fix me with a hard stare, but her eyes are struggling to focus and she almost crashes back down to the sofa.

'That we have hired a creative genius and he can stop worrying. The campaign is in good hands.'

Bearing in mind we haven't actually discussed the campaign

in any detail this afternoon, her confidence in my ability feels a little premature.

'I should be able to pull a couple of bits together to share with you by Friday,' I offer, feeling guilty that I've allowed today to escape me.

'There's no hurry. It would serve Tim well to learn a little patience.'

The last thing I want is to become a pawn trapped between the two of them, but I understand how debilitating it can feel when an overly cautious sibling smothers you.

'He only wants to protect you,' I hear myself saying, knowing how hollow the words sound.

'Yeah, well, if he spent less time worrying about me, and a little more focusing on himself, then he wouldn't be in the mess he is.'

My ears prick up at this.

'What do you mean?'

Her face reddens as she realises she's overshared.

'Oh, it's nothing to do with the business, don't worry... Sorry, I shouldn't have said anything.'

'It's okay, Lauren, I'm discreet. Whatever it is must be playing on your mind or it wouldn't have slipped out so easily.'

And I'm sure the wine played a part too, I don't add.

She raises a hand to her forehead and closes her eyes.

'What am I like? Tim is fine, and more importantly the business is in a good place. A really good place. You have nothing to worry about.'

The more she protests, the more I doubt the validity of her words. I remain silent, allowing her to fill the awkward silence.

'His wife just learned he's been cheating on her,' Lauren says, her eyes still clamped shut. 'She's taken my niece and has flown to Madrid where her parents live. She's threatening divorce, and frankly, I don't blame her. He's such an idiot!'

This is not what I was expecting to hear, and I feel like I should encourage her to sit again and make her a strong coffee, but it's nearly seven and my tenants will be knocking on my door for the meeting shortly.

'Oh, I see,' I say quietly. 'How old is your niece?'

'Five, and I think she's my favourite person in the whole world.' She pouts. 'Why are men such dicks?'

Her pout breaks into a chuckle, and I reciprocate.

'And to think they call *us* the weaker sex. Did you know he was cheating?'

She shakes her head vehemently.

'Heavens, no! If I had known I'd have told him to sort himself out. But what's worse is, he was carrying on with one of the store managers so Sophia is bound to assume I knew and kept it from her, which only makes matters worse.'

I'm not sure if Sophia is the name of Lauren's sister-in-law or her niece, but I don't ask her to clarify.

'I'm sure if you tell them the truth, they'll believe you,' I offer encouragingly. 'I'm sure they know you're not capable of such deceit.'

'That's kind of you to say, but you barely know me.'

'Maybe not, but I'm usually a good judge of character, and between the two of us, I prefer working with you over your brother. He seems so... controlling.'

'You don't know how right you are. Sophia would tell me stories about how he would insist she be home by a certain time if going out with friends, and how he used to regularly check her phone for messages from other men. And all the time it was her who should have been checking up on him. It makes my blood boil!'

I start at a sudden buzzing and then realise it's my phone vibrating on the arm of the sofa.

'Sorry, I really should let you get on,' Lauren says, collecting herself. 'Please don't think badly of our project because of what I've told you about Tim. When it comes to business he's far more organised and single-minded, so I don't want you questioning what you're getting involved in.'

The phone continues to vibrate, and I point at it.

'Relax, I told you before I know what it's like having an overprotective brother. You have nothing to worry about.'

She smiles, and I show her to the door, thanking her again for the box of cake samples, before answering Pete's call.

'I was just talking about you. Were your ears burning?'

The question seems to throw him.

'Eh? Who were you talking to?'

'A new client.'

'And what were you saying about me?'

I could be honest with him, but I'm not that cruel.

'Never mind. Why are you phoning?'

'Because when we spoke earlier, you neglected to mention that one of your tenants had died.'

My brow furrows.

'How do you know about that?'

'I just heard it on the local radio news. I can't believe you didn't say anything to me.'

I'm surprised the police would announce James's death on the radio, unless that's a sign that they really do suspect foul play.

'When we spoke first thing I didn't know James had died, so I couldn't tell you what I didn't know. Besides, you didn't know James, so what's it to you anyway?'

The phone crackles as he sighs.

'Oh, I don't know, maybe it would be nice to know my sister is doing okay despite news that one of her tenants had been murdered.'

'Wait, what? Who said James was murdered? He hung himself.'

'That's not what they said on the radio.'

'They said James was murdered?'

'No, not in so many words, but they said they are treating the death as suspicious, which basically means the same thing. Are you okay?'

'Of course I am.'

'Are you sure? Were you close to this James?'

It's my turn to sigh.

'Not particularly, but finding him hanging from a rope this morning was a bit of a shock.'

'Wait, you found him? And you didn't think to phone and let me know?'

'No, but it's been kind of a busy day with the police traipsing in and out. Believe it or not, Pete, notifying you about the passing of someone you didn't know wasn't top of my list of priorities.'

'Maybe not, but learning that my sister – who already struggles with her mental health – has now experienced an emotionally traumatic scenario would have been good. Have you spoken to Dr Winslow about how you're feeling?'

I sigh again.

'No, but I'm fine, Pete. As I said, it was a shock to find him there, but I'm fine.'

I can see he isn't going to let this drop, and will continue to badger me about my mental health when he shows up for his birthday dinner. I really don't understand why the police would leak the story to the press, particularly when Detective Atwal told me they weren't ruling anything out.

'I know you think you're tough, but that will never stop me

worrying about you,' Pete says. 'Are you sure you're safe to stay there tonight? I can collect you and take you to my place. I don't mind.'

Even if I could physically step out of the building, I don't feel unsafe staying here. I have no reason to doubt that James chose to end things, despite what Detective Atwal implied.

'I know you worry, Pete, and I don't know how many times I have to tell you that I am fine. Yes, this morning's discovery was a shock, but I'm coping fine. I haven't spoken to Dr Winslow yet, because I don't see the need.'

'Are the police still there?'

I glance out of the window, and it looks as though they've all but packed up for the day. The white canopy has now been removed from the main entrance. I step away from the window, hating myself for what I'm about to say.

'Yeah, the detective in charge reckoned they'd be here all night and for the next day or so. Probably best if we postpone your birthday dinner. Is that okay?'

If he says he's still coming over and sees the lack of police presence he'll realise I've lied.

'Sure, no worries, the last thing they need is me getting in the way.'

I resist the urge to punch the air, feeling my mood lifting.

'I could still drive over,' he adds and the breath catches in my throat. 'I could pick you up and we could go out for dinner.'

I grind my teeth.

'You know I don't want to do that.'

'Don't *want* to or *can't*?'

I groan as my frustration boils over.

'Oh my God, when are you going to get it into your thick head that I *choose* not to go out? I am not mentally unstable, I just prefer the safety and sanctity of my home. No amount of emotional blackmail will change my mind, Pete. I'm sorry that you don't like my choice, but if it's too much for you to handle, stop phoning. I don't want to lose you, but I can't bear how hard you are making this for me.'

There's silence on the line, and I double-check he hasn't hung up.

'I don't know what to say,' he eventually mumbles. 'With Mum and Dad gone, I feel responsible for you, Eve, and although you can't see it, your mental health isn't as good as you think it is. I've spoken to Dr Winslow and she's given me loads of information about agoraphobia and how it affects those who suffer with it. You describe it as a choice not to go out, but you're lying to yourself.'

I'm not convinced Dr Winslow hasn't breached doctor-patient confidentiality rules and told Pete far more than he's letting on, but I'd argue Pete's obsession with my mental state is what's unhealthy here.

'Dr Winslow was explaining the practicalities of using virtual reality headsets as a means to help sufferers overcome their trauma. I'd be happy to buy a VR headset if you're willing to give it a go. Dr Winslow says it would allow you to experience the outside world, safe in the knowledge that you're still at home and not in any danger.'

There is a knock at the door and I'm relieved I have an excuse to hang up on Pete. I tell him that my tenants have arrived for a meeting, and that I'll speak to him later in the week. As usual, Bill is the first to arrive, and when he asks if I'm okay, I collapse into his arms, and will myself not to cry.

# 17

## TUESDAY, 7.30 P.M.

With George safely secured in my bedroom, I count only five tenants in my flat. Bill is beside Chad and Jenny on the sofa, India is in my armchair, and Caz is perched on the chair I left by the window. The meeting should have started ten minutes ago, but there's no sign of Danielle, Mike, or Fi. And of course there's no James. I hadn't realised how much of an influence he had on the group, but these five have been sitting in silence since they arrived.

'Are we going to start soon? Some of us have plans for tonight.'

Jenny is shooting daggers at me as she says this, but it's a fair point.

'Absolutely. Thank you all for coming at such short notice. Some of you will probably already know, there's been a large police presence in the block today, and that's because James DeVere from Flat 4 died this morning.'

I pause, allowing the others to process my words, but there are no gasps or shocked faces, so my assumption is that all five have probably been spoken to by the police at some point today.

If Mike and Fi are still at work, then they're probably the ones who I need to speak to most.

'I wanted to gather you all to make sure you knew about James and to check how you're all feeling about the situation.'

Nobody responds at first. Chad and Jenny exchange glances, Bill smiles empathetically, but it's Caz, James's closest neighbour, who breaks the silence.

'The detective I spoke to said that James hung himself.'

'That's right. I assume you've all spoken to the police at some point today?'

There are subtle nods from the whole group.

'I'm aware that James's passing has been mentioned on the local news,' I continue, 'but from what Detective Atwal told me, they're not currently treating this as anything other than a death by suicide. So, I don't want any of you worrying or jumping to the wrong—'

I gasp at a sudden, urgent knocking at the door. Five pairs of eyes turn and look towards it. I don't immediately move, my mind whirring with possibilities as the knocking continues. It could be Detective Atwal, declaring she's come to arrest one of my tenants on suspicion of murder. Or it could be James, standing there with an aloof grin on his face, revealing that we've all been the butt of some gruesome joke and he's perfectly fine. Still the knocking continues, but it's Bill who crosses to the door and opens it.

Mike stoops as he enters, apologising for his tardiness, and my pulse slows to a more regular beat.

At six feet seven, Mike is easily the tallest person I've ever known, but for all that height he's almost stick thin, which just makes him appear more gangly and awkward. He's lost none of his West Country accent, despite living here for more than five years.

'Evening, all,' he says light-heartedly, as he joins the group. 'Sorry I'm late. Got stuck at school. Bloody GCSE students.' He quietens, gazing at each of us. 'Jesus, what's with all the sad faces? Who died?' He stops chuckling when he sees nobody reciprocate.

'I'm sorry to be the one to break it to you, Mike,' Bill says, retaking his seat. 'James passed this morning.'

Mike pulls an unconvinced face.

'Yeah, good one, Bill. No, seriously, what's going on?'

I clear my throat.

'It's true, Mike. Danielle and I found him this morning. He died by suicide.'

'What? No, don't be ridiculous, I'm supposed to be meeting him for a drink in an hour. Where is he really? Stop joking around.'

'It's not a joke,' Bill says. 'I'm sorry.'

Mike stares at us in turn, before the penny finally drops.

'I don't believe it. I only spoke to him last night. He was shouting about that bike again when I came home, so I suggested we go for a drink and chat about it. He said he had plans, but was free tonight. You're sure he's dead?'

An image of his body hanging from the rope fills my mind.

'The police are keen to speak to each of us to get a sense of how he was and why he might have made that choice,' I add.

'I wondered why he hadn't replied to any of my WhatsApp messages today, but I just assumed he was too busy. I don't understand why he'd agree to meet me for a drink if he was planning to...'

'It's a shock to all of us,' I concur. 'That's why I wanted to get you all together tonight. I wish I'd known he was struggling with his mental health, and I want you all to know that if you need to talk to anyone I'm more than happy to lend an ear—'

'Of course, we all know who isn't here tonight,' India from Flat 6 interrupts. 'If anyone's to blame for what's happened, it's Danielle and her fucking bike.'

Her outburst is unexpected.

'Actually, Danielle is working a double shift at the hospital,' I lie, feeling compelled to defend her yet again. 'I know that James was unhappy with her leaving her bike in the hallway—'

'He's not the only one,' India glowers.

'I've spoken to Danielle about her bike, and will be ordering a lockable unit for outside where she can store it in future. You'll all be able to store bikes in it as well.'

Something triggers in the back of my mind.

'Speaking of which, does anyone know what has happened to Danielle's bike?'

I study India's face, looking for any kind of tell that she might be the one who's hidden it, rather than James. She's never mentioned an issue, and as far as I was aware, James was the only one with complaint, but now I'm worried that I know far less about what's going on with my tenants than I previously thought.

'Danielle's bike was in the corridor last night when she went to bed, and this morning it was gone. Does anyone know what happened to it?'

I'm met with stony silence.

'Well, maybe if she'd taken better care of it, she'd still have it,' India says, shrugging.

'India, do you know where Danielle's bike is, yes or no?'

'No, how the hell would I know where it is? If she left it out in the open and someone's stolen it, that's nothing to do with me!'

Bill stands.

'I think we should all just calm down,' he says. 'Understandably, today's news has come as a shock, and we're all probably a bit wound up by it. Turning on each other isn't the answer.'

'Especially when the real guilty party isn't even here,' India adds.

'Danielle was with me when I found James this morning,' I say, 'and she was as shocked as I was. You can't blame James's decision on anyone.'

'Oh, she happened to be with you? How convenient!'

'India, what is your problem with Danielle?'

India clenches her jaw.

'I saw the way she led him on last year. Fluttering her eyelashes, asking him for favours, and then slamming the door in his face. It's women like her that give the rest of us a bad name.'

I hear Danielle's words in my head: *He asked me out not long after I moved in last year, and I politely declined, telling him I'd just got out of an abusive relationship and wasn't looking for anything romantic.*

'Oh, James, would you mind changing a bulb for me?' India says, putting on a whiny voice. 'Oh, you're so big and strong, would you help me move my bed?' She reverts to her usual voice. 'You act like she's sweet and innocent just because she's a nurse at the hospital, when she knows exactly what to do to get what she wants. It wouldn't surprise me if she was somehow involved in what happened.'

I'm about to correct her, when Bill speaks up. 'The police have said they're not ruling out anything at this time.'

'Wait, so they think someone helped James?'

'Let's not jump to any conclusions,' I interject. 'The police have said very little, and speculating won't benefit any of us. For now, we need to stick together and wait for Detective Atwal and her team to undertake their investigation thoroughly. I don't want anyone to leave here tonight thinking worse of anyone else. All I ask is that you all cooperate with the police. And as I said earlier, if any of you just need to chat or vent, my door is always open. I can even pass you the name of a psychiatrist should it be needed.'

I stare directly at Caz as I say this as she's hardly spoken since she arrived, and that worries me.

'And lock your doors in case Danielle is on the prowl and you're on her kill list,' India says, and I quickly glare at her.

'That kind of thing isn't helpful.'

'Oh, come on, it's what we're all thinking. She didn't like him – and made no secret of it – and if I had to choose one of us as the most likely suspect to harm James it would be her.'

There are murmurs of agreement from Jenny and Mike.

'Nobody is saying that James was killed by anyone,' I insist.

'But Bill said the police haven't ruled out the possibility,' Mike chimes in.

'And where's Fi tonight?' India asks, before I have chance to regain control of the conversation.

'Ooh, maybe Danielle has already done her in as well,' Mike says. 'Has anyone seen Fi today?'

'I didn't hear any movement inside her flat when I passed her door,' India replies. 'I assumed she'd already come up. Maybe someone should go and check.'

All eyes fall on me.

'Just because Fi isn't here, it doesn't mean anything has happened to her.' I keep speaking before anyone can interrupt me again. 'I'm sure Fi is probably just not home from work yet. Or maybe she had other plans. I'm sure she'll come and see me when she sees the note I left under the door. This gathering was very last minute.'

'So, you're not going to check that Danielle hasn't hurt her?'

I glare back at India.

'I will check on Fi later this evening, and I'd appreciate it if you stopped this witch hunt.'

'I'm only saying what everybody else is thinking. This place has always given me the creeps, weird noises behind the walls sometimes, almost as if someone is creeping about out there—'

'Oh my God, Chad reckoned I was imagining it, but I swear I've heard scuttling.' Jenny slaps Chad's arm. 'You see, I'm not making it up.'

I hope nobody has noticed the heat rising to my face. I had no idea that any of them had ever heard me before, but now I'm conscious that I'm going to have to take more care when I use the passageway. If any of them mention it to the police, they might discover the ladder leading to my flat, and I don't want to face that kind of scrutiny.

'I think we should call it a night. I will follow up with Fi once she's home so she's aware of what's happened. Please remember that I'm here if any of you want to talk further.'

'And be sure to lock your doors tonight, just in case,' India says as she marches to the front door.

I move to hurry after her, but feel Bill's warm hand on my shoulder.

'Let her be. We all grieve in different ways.'

He's right, but I don't like the weird atmosphere that seems to be growing between my tenants. Hopefully, Fi returning home late from work will quell any further talk of a killer being at large in the building.

## 18

### TUESDAY, 9.45 P.M.

I haven't been able to stop thinking about what India and Jenny said about the noises they've heard behind the walls. Nobody has ever mentioned it before, so I wasn't aware that my evening movement along the passageway has ever been noticed. Would they still be so suspicious if they understood that I only do it for *their* benefit? The way Jenny spoke made me sound like some kind of pervert, but nothing could be further from the truth. I just want them all to be happy, and I'm going out of my way to ensure that. Is that really so wrong?

It's a moot argument as I have no intention of letting any of them know it's me they've heard. I will just have to lay off my nightly checks for a few days – maybe a week – just until the dust settles and everyone stops thinking about what happened in James's flat. The sooner the place is emptied and cleaned, and a new tenant found, the better.

I pick at the lasagne meal I nuked in the microwave, my mind elsewhere. I keep looking at the clock, trying to determine when I can check that Fi is okay. It's unlike her not to attend one of the tenants' meetings, but it is possible she got held up at work.

India's voice echoes in my mind: *So, you're not going to check that Danielle hasn't hurt her?*

I don't want to contemplate the prospect that there is a killer at loose in the building, and if I was to suspect anyone, Danielle would be last on the list. But who would be at the top? In truth, I don't think any of my residents would be capable of murder. I spent a long time researching each of their backgrounds before agreeing for them to move in, and there was nothing to suggest any would be capable of criminality.

I close my eyes and picture each of the tenants in turn, starting with Bill in Flat 1, but in his seventies and without a bad word to say against anyone, he's a gentle giant. Then there's Danielle and Caz, but neither strike me as malicious or psychopathic. Heading up to the first floor, Fi is too quiet, and despite their suspicions Jenny and India are just hot-headed. And that leaves fitness-freak Chad, and secondary school teacher, Mike. And whilst there's something off-putting about Mike's gangly frame, social inadequacy and inability to read a room, I can't believe he would contemplate harming James, especially as the two of them were friends.

I push the plate of lasagne to one side, and groan in frustration. This is ridiculous! I'm allowing Jenny's and India's paranoia to permeate my own subconscious. James taking his own life is the simplest explanation for what happened last night, even if it's the most painful to accept.

It's almost ten o'clock, and with no appetite for the congealing pasta, I make the decision to go and break the news of James's passing to Fi. She must be home from work by now, but I collect my set of skeleton keys from the hook on the wall, and leave the flat. I hover at the top of the stairs, listening out for any sound, but all is eerily quiet in the building. It amazes me how quickly everyone else seems to have managed to return to their normal lives despite the day's upheaval. I wish it could be that easy for me.

The lights are already on, which means somebody has been moving about and triggered the sensor, so hopefully that means Fi has finally returned. I knock on her door, and pause, listening for the sound of movement inside. Taking a step back, I examine the carpet, looking for the telltale sign of light from beneath the door, but there is nothing. I knock again, banging harder this time in case Fi didn't hear, but there is still no sound of movement inside. I shuffle closer and press my ear against the cold woodwork, straining to hear anything over the sound of my racing heart, but if she is inside, she's doing a great job of pretending she isn't.

I knock again, this time gently calling out her name.

'Fi, it's Eve from upstairs. There's something I need to talk to you about. If you're home, can you open the door? It won't take five minutes.'

Again, I press my ear to the door, but there is no sound within. She isn't home, which is unusual for Fi. She's a legal secretary at a firm in the city centre, but their operating hours are nine to five, and I've overheard her on the phone to her mum, and the firm don't pay overtime, so I'd be surprised if she is still there. Of course, I'm forgetting that unlike me, all my tenants have lives outside of this building, so it's equally possible she's met up with a friend or someone as well.

I feel the sharp edge of the skeleton keys pressing against my thigh, and am tempted to withdraw them from my pocket. I could easily slip into Fi's flat and have a look around to check on her wellbeing. It isn't snooping when the intention is to check welfare. And there's every chance I could be in and out before anybody realises. I hesitate. I don't want to breach Fi's privacy. It didn't end well when I entered James's flat earlier, and I'm not sure my heart could take it if I found Fi dead inside.

I leave the keys where they are, and instead hurry back upstairs, in through the door and quickly raise the trapdoor in the airing cupboard. Flicking on my torch, I descend the ladder as quietly as I can, too conscious that Jenny and India could be listening for any noise. My heart is thundering in my chest as I reach the first-floor platform. It's so dusty down here with fibres from the insulation floating freely in the air. I really should think about wearing a face mask when I'm down here, as I don't want to think about what kind of shit I'm inhaling into my lungs. I lift the collar of my hoodie up over my mouth and nose in an effort to protect myself.

Something stirs over my shoulder, and I swing round, arcing the torch as I do. The wooden beams and insulation cast all kinds of strange shadows, almost as if they're dancing as I wave the torch over the area. I definitely heard something moving, but there's no obvious cause of the noise.

Probably just my mind playing tricks on me.

I close my eyes, and focus on trying to slow my breathing until the tension in my shoulders begins to ease. But then I hear a definite scratching sound and my eyes snap open. It's coming from the direction of India's and Mike's side of the hallway, and so I slowly tiptoe forwards, placing each step ever so carefully, not wanting to make a sound.

I freeze when I hear the scratching start up again. It's coming from around the corner of India's wall, so I edge closer, my pulse racing, and as I swing around the breezeblocks, it takes all my effort not to scream out loud when I see the small rodent several metres along the wooden platform. I cover my mouth and nose with my hand, pressing the hoodie against my skin, the breath warm on my palm.

The rodent stops what it's doing as it sees me, standing on its haunches, assessing whether I'm a threat. It must be at least seven inches tall with a long pink tail. I don't move for what feels like an age, a standoff between the two of us; a myriad of thoughts racing through my mind.

How did it get in here? Is there more than one? How long has it been here? Could this be what India and Jenny have heard scurrying, rather than me? How am I going to get rid of it?

Like most property owners, I understand the many issues that can come with an infestation of rodents in the home. They can cause fires by chewing through electrical cables; contaminate water tanks; not to mention spreading disease.

I know I'm going to have to act, but I can't call in a professional exterminator without having to reveal the existence of the passageway, but equally I don't like the idea of using traps and having to dispose of the bodies. And if one rodent has managed to get inside, how am I going to find and close up that entry point? I don't want to waste time getting rid of this one only for another family to move in. I could notify Pete and see what he suggests, but he'd probably tell me to hire a company to eradicate the problem.

I take a lunging step forward, and am relieved when the rat scurries away and doesn't engage me. But as I'm recovering my breath, the torchlight catches something shiny poking out of the floor insulation beside where the rat had been standing. I tiptoe closer, unable to work out what it is at first. And it's only when I'm standing directly over it that I realise what I'm looking at. Bending over, I pinch my fingers and pull it out. The plastic end has been chewed – presumably by the rat – but I can't understand why there would be a crushed bottle of mineral water hidden in the insulation. The bottle design isn't old, so I can't imagine it's been down here since my dad first had the property insulated. And I've never brought a drink down here with me as I've always wanted to have a free hand to stop myself falling.

A shiver runs the length of my spine: someone else has been in here.

They must have left the bottle here but I don't know who or when.

I can hear the sound of voices beyond the wall as I straighten, and push my ear against the cool breezeblock, trying to work out who India is speaking to. It wouldn't surprise me if she and Jenny had got together after the meeting to discuss their conspiracy theories, but then I realise it's a man's voice I can hear.

It takes a moment to realise that I'm not listening to a conversation but a television report of some kind. I vaguely recognise the tone of the presenter, and deduce that India must be watching the local BBC news. I'm about to head away when I hear the presenter mention James DeVere by name. It's hard to make out specific words through the barrier of the wall, but I start when I hear him say it isn't the first suspicious death to occur within the building.

## 19

### TUESDAY, 10.48 P.M.

I've been online searching for news stories about this address since I clambered back through the trapdoor, but haven't found anything but property rental sites coming up in my feed. Even when I add the word *murder* to the filter, I can't find anything.

I think back to how the news presenter described it. He said it wasn't the first suspicious death in the building, and maybe it's just my own paranoia that assumed that would mean murder. I try adjusting the search to include suspicious deaths, but the first dozen or so hits still miss the mark.

Surely I would know if the building I inherited had a dark history. Dad would have mentioned it, or it would have come up in conversation with Pete, and I can't trace any memory of it.

I tip the remains from the bottle into my glass, and when I search for a refill, find the panel in the fridge door frustratingly empty.

I hear Dr Winslow's words in my head as I stand in the glow of the fridge light: *And how is the drinking?*

I know I shouldn't drink as much as I do, but it's not like it's my first thought when I wake up in the morning. I can get through the day without having a drink. I've done it plenty of times, and I resent anyone judging me for enjoying the pleasures that a large glass of wine at the end of the day can bring. It doesn't make me a bad person, but Winslow and Pete don't see it like that. But if they spent less time trying to fix me, they'd see I'm perfectly fine.

I fill my glass with water from the tap and carry it back to my laptop. I shouldn't have started searching for information this late in the day; my mind is never as productive as it is during daylight hours. And given everything that's happened today, there's every reason for my mind not to be functioning at an effective level.

I stare at the screen and then remove the address from the search box, and look for suspicious deaths in the area instead. Various articles from news websites appear, but all are from the last couple of years, and if any of these events had happened in the building, I'd be aware of them. I need to go back further, but the question is how far. I was born in 1994, so I adjust the filter to show suspicious deaths prior to 2000, but there are still so many results to sift through and half an hour quickly passes as I skim read the headlines, finding no mention of this address.

My eyes are heavy, and I'm about to give up when I find a Wikipedia page listing unsolved murders in the county. I open the page, which lists murders in the city in date order going back to the start of the twentieth century. There are only a handful of unsolved crimes listed, and none that mention the road or wider area, but there is a link to solved murders that I click on. The list is much longer and as I skim through dates and names, I stop when I see the words *Freemantle Hotel*. A bell rings in the back of my head, and I try to pluck out the memory. I can't say why but I have a vague memory of someone – maybe my dad or Bill – saying this building was a hotel before it was converted into flats.

I open a fresh page and type the words *Freemantle Hotel Death* in the search bar, and am stunned by the number of hits generated. I click on the first and a sepia-coloured photograph appears on the screen, and my mouth drops at the familiarity of the building. It doesn't look quite right, with a green awning hanging over the front entrance, emblazoned with the hotel's name, but I'd recognise the first-floor layout anywhere. The site I've opened is a page on the *Daily Echo*'s website dated July 1975.

Hotelier John Samuel Cooper, 46, will today be sentenced following his conviction on five counts of murder during a spree lasting fifteen months in Hampshire. Cooper, who denies the charges, came to the attention of senior detective Reg Dixon when it was discovered that each of the female victims had stayed at or within the vicinity of the Freemantle Hotel where Cooper worked. Cooper was arrested in November 1974 for the murder of Miss Patricia Robinson, 24, a singer and dancer aboard cruise ships. Miss Robinson spent a weekend at the hotel in the days prior to her body being discovered on Southampton Common.

Cooper, born and raised in Southampton, initially told police that he'd witnessed Miss Robinson being collected from the hotel by an unidentified male in a sports car, but no other witnesses could corroborate the story. The arrest led police to consider Cooper's involvement in other unsolved murders in the county, and they identified four such victims known to have also stayed at the Freemantle Hotel.

A search of the hotel uncovered blood stains on the carpet in Cooper's own room. The blood belonged to victim number two, Miss Caroline Finneran, 21, who was on holiday in the city in August 1974 but never returned home. Her body washed up on the shore in Hythe in September 1974. Cooper initially denied knowing Miss Finneran, but later admitted to buying her dinner at a local Italian restaurant while she was staying at the hotel. Miss Finneran's widowed mother attended the trial at Winchester Crown Court and applauded the jury's verdict when it was read out.

Cooper's third victim was Miss Tania Denby, 19, a barmaid at the Freemantle Arms pub a short walk from the Freemantle Hotel. She was last seen following her shift at the pub. Her walk home took her directly past the hotel, and it was confirmed Cooper was working the night she disappeared. Police initially suspected Miss Denby's boyfriend of the crime, but he was provided with an alibi by his brother. Cooper only became a person of interest to police in the case following his arrest for Miss Robinson's murder.

Cooper was also found to be working at the hotel the night that Miss Sally Edmunds, 26, visited a guest at the hotel. Miss Edmunds, a known prostitute in the area, left her client's room at 2 a.m., but did not return to meet her friends as previously arranged. The client, Mr Tristan Partridge, 54, was arrested by police following reports of Miss Edmunds's disappearance, and although he admitted to paying for sex with her, he denied any knowledge of her whereabouts. Her mutilated body was found in woods near Romsey in the north of Hampshire a few days later, and Mr Partridge's car did not leave the hotel car park at any point after his arrival. He remained a person of interest until Cooper's arrest.

The final victim, and possibly Cooper's first murder, was that of Miss Valerie Windermere, the sister of Cooper's best friend. Her body was found in Ryde on the Isle of Wight while Cooper was staying with the Windermere family. Her death was initially ruled as suicide as an empty bottle of painkillers was found near the body. Police dismissed bruising around her wrists, and it was only when her brother Lucas Windermere accused Cooper following his arrest that a full postmortem was ordered.

Cooper admitted to sleeping with Miss Windermere whilst he was in Ryde, but denied any involvement in her death. Police believe the bruising to her wrists was caused by Cooper while he held her down and forced her to swallow the pills. Similar bruising was discovered on three of the other victims, and nobody could provide Cooper with an alibi for any of the times of death.

Police claim Cooper fantasised about the young women who would visit the hotel, believing they were beckoning him to pursue them. In his twisted psyche, they wanted him to have violent sex with them, ending in their deaths. Despite a thorough review of Cooper's mental capacity, he was deemed fit to stand trial, and now faces the prospect of five life sentences.

The Freemantle Hotel has been put up for sale by the owners who no longer see it as a viable business. It is thought the land may be purchased by local developers and the murder building knocked down, but bidding is yet to begin.

I sit back from the screen, my head spinning and an uneasy feeling in the back of my throat. I don't want to believe that such horrific crimes occurred here, nor how ignorant I've been. It's been fifty years since Cooper's trial, which is probably why nobody else seems to be aware of the building's history. There was certainly no mention of it at the reading of Dad's will. I can't believe he didn't know something of the history. And yet, rather than knocking it to its foundations to wipe the slate clean, he simply slapped on a mask and pretended it didn't happen.

The article said the police found Caroline Finneran's blood

on the carpet in Cooper's room, but which room was his? My eyes drop to the carpet around my chair and I pull up my legs in revulsion, even though this carpet was fitted when I moved in. My head then snaps around to the airing cupboard. I've always wondered why there is a trapdoor leading to the passageway, and now it makes sense. It's possible Cooper used to use them to creep about and observe his guests, hunting his next victim.

I leap out of my chair and run to the kitchen sink, expelling the contents of my stomach. My eyes close as I retch, the smell permeating every pore of my body, but in the darkness all I can picture are the ghosts of Cooper beating and cutting into his victims in this room. I continue to retch, even when there is nothing left, and eventually I run the tap and squeeze my fingers into the plughole until it clears, before filling a mug with fresh water, sipping it. My whole body is trembling with shock, and it feels like a wrecking ball is swinging freely behind my eyes.

Cooper's exploits must be the reason why Detective Atwal is so open to the possibility that James was murdered. The article said Valerie Windermere's death was initially ruled as death by suicide, but it didn't mention whether she had known mental health issues. But then, fifty years ago, it probably wasn't considered as it would be now.

There is a part of me that wants to phone Pete and ask him what he knows about Cooper's activities, but he's probably either out celebrating his birthday or already tucked up in bed. It's late but I can't go to sleep without answers, and I immediately picture someone who might be able to provide them. I grab my keys and my phone, and head out of the door, feeling unsteady on my feet as I descend the stairs. It suddenly feels so much colder in here, but I can't tell if that's just my imagination now considering my home in a different light.

I reach the door to Flat 1, and take a deep breath before

rapping my knuckles against it. I hear the sound of the security chain being unlatched and a moment later, Bill's face appears in the gap.

'Hey, kiddo, what can I do for you this late?'

He glances at his watch as he says it, before stifling a yawn. The fact that he's in a buttoned shirt and tank top tells me I haven't dragged him out of bed.

'I want to know about John Samuel Cooper.'

I'm hoping he'll feign ignorance and send me on my way, but instead his brow furrows with what I can only describe as a look of resignation.

'You'd better come in.'

## 20

### TUESDAY, 11.27 P.M.

I follow Bill through to his living room, and am immediately hit by the obvious stench. It's a rancid combination of damp and body odour, and I can't tell whether Bill is aware of it. One of the double-glazed windows is fogged up where the seal has blown, and there is a portable electric heater glowing orange in the corner of the room. Bill hasn't mentioned any issues with damp or the window, but I make a mental note to have it replaced.

'Please take a seat,' he says, lifting a pile of folded clothes from one of the two armchairs and carrying it out of the room, presumably to his bedroom.

I sit in the chair, wrestling a sock from beside the seat cushion, and leave it on the small, round wooden coffee table that sits between the two armchairs. It is littered with cellophane sweet wrappers and there are three lemon bonbons left in an open packet on the table.

It's been weeks since I've been down to visit Bill, even longer since he's invited me inside his flat. He usually pops up to see me on the rare occasions there is anything he requires my help with. Of all my tenants, Bill has lived here the longest and is the least demanding. I suppose that's why I feel less like I need to check up on him as much as the others.

'I was about to fix myself a nightcap,' he says, striding back into the room, his tall frame now wrapped in a thick woollen cardigan. 'Can I pour you a glass too?'

He lifts a bottle of Scotch from beside the other armchair, and I'm about to politely decline when he interrupts my thoughts.

'You look like you could use a drink after today.'

I end up nodding and watch silently as he selects two glasses from the wooden cabinet beside the large box television on a stand nearest the window. He pours large measures of caramel-coloured liquid into both and hands me one of the glasses.

'I have no ice, I'm afraid.'

'That's fine,' I tell him, accepting the drink and raising it in toast to him.

The Scotch burns the back of my throat as I swallow a sip of it, and I quickly place it on the small table, the smell immediately going to my head. Bill takes a much larger drink, but doesn't even wince when he swallows it.

Bill was already living here when I took ownership of the building, so I don't understand why I feel so awkward sitting here in his poky flat. I know what I want to ask him, but I can't bring myself to say the words. His acknowledgement of John Cooper's behaviour fifty years ago has thrown me. Suddenly it feels as though Bill – potentially along with my father and God knows who else – has been conspiring against me. They've kept this sordid secret, and even though I've caught them red-handed, it still feels like he holds all the cards.

'I didn't expect to see you up so late,' Bill says to break the awkward silence.

I shrug.

'I wasn't sure you'd be up this late either.'

'Always been a bit of a night owl, me,' he says nodding, as if replaying some distant memory in his head. 'Got a bladder like a colander, so I've never managed more than a few straight hours of undisturbed sleep, so now I just nap when I feel tired. Over a twenty-four-hour period I'd say I get maybe five or six hours, but it comes at different times. I probably sleep more in this chair than I do in the bed next door. Power napping, Elsie used to call it.'

I don't know why this makes me feel so sad; between stalking the passageway and drinking until I pass out, I'm probably not getting nearly as much quality sleep as Bill. I reach for the glass and take a second, longer sip, the burn not nearly as bad this time.

'You wanted to ask me about John Cooper,' Bill says, reading my mind. 'I figured it was only a matter of time before someone raised it after what happened this morning. What do you want to know?'

There are so many questions racing through my mind, but with the tremor of the Scotch now mixed in, I don't know where to begin.

'Why didn't Dad tell me about the history of this place?'

Bill takes a deep breath in and loudly exhales it.

'It was a long time ago, and not something anyone wanted to remember. John Cooper was charged and sentenced to spend the rest of his life behind bars for his crimes.' He pauses. 'Would it have made a difference if you had known?'

The question throws me. When Dad passed, I was heartbroken, and his bequeathing the building to me felt like something I had to do to honour his memory. I don't know how I would have reacted had there been a footnote at the end of the will listing Cooper's crimes.

'At least I would have had all the facts at my disposal to make a more informed decision,' I say evenly, avoiding answering the question directly.

He studies my face.

'Those five women died because of a human being. It had nothing to do with the static bricks and mortar that create this wonderful home. Sure, it's horrific to think about what might have happened inside, but there have been more murders committed on the city streets than behind these windows and it doesn't stop you walking them, does it?'

He catches himself.

'Well, obviously that doesn't apply to *your* situation, but prior to your attack, it never bothered you to think about how many innocent people had suffered on the very pavements you were treading on.'

'But he physically murdered those women in here. There was blood found on one of the carpets.'

He raises a finger.

'Ah. Now. Well, hold on. You're right that blood from one of the victims was discovered inside the hotel as it was then, but she was the only one.' He closes his eyes and raises his face to the ceiling. 'Oh, what was her name? It's been so long since I've thought about it.'

'Caroline Finneran,' I say quietly, picturing the article I read.

Bill nods, and takes another drink.

'That's right. I still remember how broken her mother was at the trial.'

'You were at the trial?' I ask, unable to keep the surprise from my voice.

He nods again.

'Had to be as I was one of the officers involved in the investigation. Most of the force was at one point or another.'

I blink several times, trying to process this new information. Did I know Bill used to be in the police? I didn't start researching my tenants until after the night I was attacked, and Bill was already here so I didn't dig into his background.

'I didn't realise you were involved in Cooper's arrest.'

'He really was a nasty piece of work. The images of his victims are seared on my memory. Even though I had to retire early on medical grounds, I can still see them now.' He pauses. 'That's when I first met your dad.'

The folds in my frown deepen.

'Dad wasn't in the police.'

'Oh, no, that's not what I meant,' he says, quieter now as if carrying the weight of the world. 'No, I met your dad whilst I was serving in the police. He hired me to do a bit of security for him from time to time. That's what I meant.'

'I don't understand. Dad was an investment banker. Why would your paths have crossed?'

He doesn't answer at first, draining his glass instead.

'Can I top you up?'

I place my hand over the top of my glass and shake my head. Bill groans as he stands and shuffles back to the cabinet, pouring himself another large measure and then shuffles back to his armchair. He takes a sip from the glass but makes no effort to answer my earlier question.

'Bill, how did you come to meet my dad?'

'I interviewed him in 1974.'

'About what?'

He lowers his face, as if wrestling with his words.

'Your dad was a good man. A great man. Remember that. But, back in seventy-four, we were hunting for a serial killer. We had a huge list of potential suspects, ranging from family members of the victims to their friends and known acquaintances. We interviewed your dad because he was a friend of the singer from the cruise ships. Sorry, I forget her name.'

'Patricia Robinson.'

'If you say so. Anyway, he had dinner with her the night before she disappeared, and so we had to interview him. Bear in mind this was long before he met your mother, so don't think badly of him. He was a person of interest to us, but was ruled out as she was seen alive the day after their date.'

I think back to the article, the words now ingrained in my mind's eye.

'Cooper claimed she was picked up by a man in a sports car.'

'He did claim that, you're right, but it was determined that he'd made that up to try and cover his tracks.'

'Was my dad the man in the sports car?'

Bill frowns at me.

'That man didn't exist. Cooper invented him.'

'What car did my dad drive at the time?'

I recall the picture of Dad that used to hang in our dining room. He's in a green Jaguar E-Type, the roof down and is holding a flute of champagne up to the camera. It was given to him by a generous client when Dad closed a multimillion-pound deal. He used to tell me how much he wished he'd kept the car as it would be worth a mint to collectors.

'I honestly couldn't tell you, but it isn't important. Your dad was ruled out of the investigation prior to Cooper's arrest.'

'A little convenient that he ended up buying the building though.'

'I disagree. Your dad was an astute businessman. He saw the potential of converting the hotel into affordable housing. Although the outside shell remained, much of the interior was gutted and decorated. Look around you, it's virtually impossible to see where the hotel rooms were divided once upon a time.'

'And it didn't bother you to move into a place where a serial killer once resided?'

'Absolutely not. I needed somewhere to live and because I was doing occasional security jobs for your dad, he gave me a discount on my rent.'

'The article I read said Cooper never confessed to any of the crimes.'

'John Cooper was a despicable human being. He was a narcissist who enjoyed manipulating and hurting others. People like that never admit their crimes.'

'But what if he's out of prison and has returned to wreak havoc again?'

'Cooper died in prison in the late eighties. Cancer. There's no way he had anything to do with what happened here last night.'

'But you still think that James didn't hang himself?'

He takes another drink.

'What do I know? I've been retired for thirty years. Leave it to the professionals. They'll find out what really happened in that room.'

'You must have a hunch though? You were in the police and trained to spot liars, no? Do you think someone here could have killed James and staged it to look like something else?'

He finishes his drink, buying himself time.

'The markings on his wrists suggest he was tied up at some point. It could have been before he made the decision to tie the noose, but if it wasn't then how did he get his hands free and what happened to whatever made those markings? It's possible that somebody else was involved, but if you're asking whether one of the tenants could have... I honestly don't know.'

A shiver ripples down my spine.

'Do you think Cooper murdered those five women?'

'I must admit that I had my doubts when he was first

arrested, but I saw every piece of evidence that was presented at the trial, and it was enough to convince a jury of twelve independent people.'

'What sort of doubts?'

'Doubts is probably the wrong word. What I mean is I wasn't totally convinced that he was guilty of all five murders. Once he was arrested for the singer's murder, it felt a little bit like they tried to pin as many other unsolved crimes on him as they could.'

'So, is it possible someone else could also have been involved?'

He raises a finger of warning.

'I knew your dad for a long time and I can hand-on-heart say he wasn't involved. You need to banish any such thoughts from your mind. He didn't tell you about what happened here because he was trying to protect you. Don't think ill of him. On his deathbed, he asked me to keep you safe. That's why I've continued to live here, even after Elsie's passing. And I will continue to protect you until my last breath. You have my word.'

I'm tempted to ask Bill whether he knows of the passageway, but I don't want to let on that I know. Despite his reassurances, I can't stop picturing Dad in that green Jaguar, and wondering whether he did get away with murder.

## 21

### WEDNESDAY, 7.05 A.M.

Something stirs me from my slumber and I groan when I see the time on my phone. It feels like I only just fell asleep, and even then I don't think I went more than a few minutes without my mind kicking into action. I kept seeing snippets of the John Cooper article with my inner monologue asking unhelpful questions.

*Why didn't the police follow up on Cooper's claim about the man in the sports car? Dad lived in the area and must have known about the hotel, so what if he was also there when Caroline Finneran visited the city in August 1974? He said he married Mum because he was enamoured by her Cork accent; what if she wasn't the first Irish woman who enchanted him? And if he frequented the Freemantle Arms, then he must have spoken with Tania Denby who worked there.*

The rational part of my brain knows Dad was a kind and generous man, and didn't have a murderous bone in his body, and yet I can't stop picturing him in that green Jaguar. And I can't believe he never mentioned being considered a suspect in a murder investigation.

Pete once told me that Dad came down on him like a tonne of

bricks when he caught Pete with a packet of cigarettes when he was fourteen. Pete said he felt pressured to be like his mates, but Dad went ballistic, warning him not to fall in with those kinds of groups because he didn't want to see Pete fall foul of the police. He could have shared his own experiences of being questioned and held in a cell to emphasise the point, but he didn't. Mum never mentioned it, but Bill said he didn't meet her until later, so maybe she never knew either. And realistically, I doubt Bill would have worked for him and become friends if he suspected Dad's involvement in what happened at the hotel.

Looking around my bedroom, I can't help searching for anything that shows this flat was once a hotel room or two. For all I know I'm breathing some of the same air that Cooper did in this very room. I detest the thought that this is where he lured Caroline Finneran before butchering her to death. Maybe it's the scent of death that always makes this place feel so cold.

I reach out a hand and feel along the top of the duvet for George's warm and calming fur, but he's not at the foot of the bed where he usually is most mornings. I run my hand over the other, narrower side of the duvet, but can't feel him there either. I raise my head and open my eyes, frowning when I can't see him on the floor either. Maybe it's too early for him to come in here, and he's still dozing in his basket in the living room.

I push the duvet back and swing my legs over the side of the bed, sliding into my slippers and rub sleep from my eyes as I head out of the room and into the kitchen, filling the kettle and putting it on to boil. I glance over the edge of the counter but George's bed is empty.

'George,' I call out. 'Where are you, young man?'

I wait to see if he appears from wherever he's hiding, but I don't hear the patter of feet. I check by the front door, but he isn't there. I do spot an envelope poking beneath the bottom of the door, and I stoop to collect it, seeing my name on the front but no designated flat number. One of my tenants must have received it in their post box downstairs and slipped it under my door. I don't recognise the handwriting on the front, and slide my index finger beneath the lip and open it.

There is an embroidered piece of card inside, and at first I assume it's a wedding invitation, though I can't think of anyone I know who's getting married. But then I read the calligraphy, and roll my eyes when I see the words 'school reunion'. It's an invitation back to the place I swore I would never visit again after what happened. I can't imagine who in their right mind thought it would be a good idea to reach out to me. At the bottom of the card is the name of the reunion organiser, but I don't recognise it. If she was in the same year as me, we certainly didn't take any of the same classes.

Even if I could attend such an event in person, I'm not sure I'd want to. I've tried to bury all the awful memories after what happened, and I'm not in the right frame of mind to be dredging them up now. I leave the card and envelope on my desk in the living room and return to the kitchen.

Opening the cupboard by the fridge, I pull out a pouch of George's food and give it a shake, knowing breakfast is the one thing he'll never ignore, but he still doesn't appear. Opening the packet, I tip it into his bowl beside the litter tray, the hard nuggets clanging against the metal rim of the bowl, but he still doesn't materialise.

'George, come on, breakfast,' I call out, louder this time in case he can't hear over the sound of the kettle.

George is a house cat, partly because I don't want the tenants to know about him, and also because if the outside isn't safe enough for me, it's even worse for him. He's never been outside since I brought him back to the flat before the pandemic, and unless he's worked out how to unlock and open the front door, he has to be around here somewhere. I move to the living room and check both sofas, even looking beneath and behind both in case he's become trapped, but I don't find him. I check in the washing basket, on my office chair, and even head into the bathroom but there's no sign. I double-check my own room again but he isn't under the duvet or the bed. I call to him again, but am met with silence.

*Where on earth could he be?*

My eyes fall on the door to the airing cupboard. It's ajar, and I realise he must be asleep on the towels beside the water tank. I've caught him there before. I pull the door wider. The towels are untouched, but the hatch in the floor is open. I stare at the dark hole in disbelief. I'm sure I closed it after I last went down to check on Fi's flat, but I must be mistaken if it's open now.

I rack my memory for whether I went back down last night after returning from Bill's. I can see myself stumbling back in through the door, and my keys clattering to the floor when I was trying to hang them on the peg and failed. Under the influence of Bill's Scotch I was in no state to be stalking along the passageway, but there's no other explanation for why the hatch would now be open. The question is how long George has been missing. I don't remember seeing him when I returned last night but it's hard to recall anything through the black cloud in my head.

*What if I only thought I'd closed the hatch after checking on Fi, and George went into the cupboard searching for the warm spot on the towels and fell through the open hatch?*

I switch on the light on my phone and shine it down into the darkness, but there's no sign of him at the foot of the ladder.

'George,' I call out in a loud whisper, conscious of being overheard by the tenants on the first floor. I make kissing noises as well, but I don't hear the jangle of his collar bell.

Crouching, I push my feet through the hole and swiftly clamber down the ladder, shining my torchlight in an arc, searching for where he could be. To my relief there's no sign of blood, so wherever he is, hopefully he isn't injured. I call his name in a loud whisper again, and make the same kissing noises as I tiptoe towards Fi's flat. There's no sign of George, but I spot the discarded water bottle again. It doesn't look as though the rat has been back to chew on it.

An image of George chasing around down here after the rat pops into my head. One misplaced paw and he could crash through the insulation and plasterboard of the ground-floor flats. Maybe that's why he can't hear me.

I place my ear to the wall of Fi's flat, listening for any sign that she's finally returned home, but I can't hear any movement, music or television from within. I'm sure she didn't mention going away on holiday, and it's unlike her to stay out all night, but then I'm learning so many new things about my tenants this week that nothing should surprise me.

'George,' I try again, as I retrace my steps back towards Jenny's flat. 'Where are you, my boy?'

I freeze when I hear raised voices coming from beyond the breezeblocks. Jenny is shouting at Chad, and as I lean closer, the rough edge of the stone feels cold against my ear.

'I don't believe you,' Jenny shouts.

'Babe, you're putting two and two together, and coming out with five. I'm telling you there is nothing going on between me and Eve.'

I freeze at mention of my name.

'I've seen the way she looks at you, Chad. I'm not blind! If you want to screw her, then just be honest with me. I'm too old to be playing games.'

'Listen to me, Jen, I am not having an affair with Eve. She isn't my type.'

I try not to take it personally and continue to listen in.

'Then explain where you were on Monday night.'

'What are you talking about? I was here with you.'

'Bullshit! I woke up at four and you weren't in bed. I checked the flat and you were nowhere to be seen. You told the police that you were here with me all night and I lied and said you were. Maybe I should phone that detective and come clean.'

There's a pause as my imagination goes into overdrive.

'Wait, Monday night? You mean Tuesday morning, right? I remember now, I was struggling to sleep, so I decided to go for an early-morning run. I would have said something sooner but I figured you wouldn't have noticed.'

'You were out running at four in the morning?'

'Sure. I've got that 10K coming up in a couple of weeks and I figured the streets would be quiet at that time.'

'So, you weren't upstairs shagging Eve?'

'Babe, please, you know you're the only woman for me. I love you.'

I've heard enough, and continue along the wooden board until I reach Mike's flat, but I can't see any sign of George. It's possible that he followed the rat down to the ground floor, but it's not safe to be shuffling along these boards in my slippers, so I return to the ladder and clamber up, making sure I lower the hatch once I'm inside. I return to the kitchen to make tea, and am about to go and get dressed when I hear a faint scratching noise. I strain to hear, crouching and then crawling along on my hands and knees.

'George? Is that you? Can you hear me?'

I follow the sound towards the hallway, and stop when I hear the scratching coming from the other side of the front door.

Leaping to my feet, I grab my keys from the peg and unlock the door, relief flooding my body as I scoop George up and into my arms.

'There you are,' I say, nuzzling his fur against my nose and kissing his head. 'You scared me.'

I close the door and return the keys to the peg, carrying George over to the sofa and keep him in my lap while I stroke and play with him.

'How on earth did you get outside?' I ask playfully, as something scratches at the back of my mind. 'I've looked everywhere for you. I was scared I'd never see you again.'

He jumps down from my lap and patters into the kitchen and munches his breakfast whilst I stand and look back at the front door. I definitely didn't see George slip out of the door when I came back last night. I'm always so careful when opening and closing it, even in a drunk state, and George knows better than to venture outside.

My eyes fall on my keys on the peg. I remember them clattering to the floor, but made no effort to try and put them back on the peg. I definitely remember crawling into bed and thinking I would pick them up in the morning. So how would they have returned to the peg if I didn't do it?

My gaze switches back to the closed airing cupboard door, and the breath catches in my throat. The hatch was open when I was sure I'd closed it, my keys miraculously appeared on the peg, and George was left outside the flat. Someone else has been inside my flat.

## 22

WEDNESDAY, 9.15 A.M.

I have searched every inch of my flat and there is nobody in here but me and George, and yet I can't escape the feeling that I've been violated. Only my brother has a spare key for my flat, and although he had spoken about coming over last night, he knows better than to turn up unannounced. And given we'd spoken earlier about the police presence and hassle downstairs, I don't think he would have come here. And he lives on his own – ironic that he accuses me of being antisocial – so I can't see how anyone else could have used his key.

All of my windows are closed and locked, and I keep the keys hidden beneath plant pots on each of the windowsills, and neither plant looks disturbed; no telltale signs of spilled soil. So, the only other entry point to my flat is through the hatch that was open when I woke this morning.

A shiver ripples the length of my body as I picture some faceless person roaming about inside here while I slept, oblivious to their presence. For all I know, they came close enough to feel my breath against their skin. I shiver again, trying to force the terrifying images from my mind. I've now put a set of dumbbells on top of the hatch to make it near impossible to get through from the passageway, but even with that deterrent I don't feel brave enough to shower.

The thing I can't explain is why they were careless enough to leave the trapdoor open. If I was trying to sneak into someone's home, I'd do my utmost to make it look as if I hadn't been there. Yet the fact the hatch was left open, the keys were returned to the peg, and George was evicted, all point to the fact somebody has been inside my home, and they want me to know it. If I'd stirred and disturbed an attempted robbery, I'd have assumed they would head back down the same way they came in, and maybe they did, but that would mean they're still down there, which is the reason I've tried to secure the hatch as best I can.

The image of the rat-chewed plastic bottle on the first floor flashes before me. It was a red flag that somebody else had been down there, and I chose to ignore it. For all I know, someone could have been living in the passageway for some time, and last night may not have been their first visit to my flat.

I hurry to the bathroom, and dry retch into the sink, but I've had no appetite since I woke, so nothing comes up. I look up to the mirror and see a haggard, pale face staring back at me. The dark circles beneath my eyes are in stark contrast to the pasty skin around them. For the first time I can see why Pete is permanently worried about me. I do look ill.

I start at knocking on my door, and quickly splash some water on my face, reaching for my dressing gown and tying it around myself. I've never felt the need for a security chain, but after last night, it is something I should invest in. Standing by the door, I look for anything I can quickly grab and use as a weapon, but the only thing I can find is an old golfing umbrella hanging on one of the coat pegs.

'Who is it?' I say.

## The Tenants

'Good morning, Eve. It's Detective Sergeant Kim Atwal. I have a couple of follow-up questions to ask.'

I close my eyes and sigh with relief, unlocking the door and opening it wide for her.

'Oh, I'm sorry, did I wake you?' she asks, eyeing the robe.

'Oh, no, I... was just about to shower.'

The rational part of my mind suggests I tell her the truth about my morning and the intruder in my home, but apart from the moved keys and George being left outside – for which I am the only witness – there is no evidence that anybody was in here. I can't tell her about the hatch because that will lead to all sorts of other difficult questions. George and the keys are circumstances that can easily be explained by the fact that I was drunk when I returned last night and could have misremembered the incidents. If I tell her what I'm going through I'll sound paranoid.

'Would you like a cup of tea?' I ask instead, ushering her through to the living room.

'I'm fine, thank you. Shall we sit down?'

My head feels as though I've gone ten rounds in a boxing ring, but I plaster on a smile and sit across from her.

'Thank you for making the time to see me,' she begins, in a tone that is probably designed to make me feel more at ease, but does quite the opposite. 'We've had difficulty trying to get hold of Fiona Erskine in Flat 5. Do you have any idea of where she might be?'

'No, I don't, I'm afraid. I invited all of my tenants to a meeting last night but she didn't show up, which is quite unlike her.'

'Can you remember the last time you saw her?'

I try to think but it's almost impossible to recall anything through the thick fog in my head.

'Um, I'm honestly not sure.'

'Have you seen her in the last twenty-four hours?'

I shake my head.

'How about the last week?'

I desperately scramble for any memory involving Fi. I don't remember seeing her face to face since last month's tenants' meeting, though I have heard her via the passageway.

'Yeah, I think I saw her coming in from work last week.'

'What day?'

*When did I last hear her inside her flat?*

'Um, Thursday, I think. Sorry, I have a banging headache, and I'm struggling this morning.'

'Heavy night?'

The question puts me instantly on alert.

'No, I just didn't sleep very well. That's all.'

She fixes me with a hard stare.

'No judgement. If I'd found one of my neighbours' bodies, I'd have probably needed a stiff drink for shock.' She glances down at the notebook she's been scribbling in. 'Whereabouts did you see her on Thursday?'

'What, sorry?'

'You said you saw her coming home from work on Thursday, but where did you see her?'

'Um, in the corridor.'

'Which corridor? Ground floor? First floor?'

'Um, ground floor.'

'And were you on your way out, or just returning from somewhere?'

'What does that have to do with anything?'

'I'm just trying to paint a picture in my mind. I'm a bit of a sponge when it comes to detail. It helps me see all the angles and permutations.'

I don't like her tone, but I've learned it's best to pick your battles in a police interview.

'Um, I don't ever go out anywhere. I think I was downstairs checking the post box for new mail when she came back. She didn't stop to speak before hurrying up the stairs to her flat.'

'So, you didn't see her face? How can you be sure it was her?'

'I saw her face when she came through the door, and then she brushed past me on her way up the stairs.'

I can feel beads of sweat pooling at my hairline. I can't believe I'm tangling myself up in knots over something so irrelevant.

I stop, as my brain slowly kicks into gear.

*Unless they think that Fi was involved in what happened to James...*

'Do you know where Miss Erskine works? We asked her next-door neighbours but they said they didn't know her profession.'

'She's a solicitor, works at a firm on London Road.'

'Do you happen to know which one?'

I shrug apologetically, and she narrows her eyes.

I hear Mike's Bristolian voice in my head: *Ooh, maybe Danielle has already done her in as well.*

'Wait, you don't think something bad has happened to her, do you?' I ask before I can keep my mouth shut.

'What makes you ask that?'

I don't want to reveal the accusations that were being thrown about at last night's meeting.

'Just the way you're asking all these questions.'

'I'm merely trying to establish where she is so we can ask her whether she witnessed anything odd about Mr DeVere's behaviour in the last couple of days. It's quite a leap to suggest that something ill may have befallen her.'

'Is it? I heard on the news last night that you have yet to confirm James died by suicide, which means you think someone else is involved, and if they were, he might not be the only tenant attacked.'

I know I'm spiralling, and that my attempts to dig myself out of this hole are only making matters worse. And the way she's looking at me right now, the mask of pleasantries has slipped.

'Remind me where you were on Tuesday night.'

'I was here all night.'

'And were you with anyone?'

'No, I told you I was alone.'

'That's right, but you just *happened* to go downstairs to speak with Mr DeVere and just *happened* to see a mysterious dark-haired woman go into his flat with him. A woman that nobody else saw or can account for.'

I don't like the insinuation, but that isn't what raises the hairs on the back of my neck. I see the words from the newspaper article floating in the air above Atwal's head: *Cooper... witnessed Miss Robinson being collected from the hotel by an unidentified male in a sports car, but no other witnesses could corroborate the story.*

They didn't believe him, and Atwal isn't hiding her own incredulity right now.

'I did see a woman with dark hair,' I say firmly. 'I'm not making it up.'

She sits there staring at me.

'Why don't we go and check on Fi? I have a set of keys to her flat and we can make sure nothing untoward has happened.'

She frowns.

'You have keys to all of the flats?'

'You know I do. That was how I was able to get into James's flat and find him...'

'Okay, then let's go and check on Flat 5,' she says, standing, urging me to lead the way.

I collect the keys from the peg, with a growing sense of dread about what we might find. My paranoia is spiking and all I can think now is that a killer entered my flat through the hatch last night, stole my keys to go and attack Fi, before putting everything back, knowing I can't prove it.

I feel as though I may retch again as we head down the stairs to the first floor and along to Fi's front door.

'I'm required to knock and let her know I need to come in,' I say, as a single bead of sweat drips into my eyes, causing me to blink it away.

I knock twice and clear my throat.

'Fi, it's Eve. If you're home, can you let me in as there's something urgent I need to speak to you about.'

Atwal leans closer to the door, listening before nodding at me to use my keys. My hands tremble as I try to locate the correct one and fit it into the lock. The tremors are so bad that the keys fall to the floor, but Atwal is the one who picks them up and inserts them into the lock. She cracks the door open.

'Fiona Erskine, my name is Detective Sergeant Kim Atwal, and I'm part of Hampshire Constabulary. I'm entering your flat, and don't want you to be alarmed.'

She nudges the door open with her foot and slowly enters, keeping one eye on me as she proceeds into the living room. I can't ignore the dread at what I'm about to see but I follow her inside, so relieved when I don't see her hanging from the ceiling. Atwal proceeds to check the bedroom and bathroom, but Fi isn't here.

'Toothbrush and shower gel are still here, and it doesn't look like she's taken clothes from the wardrobe in the bedroom. So where is she?'

'I don't know.'

'What are you hiding, Eve? My intuition is pretty good, and I know you're holding something back. It would be better and easier for everyone if you just told me.'

'I'm not hiding anything,' I reply, taking an unsteady step backwards.

Atwal surveys the room until something catches her eye. Crossing the living room she stabs her finger against the phone dock that I see now is flashing.

'There is one new message,' the digitised voice announces, 'left at 3.17 p.m. on Tuesday.'

There's a pause and then a voice from the grave speaks.

'Hey, Fi, I'm so sorry but I'm running late for our dinner. I've got something to sort at work and then I'll head straight to the restaurant. I should make it by eight o'clock at the latest. Any problems, just give me a call. Love you.'

My mouth drops, and Atwal stares back at me with suspicious eyes.

'So, James DeVere and Fiona Erskine were an item. Why did you choose not to disclose that?'

'I didn't know,' I mouth, but it's barely audible.

*How could I not know that the pair were seeing one another? How could I have missed that?*

'I'm asking you directly, Eve: was Fiona Erskine the woman you saw entering James DeVere's flat on Tuesday night? Is that what you've been holding back?'

I shake my head, but she isn't waiting for an answer, pulling out a radio and requesting an APB and phone trace on Fi.

## 23

WEDNESDAY, 9.53 A.M.

Detective Atwal doesn't hang around, and her presence here has left a nasty aftertaste. When we found James yesterday, it seemed obvious that he'd chosen to take his own life, even though I couldn't understand his motivation for doing so. Yet the way Atwal was questioning me, and then her reaction to the answerphone message in Fi's flat, suggests she believes James didn't act alone.

Fi has blonde hair, cut into a short bob, and she's not much taller than me so I am certain it wasn't her I glimpsed heading into James's flat on Monday night. But if he was supposed to be meeting Fi for dinner that night, and was in love with her, why did he return to his flat for sex with another woman?

I should be working on the advertising pitch for Lauren's bakery, but my brain is screaming out for answers, and I can't concentrate. I have kept such a close ear on my tenants and yet I had no clue that James and Fi were romantically involved. I'd have said there were no signs or clues that they were together, but maybe my instincts aren't as entwined with my neighbours as I hoped. I'm trying to replay the last few tenants' meetings in my head to see if there were any furtive glances between the pair that I might have overlooked, but it's no good.

I stare at the laptop screen, the blank page before me seeming to mock me for my inability to create. My appetite has yet to return and whilst there's part of me that wants to go into the passageway in search of whoever locked George out, I don't know what I'd actually do if I came face to face with that person. If they killed James, would they think twice about killing me too?

I check the dumbbells haven't been disturbed, and then I throw on jogging bottoms and a hoodie and head out of the flat and down to the ground floor. Although there is a band of police tape across the front of James's door, and occasional dashes of fingerprint dust along the walls, there's no other sign that the police were here. The temporary white canopy is now gone from outside and there is no uniformed officer guarding the entrance. I knock twice on Danielle's door and when she eventually opens it, she's rubbing her eyes, dressed in satin pyjamas.

'Oh, shit,' I exclaim, 'I didn't think. Sorry, were you asleep?'

She stifles a yawn while nodding.

'It was a manic one in A&E last night. It's true what they say about the full moon bringing out the crazies. Do you want to come in?'

I feel guilty for disturbing her sleep, but I haven't managed to speak to Danielle since we found James yesterday, and I want to check how she's coping, and to find out if I was the only one ignorant of Fi's and James's relationship.

'Only if you're sure?'

'It's fine, Eve. I'm not due back in until tomorrow. Do you want a cup of tea or coffee?'

'Coffee. Thanks.'

Danielle heads into the open-plan kitchen and prepares drinks whilst I sit at the small square table and try to compose the questions in my head. She carries over two mugs and a packet of chocolate digestives, offering me one. I take a biscuit in an effort to rid myself of the bitter taste in my mouth.

'Sorry I didn't make it to last night's tenants' meeting,' she says. 'I saw the note you put under the door when I got back this morning.'

It's probably just as well she wasn't there to hear India's stinging attack: *If anyone's to blame for what's happened, it's Danielle and her fucking bike.*

'No worries, it was last minute, and I figured you were probably at work. I just wanted to make sure everybody knew what had happened and to offer my support.'

'How did the rest of the group take the news?'

I'm not going to mention India's and Mike's accusations.

'Everyone was as shocked as you and me.'

'I still can't believe he's gone. When you knocked this morning I couldn't be sure if it was all just a bad dream.'

'What did the police ask you about what happened?'

She takes a sip from her mug.

'They just wanted to understand our exact steps and why we were in his flat that morning.'

'And what did you tell them?'

'I told them the truth. I said my bike was missing and I was convinced James was the one who'd taken it, and that's why we went in when he didn't answer the door.'

'Did you mention the argument on Monday night?'

She frowns slightly.

'I wouldn't describe it as an argument. I told them he'd kicked off about the bike being in the hallway again, but that you were taking steps to resolve that. Turns out he probably had nothing to do with the bike going missing.'

It seems an obvious statement to make given we didn't find the bike inside his flat, but I don't understand why she's added it.

'You weren't so sure yesterday.'

'Ah, but the police have recovered it. They found it a couple of streets over apparently. Dumped, but not damaged in any way. They've confiscated it to check for forensics or something.'

If Atwal is so convinced James didn't die by suicide, then maybe she suspects the killer made their escape on the bike.

'Well, that's good news, I suppose. At least you won't have to replace it.'

'It doesn't explain who took it and dumped it. It has to be someone from in here though, don't you think?'

'Why?'

'Because it was just outside my flat on Monday night. Nobody can get through the front door without a key, so whoever took it had access to this building. It wouldn't surprise me if it was one of those lot from upstairs.'

'Who are you accusing?'

'Could be any of them. India has looked down her nose at me since I moved in. They all put on an act when you're around, but when you're not, there's no love lost between the two floors.'

I'm winded by the statement. I've worked so hard to make sure everyone gets along – these people are my family – and to hear they're all pulling the wool over my eyes stings.

'I'm sorry, Eve. Listen, it isn't my place to say anything, and I know you try your hardest to keep things pleasant, but one or two of them really should look for alternative accommodation.'

I hear India's voice in my head: *She knows exactly what to do to get what she wants.*

Is that what Danielle is doing now? Should I be taking her comments with a pinch of salt?

'What about Fi?' I say, my mind coming back to the real reason I knocked on her door. 'Do you get along with her?'

She wrinkles her nose.

'I don't have any problems with Fi, but I don't really know her. She's usually out when I get home or vice versa, so I very rarely see her.'

'Can you remember the last time you *did* see her though? I haven't managed to speak to her about what happened to James, and I'm now wondering if maybe she's away for a few days.'

'I can't really remember, to be honest. I tend to keep myself to myself most of the time. Working at the hospital can be so draining that it doesn't leave much time for being sociable.'

'So you weren't aware that James and Fi were involved romantically?'

She raises her eyebrows.

'Really? No, no clue whatsoever.' She pauses, considering it. 'I suppose I shouldn't be surprised, given how he pursued me when I moved in. I'm just amazed she'd fall for his charms.'

I was also stunned by the message he left on her answerphone, but it's been that long since I was in a relationship that there's probably a good reason I missed the signs. At least I'm not the only one who hasn't seen Fi, although I can't imagine that she could be responsible for what happened to James.

'I should let you get back to bed,' I say, draining my coffee. 'Do me a favour, though, yeah? Keep your door locked and keep your eyes peeled when you have to go out. I've said for years that the outside world isn't safe, and I'd hate for anything bad to happen to you too.'

Danielle promises she'll be careful, and shows me out.

I hear India's words in my head as Danielle closes and locks the door: *It wouldn't surprise me if she was somehow involved in what happened.*

But I shake the thought away dismissively. If Danielle is right about India looking down her nose at her, then it makes sense that India would try and throw her under the bus, but could she have another reason for doing so?

This is the question I'm pondering as I head back towards the stairs when I hear a voice that makes the hairs on the back of my neck stand. I hurry along the corridor and look around the corner, my mouth dropping when I see James pulling the strips of police tape from the doorway of Flat 4.

## 24

### WEDNESDAY, 10.22 A.M.

I double-take at the figure. I know it can't be him, and yet...

'James?' I call out, and the figure slowly turns and stares back at me, his face clouded with confusion.

Heat rises to my cheeks as I realise my mistake. The man clearly isn't James now that I can see his face, though his height and figure match.

'No, I'm Ethan,' he says, moving closer and as he steps into the light he is much younger than I realised. 'I'm James's brother.'

He holds out his hand, and I feel compelled to shake it.

'I'm Eve. I'm the landlady here. I live on the top floor.'

I don't know why I've given him that information so freely, and I realise now that I've been staring into his dark brown eyes for too long and avert my gaze.

'Ah, the infamous Eve,' he says, a smile breaking across his face. 'James mentioned you looked after him. He never said how pretty you were though.'

My cheeks redden further. His nose isn't bent out of shape like James's was, and his hairline isn't receding in the same way, but the jaw structure is very familiar. I can't be the first to have mistaken one for the other. He really does look like a younger version of James.

'I'm sorry, I didn't mean to make you blush. I always find small talk so challenging that I blurt things out.'

I take a breath and compose myself.

'I'm sorry about your brother. It was such a shock. To all of us.'

'Thank you. Yes, for us too. The police asked if I could come and look over his flat to see if anything is missing.'

'Of course. That makes sense. If there's anything I can do to help, please just shout.'

I turn to leave.

'Actually, there is something you could do,' he says, and I turn back to face him. 'The police didn't leave me a key to gain access, and the door is locked. I don't suppose you have a spare?'

I reach into my pocket and extract the set of skeleton keys. I'm surprised Detective Atwal didn't warn me that Ethan would be coming here today. And I'm also surprised they wouldn't insist on chaperoning a visitor too.

'I can let you in,' I say, crossing to the door and unlocking it.

He pushes the door open and ducks beneath the remaining piece of tape. Although I've no doubt that Ethan must be related to James in some way – and I've no reason to doubt he is who he says he is – the police haven't told me I should allow anybody inside Flat 4, so I follow him in, just in case I'm mistaken and he wants to steal something.

My pulse quickens as I near the door to the living room and I'm temporarily transported back to the moment when Danielle screamed as she entered. Ethan makes no such outburst as he enters and surveys the room. The rope has been removed from the ceiling rose, and but for the fingerprint dust, you'd never know this was a crime scene.

'Is this where you found him?' Ethan asks, standing beneath the light fixture, and I nod, unable to look at it directly without picturing James's body swinging there. 'Did he seem down to you in the days leading up to this?'

'Not that I knew of,' I say honestly. 'I wish he had said something though. I've had issues with my own mental health and I understand how difficult things can seem.'

I catch myself, again surprised at how open I'm being towards a man I've only just met.

'I wish he'd phoned me,' Ethan says, his lips downturned, 'but we weren't that close. I mean, we were brothers and I loved him, but he had his life down here, and neither of us was good at checking in on the other. After our parents passed... we drifted apart, not that we were particularly close before that. Do you have any siblings?'

'An older brother too. Pete.'

'Do you see much of him?'

Too much, I don't say as I'm sure Ethan would do anything to see James again one more time.

'He lives locally so we speak often,' I say empathetically. 'Whereabouts are you based?'

'From Manchester originally, like James, but I live in Birmingham now.'

'And you travelled down today?'

He nods.

'Yeah, drove down first thing. My boss has said I can take a few personal days to sort out funeral arrangements and the like. Actually, that's something you could help me with if you don't mind? I don't know the area at all, would you be able to help me find a funeral director to help?'

'Absolutely,' I say, though I don't know the first thing about how to act when a family member dies. Pete handled all of the arrangements for Dad. I can probably call him for some guidance.

'Thanks.' He continues looking around the living room before heading into the bedroom. 'Do you know if James had a girlfriend or was dating anyone?'

I don't know whether I should mention the answerphone message Atwal and I heard this morning, as she may not want it broadcasting.

'Not that I was aware of,' I say instead.

'The police told me someone thought they saw him returning home with a woman the night it happened.'

This is awkward as it's now going to appear like I just lied to him.

'Yeah, that was me actually. Sorry, I should have said when you asked. I don't know who the woman was or whether they were seeing one another properly.'

His head appears from behind the bedroom door, and he looks confused.

'Oh, maybe I misunderstood then. The police said you told them you heard them having sex. Or was that someone else?'

I picture myself with my ear pressed to James's wall: *When my friend said you liked it rough, I didn't think she meant it.*

'No, that was me, but I can't really be sure what I heard. There was banging about and giggling. I don't know, it just sounded like two people tearing each other's clothes off.'

I'm blushing again, but if he notices he doesn't say.

'Do you often listen in on what your tenants are getting up to?'

'What? No! Why would you ask that?'

He raises his hands into the air as if I'm holding a gun.

'Whoa, Eve, I'm sorry, I was just joking.'

My breathing is coming in short, rapid bursts, and I dread to think how crazy Ethan must now think I am.

I laugh falsely, but I'm not sure I've covered my tracks sufficiently.

'Sorry, James always used to tell me my sense of humour wasn't to everyone's taste. I tend to use humour as a defence mechanism. Forgive me.'

'It's fine,' I say quickly. 'When was the last time you spoke to him?'

He looks wistfully towards the window.

'I'm embarrassed to say that I don't think we've spoken since Christmas. Doesn't that make me an awful brother?'

'You don't need to explain how challenging sibling relationships can be. I'm already a member of that club.'

I've no doubt that Pete will be around later to check my flat for signs of overreliance on alcohol, examining every item of food in my fridge for its nutritional impact.

'When we were kids, my parents sent us to boarding school. Dad justified it as he was always travelling for work, but Mum was at home and could have looked after us. It was how he was raised, and she wasn't strong enough to stand up for herself. James was six years older than me, so he had little interest when I joined the school, preferring to hang out with his own mates and not wanting a little brother hanging around. It's no wonder we turned out as badly as we did.'

I don't tell him that I also boarded at school, albeit only Monday to Friday, returning home each weekend. I understand how tough it is though. James never shared any of that detail with me. When he first applied to move in, he was warm and charming, but I saw less and less of him after the first couple of months and he seemed to have no interest in nurturing a personal relationship.

'Let me thank you for keeping an eye on him down here,' Ethan continues. 'I'm going to go as I have no clue what I should be looking for anyway. Can you see anything obvious missing?'

I can't honestly remember the last time James invited me inside, and shake my head apologetically.

'Would it be okay if I called you later on? To discuss funeral arrangements, I mean.'

'Of course,' I say, reciting my mobile number to him which he types into his phone.

'And will you attend the funeral?'

I've been so open with him until this point that I should just tell him about my agoraphobia and that attending the funeral will be impossible.

'I'll try my best,' I say instead.

'Great. It would be nice to have a friendly face there.'

He smiles and I find myself smiling back. We head out and I pull the door closed and lock it, and when I look up, Ethan has already disappeared. I hear the front door open and close, and take a moment to compose myself. He seems like a nice guy but he's only passing through so there's no point in fantasising it could be anything more.

Straightening my hoodie, I climb the stairs to the first floor and try knocking for Fi once again. I bash my hand against the door twice and am about to give up when I'm sure I hear a thump inside.

## 25

### WEDNESDAY, 10.47 A.M.

I press my ear to the door of Flat 5, uncertain whether I imagined the noise and trying to work out the cause. It sounded like something heavy falling to the floor. If a window was open, a breeze maybe could have caught hold of something on a bookshelf, but I know I'm reaching because the windows were definitely closed when Detective Atwal and I entered earlier this morning.

I knock again.

'Fi? Is that you? It's Eve. Can you let me in, please?'

My request is met with silence, but I keep my ear pressed to the door.

There. I heard something. A scuff mark of some kind, like a shoe scraping against carpet. I strain to hear anything else, holding my own breath so it's only my beating heart that I can hear out here.

It doesn't sound like Fi is making any attempt to come to the door if she is indeed inside, but I have to know one way or another. I remove the keychain from my pocket, and insert it into the lock. I turn it, and hear what sounds like a squeal as I do.

'Fi, are you okay?' I ask as I push the door open and enter. 'I'm coming in.'

My ears are poised for any trace of sound, but I don't hear any other pained cries or thumps. The door to the living room is ajar, and I'm sure it was wide open when Atwal and I left; a sign that Fi has finally returned home?

Maybe I should have phoned Atwal and told her I heard movement, rather than entering alone, but it's too late to worry about my impulsivity. I nudge the door open with my foot.

'Fi? Are you home? It's Eve and I need to speak to you urgently, which is why I've let myself in.'

The door swings open, but there's no sign of anyone inside. There's an upturned picture frame beside the large bookcase against the far wall, and if I had to guess I'd say that was probably the thump I heard from outside. But the windows beside it are closed, so it isn't obvious what caused it to fall. I move further into the room when I feel a breeze brush against my face. My eyes divert to the open bedroom door, and that's when I see the net curtains dancing freely in front of the open bedroom window.

I freeze. The window definitely wasn't open when I was last in here. I didn't imagine the noise in here. Fi has definitely been back, but where is she now?

'Fi? You can come out. I know you're here.'

There's no reason for Fi to be hiding from me. We have a good relationship as far as I know. She's never complained about the living arrangements. My eyes fall on the answerphone and I replay James's message in my head: *Hey, Fi, I'm so sorry but I'm running late for our dinner. I've got something to sort at work and then I'll head straight to the restaurant. I should make it by eight o'clock at the latest. Any problems, just give me a call. Love you.*

She must know about James's passing by now. It's been

## The Tenants

reported on the national news, which means it's bound to have made the local newspaper as well. Fi would have to have been living under a rock not to know what has happened. And I suppose if they were romantically involved, maybe the news has hit her harder than the rest of us.

The bedroom and bathroom are both empty when I check them, so Fi isn't here now, but I'm sure I heard movement inside. I look inside the wardrobe and beneath the bed in case she is hiding there, but the flat is empty. I sit up and stare at the bed. It doesn't look slept in, but now that I'm at eye-level I can see two indents at the side of the bed nearest the window. I lean closer and unless I'm mistaken they resemble footprints.

I quickly stand and hurry to the window, raising the net curtain and staring down. For the briefest second I see Simone's lifeless corpse staring back up at me, her blood streaming across the cobbles, but when I look again I see only the green lawn below. It must be three metres or so down to the patch of grass that runs the length of the rear of the building. There's nobody down there now, but I can't stop thinking that whoever was in here might have jumped out of the window when they heard me enter, but there's no reason for Fi to make such a desperate escape, so who was in here and what did they want? Did I disturb a burglar?

I may be jumping to wild conclusions, but given what I discovered in my own flat this morning, it isn't beyond the realms of possibility. I need to report this to Atwal. And I should also warn the other tenants that we've had an intruder and they should keep their doors and windows locked, despite the summer heat.

I shouldn't disturb the scene any more than I already have, so I tiptoe back to the front door and slip out.

'What the hell do you think you're doing?'

I turn at the ear-splitting shriek, and see Jenny standing behind me, incandescent.

'What were you doing inside Fi's flat?'

'I was just checking in on her.'

'She's back? Good, I've been meaning to speak to her.'

She leans past me, almost catching me in the face as she knocks on the door.

'Fi isn't home,' I say, knowing how she's likely to react to the next part.

She frowns in confusion.

'But you just said she was.'

'No, I didn't. I said I was checking in on her. I thought I heard her moving about inside, but when I went in, she wasn't home.'

'How did you get inside then if she wasn't there?' Her eyes drop to the ring of keys in my hand. 'Oh, I see, well, that's a revelation. I never realised you had a key to every flat.'

'It's just a safety precaution in case a tenant accidentally locks themselves out.'

'Ha,' she scoffs, 'and you expect me to believe that? How many of our homes do you go sneaking about in when we're out?'

I'm trying to remain calm and not raise my voice as she is because I don't want anyone else to hear. Although Mike and India are probably at work, I don't know for sure and neither of them need encouragement to question my motives.

'Jenny, please, can we take this conversation elsewhere? Maybe we can go in and talk quietly in your flat.'

'Why?' she says, even louder. 'Are you worried the rest of the building will learn how you've been spying on us?'

'That's not what this is,' I say between gritted teeth. 'I heard movement inside Fi's flat and wanted to check how she was, but she wasn't inside and I now believe I disturbed an intruder.'

'Oh, pull the other one!'

'It's the truth,' I almost scream back. 'I found foot indents on the side of her bed and the window was wide open. I think whoever I disturbed jumped from the window.'

'Jumped from the first floor? Well, why don't we go downstairs together and see if their broken leg requires an ambulance.'

'There's nobody outside. I already checked.'

She crosses her arms over her chest and looks at me sardonically.

'Let me get this straight: the *intruder* you claim to have heard inside Fi's flat escaped by jumping from the first floor and escaped unscathed.'

Hearing it said in that tone highlights just how ridiculous it sounds.

'It's the truth. I swear.'

She shakes her head.

'No, the truth is you're a sick woman who sneaks about the building spying on each of us. You can deny it all you like, but there's no way you could always know what's going on unless you've hidden microphones and cameras in all of our flats.' Her eyes widen. 'Oh my God, that's it, isn't it? You've bugged our homes and you were just removing the ones in Fi's flat in case the police find them and realise what you're up to.'

Mike and India haven't appeared from their flats, so thankfully it appears I was right about them being at work.

'Do you see any cameras or microphones on me?' I say dismissively. 'Let's just go and talk in your flat and I can explain what's going on.'

She makes no effort to move out of my way.

'Wait, you let yourself and Danielle into James's flat yesterday morning and now I've caught you sneaking out of Fi's flat as well.

Have you also been in mine when I'm not home? I'm right, aren't I? You *are* the one Chad has been screwing behind my back.'

*Not this again!*

'Jenny, I am not having an affair with Chad. I have no interest in him whatsoever. I have never instigated a relationship with any of my tenants because it would just make things awkward.'

'You must think I'm really stupid. I know he's not really going out running when he claims to be. He says he's running several miles every day, yet he doesn't look any fitter, and when he returns his clothes are barely damp, let alone soaked through with sweat. You both think you can pull the wool over my eyes, but I'm onto you now.'

'If Chad is having an affair, it isn't with me,' I yell, finally yielding to my growing anger.

Her bottom lip is wobbling and for the first time I can see how vulnerable she really is. It saddens me to see a grown woman with so much self-doubt. Maybe that's the price she feels obliged to pay for dating a younger man.

'You're really beautiful, Jenny,' I say with empathy, 'and I'm sure you have nothing to be paranoid about. Chad loves you, and he'd be a fool to throw away what the two of you have.'

She doesn't respond, but I sense she is finally listening to me.

'I reckon you could go after any man you wanted, and Chad is lucky that you've chosen to commit your time and love to him. He probably knows how lucky he is.'

Her eyes narrow.

'You must take me for such a fool. I see what you're doing, Eve. Trying to butter me up so I turn a blind eye to what you've been doing, but it won't work. I'm on to you, and I will expose you for the wretched and unstable woman you really are. In fact, I'm going to phone that Detective Atwal and tell her all about your snooping. The rest of us were assuming it was Danielle who went after James, but I can see the truth now. It was you, wasn't it? Wormed your way in and made him feel like he had no choice but to end things.'

I reach out a hand to try and make her see sense but she takes two sudden steps backwards. I close the gap, but she hurries back until she crashes into the wall.

'Don't come near me. I'll scream.'

I'm not expecting this reaction, and quickly raise my hands in a pacifying manner.

'I don't mean you any harm,' I say.

'Sure, I bet you said the same thing to Fi and James before you killed them.'

I'm about to defend myself when I hear footsteps on the stairs.

'Hey, hey, what's all the shouting for?'

We both turn and stare at the voice of the man who's just turned onto the corridor. Pete looks from me to Jenny and back again, his eyes demanding an explanation.

'It's nothing,' I say quickly, willing Jenny not to repeat her accusation in front of my brother.

We both look at her, but her tone changes in an instant.

'I don't believe we've met,' she says, extending her hand towards Pete. 'I'm Jenny.'

He takes her hand awkwardly and shakes it.

'I'm Pete, Eve's brother. It's nice to meet you too.'

Jenny turns to face me, her cheeks no longer red with anger, her eyes more playful and a huge smile breaking across her face.

'I didn't know you had a brother, Eve. Where have you been hiding him all this time?'

Is she trying to flirt with him? Only seconds ago she was revelling in jealousy about Chad, and now she's acting like we're best friends.

'What are you doing here, Pete?' I ask, certain he hasn't phoned today.

'I just wanted to pop by and see how you are after what happened yesterday.'

'Oh, aren't you the sweetest brother,' Jenny coos, and it almost makes me want to vomit.

'I'm fine,' I tell him. 'Do you want to come up for a coffee?'

He nods and moves towards the stairs.

'It was so lovely to meet you, Pete,' Jenny calls after him. 'Hopefully, this won't be our last meeting.'

She practically skips back along the corridor, staring after him as he ascends and only pausing when she gets to the door of Flat 7 to glare back at me before disappearing inside. I let out a sigh and make my way towards the stairs, feeling as though I've leapt out of the frying pan and into the fire.

## 26

### WEDNESDAY, 11 A.M.

Pete is waiting at the top of the stairs for me.

'Is everything okay?' he asks.

'Sure, I'm fine,' I reply quickly, my mind already trying to recall whether the inside of the flat is tidy.

'I thought I heard you arguing with that woman down there.'

I can't be sure how much he heard of what Jenny was saying. I really don't want Pete to know I've been snooping in my tenants' flats, even though my motive was pure on each occasion.

'Oh, that was just a misunderstanding. Nothing to worry about.'

He looks pensive, as though seeing straight through the lie, but he doesn't utter a challenge. Instead, I unlock the door and invite him in. George immediately runs over, and slinks between my legs while I walk to the kitchen to observe the damage. To my relief there are no used bottles anywhere, and only a couple of plates stacked beside the sink in need of cleaning.

'I see the police have gone,' he says next, watching me while I fill the kettle.

'The forensics team has gone, but I don't think they've reached a conclusion on what happened to James yet.'

I don't add that Detective Atwal has now issued an APB on Fi or the fact that she could be involved in James's passing.

'I couldn't believe it when I heard the report on the news. I was half-expecting some soundbite from you reassuring everyone that everything is okay.'

'I've kept myself well away from any of that. I'm sure it will be yesterday's news soon enough. Do you want tea or coffee?'

'Neither, thanks. I can't stay long. I only stopped by because I'm meeting a client for lunch nearby and it seems like an age since I last saw you.'

I don't remind him that it's been less than a week, nor that he's phoned me every day in between.

'What did you do for your birthday in the end?' I ask, instantly regretting the decision when I remember I forgot to send him a card or gift.

'I had a quiet one at home. A pizza and a couple of lagers and I fell asleep in front of the television.'

'You're still welcome to come round for dinner one day soon,' I say, the guilt eating me up inside. 'I'll cook you something. You always used to love Mum's lasagne, and I'm pretty sure I can remember how she made it.'

'That would be lovely. When?'

'Well, I'll need to order in the ingredients, but how about Sunday night?'

'Sounds perfect! Oh, I meant to say your card did arrive yesterday in the end. It was trapped between two other envelopes and I hadn't noticed it. Thank you.'

I look away as the kettle boils, grateful for a distraction. We both know a card didn't arrive yesterday, but if I now come clean and reveal I forgot to send one I'm going to make us both look stupid.

'You were right: damned postal service!'

I can't believe he would lie to protect my feelings. It makes the guilt hit home even more, and I make a vow I will order him a card and present this afternoon and pay for expedited delivery. I'm annoyed at myself for not ordering it as soon as I realised my mistake yesterday. It's yet another thing that has slipped from my mind in recent weeks. I always used to be so on the ball and organised, but lately it's just felt like I'm operating with one hand tied behind my back.

'Oh, I see you've been invited to a school reunion,' I hear Pete say and turn to face him.

He is standing beside my desk and is holding the embroidered card I left there this morning. 'Are you planning to go along?'

'Probably not,' I say.

'You should! It might be good for you to catch up with old friends and find out what they're now up to.'

An image of the gothic building flickers through my mind and I have to suppress the feelings itching to get out. He has no idea how bad things were when Dad eventually allowed me to leave. Every now and again, I still wake screaming as the memories of what happened to Simone that night puncture my nightmares. I fight the urge to tell him the real reason I had to return home.

'I'd be happy to go along with you for support. If you want, that is.'

Always my knight in shining armour, but maybe doesn't realise how it would be even worse to turn up there with my older brother beside me. Most of the girls from my year are probably now married with children and business empires, and then there's me living in a flat I inherited and a graphic design business that barely keeps me in groceries.

'I'd be happy to drive us both,' he continues, either missing or ignoring my discomfort.

'I'll think about it,' I say in an effort to shut him up.

'You can't keep pushing me away, Eve. I only want what's best for you. You must see that, surely? I could collect you from the front door of this place, drive you there and drop you at the door. You wouldn't technically be outside and alone for more than a couple of seconds. And I'll be there to look after you.'

'I said *I'll think about it*, didn't I?'

'Yeah, but we both know what that means.'

I close my eyes and try to focus on my breathing. I don't want to argue with him.

'You don't understand what I went through. School was bad enough, but when that man jumped me... until you feel your life fractured into a million pieces, you can never truly understand.'

He moves to the counter between us, and lifts his briefcase onto it, popping open the locks.

'I hate what happened to you,' he says quietly. 'I hate that I wasn't there to watch out for you. I promised Dad I would keep you safe, and it kills me that I failed—'

'It wasn't your fault, Pete, and I don't blame you. That piece of shit could have attacked any woman that night, and I just happened to be the unlucky one. And it terrifies me that I froze in that situation. My fight or flight failed me, and I will not allow myself to be in that situation again.'

He considers my answer, before reaching into his pocket and pulling out what resembles a car key on a keyring.

'There are tools that can help make you feel safer,' he says, holding out the device.

I take it and turn it over in my hands.

'What is it?'

'A personal alarm. If you press that little button, it emits a 150dB siren to attract attention. And it's rechargeable.'

'A rape alarm, you mean,' I say, shaking my head. 'This wouldn't have helped me five years ago. An alarm is great when there are people around to hear it. But where I was attacked, there was nobody around. No one would have come to my rescue, so what's the point?'

He narrows his eyes, and then gently lifts the lid of his briefcase.

'There are other personal protection tools available. Now, I've done my research and in the UK it is illegal to carry around cans of pepper spray and electronic taser devices.' He pauses and lifts out a small can of what looks like aerosol deodorant. 'However, if it would make you feel safer, you could still carry this with you.'

He hands me the small can of pepper spray.

'To the untrained eye it looks like any regular can of antiperspirant, but squirted in someone's face and they'll be temporarily blinded – incapacitated – whilst you beat a hasty retreat. You would face arrest if the police found and tested it, but hidden discreetly in a handbag, there's no reason anyone would know.'

I don't know what surprises me more: that he's been researching such tools, or that he's ordered them despite the potential legal ramifications. I've often replayed that night in my head. I don't remember all of it, but I remember the man rugby tackling me to the wet pavement, and then dragging me into the leafless trees. He was wearing a balaclava and it was too dark to see his eyes, but I've imagined squirting something into his face and escaping unharmed.

'I also ordered this,' he says, and I see him holding out a small black box with two metal prongs on the end. 'Go ahead. Take it.'

I place the alarm and deodorant can on the counter and accept the device, feeling the cool plastic in my hand. I press the side trigger and it whirs and crackles as the prongs glow. I feel a power I haven't felt in a long time.

'Bloody hell.'

'Exactly. This is 100 per cent illegal to carry unless you're a trained police officer. You'd definitely be in trouble if caught in possession of it. I'm pretty sure I'd also be in trouble for ordering it from overseas, but I used a VPN so they shouldn't be able to trace the origin. If this is what it will take to give you the confidence to reclaim your life, then I want you to have them.'

I place the device on the counter and move away from it.

'You need to get those things out of my flat,' I say firmly, crossing to the sofa and holding a pillow across my chest, my legs curled beneath me.

'What's wrong? I thought you'd be pleased.'

'Pleased? Didn't you hear what I said earlier? The police aren't finished with this building. What if the lead detective arrived now and found us with these?'

'That's why I bailed on coming over last night. I was going to show these to you then, but worried that they might want to look in my briefcase. But there are no police here now, and I think you're being a little paranoid.'

He wouldn't be saying I'm paranoid if he knew that Atwal has visited me twice already.

'Where's your regular handbag? I can help you hide them, and then when you're feeling braver, you can take them with you. Maybe a short walk to the local supermarket or petrol station. You'll see that the man who attacked you is no longer out there, and in the highly unlikely event anyone else comes for you, you'll be prepared.'

'Just stop it, Pete! Please? I don't want to run the risk of ever being anywhere near that situation again.'

He sighs in frustration and closes his briefcase, leaving the three gifts on the counter.

'I don't want to force you to do something you don't want to do, Eve. All I want is for you to feel safer. It's my job. It's what I promised Dad, and I won't ever stop trying...'

His words trail off as the intercom buzzes. My eyes widen, instantly picturing Atwal at the front door demanding to come up.

'Are you expecting anyone?' Pete asks, maybe following the same trail of thought.

'No, I'm not,' I confirm.

'Do you want me to answer and tell them to go away?'

I shake my head.

'No, you hide those things, and I'll see who it is.'

I move past him to the front door and lift the receiver to my ear.

'Hello?'

'Tesco delivery for an Eve Pennington.'

'I'm Eve Pennington, but I didn't order any food.'

'Well, I've got three crates here that would beg to differ.'

My brow furrows. Did I order something and I've just forgotten about it? I had a delivery on Monday, so can't see why I would have ordered more food. I'm so confused, but Pete is looking at me with real worry, so I tell the driver I'm on my way.

## 27

### WEDNESDAY, 11.20 A.M.

Why did this misunderstanding have to happen while Pete was here? Despite my reassurances, Pete has insisted on coming down to the front door with me. I dread to think what's going through his mind right now. He'll probably be on the phone to Dr Winslow as soon as he gets out of here to ask whether his sister has lost the plot.

I can't bring myself to say anything to him as we head down the stairs. Could he be right and I am losing my mind? Even placing one foot in front of the other feels like a challenge as my vision blurs in and out. But this isn't like when I have an anxiety attack; this is something different.

I make it to the bottom stair and finally release the handrail. I can see the driver's blue uniform through the glass of the door, and as we reach it, I can see now it is the same woman with hair tied in a messy bun who was here on Monday.

I open the door, and I'm sure I see her shoulders tense when our eyes meet, but maybe I'm just imagining it. Her name badge shimmers in the morning sunshine. I still can't get over how someone my age can be called Joan.

'I think there's been some kind of mistake,' I say firmly. 'You already delivered the last food order I placed on Monday. Surely you remember bringing it to me?'

Her eyes answer, but she unlocks her tablet and scrolls the screen.

'Are you Eve Pennington?'

'Yes, I am.'

'Can you confirm your email address to me?'

'Eve dot Pennington at Vector underscore Designs dot com.'

'Well, that's the email address linked to this order, which means it was placed from this account.'

'But there must be some kind of mistake, because I didn't place an order.'

'Listen, lady, I don't have time to argue. You either want the food or you don't.'

I take a deep breath, desperately trying to remain composed.

'I understand what you're saying and I'm not trying to be difficult, but I think there must be some kind of error at your end, because I haven't placed an order since the weekend. Can you check what date the order was placed, please, as it's clearly some kind of duplicate. I've already received last week's order. A system glitch of some kind, I suppose.'

She studies the screen.

'This order was placed at eleven fifty-nine last night. You paid for expedited delivery.'

I frown at this.

'There must be some kind of mistake. Can you check again?'

She turns the tablet to face me and shows me the order date and time, and the last four digits of my credit card. It can't be right, and yet there it is in black and white. I bite the inside of my cheek in case I'm dreaming, but I don't wake.

'I'm Eve's brother,' Pete announces from over my shoulder.

'What seems to be the problem here? Eve said she didn't place any order.'

Joan shows him the screen, and he looks at me.

'Eve?'

'I swear I didn't place an order last night...'

My words trail off as I search my memory for any flash of me sitting at my laptop last night, but my mind is blank. I barely remember returning from Bill's save for the keys dropping to the floor. I assumed I'd just crawled into bed and passed out, and I would have been in no state to order groceries.

'Listen,' Joan says, breaking the awkward silence. 'You've got two options: accept the order, or refuse it and I'll take it back to the shop, but you'll have to take it up with the customer care team to request a refund. I can assure you that I've never heard of an order being duplicated, and this order was definitely placed from this account last night. Is there someone else who lives with you who could have placed it?'

'No, I live on my...'

Again, I can't finish the sentence, as I recall the blind panic this morning when I couldn't find George, and finding the hatch raised.

'What time did you say the order was placed?' I ask.

'Eleven fifty-nine last night.'

I would have been back from Bill's at that time, but if I can't remember logging in to my laptop, maybe the intruder did. But why would they break in to order groceries? It makes no sense.

I can feel Pete's stare burning into me. This situation isn't helpful when he already thinks I'm not coping. I'm just going to have to accept the order and figure it out once he's gone.

'You're not going to cause a scene like you did the other day, are you?' Joan asks, also now staring at me with a worried expression.

Her lack of empathy towards my passing out speaks volumes, and I feel the heat rise to my cheeks in an instant.

'What are you talking about?' I hear Pete interject before I can figure out how to defuse the situation. 'What happened the other day?'

She glances at me before continuing.

'Look, I explained to your sister that it's company policy that I only bring the food to the door. That's what I've done. I'm not allowed to carry it inside.'

Three crates are already stacked up on the pavement outside the door, just out of my reach.

'That's fine, I can lift the food in,' Pete says, stepping forward.

'And you're not going to start shaking and then collapse like your sister did?'

He looks thrown by the question, but proceeds to lift the first crate inside.

'You know, it's lucky that old man came by when he did,' Joan continues. 'I didn't know whether I should phone for an ambulance or what. Really freaked me out, it did. Never had someone faint on me before.'

'Wait, you passed out?' Pete asks, as my fight or flight fails me again.

'Made me late for my next delivery,' Joan continues, ignorant of how much worse she is making things, 'but thankfully I was able to make up time in the afternoon.'

Pete places the first crate just inside the door and lifts out the two carrier bags, before returning with the second crate. Something audibly rolls around inside, and the glass-on-glass collision is unmistakeable. He lowers the crate to the floor and lifts out the single bag, studying the contents before raising his eyebrow in my direction. He shakes his head as he carefully places the carrier bag on the floor and lifts the final crate into the hallway. More bottles collide as he carries it over the threshold.

He passes the three crates back to Joan, who holds out the tablet.

'Which of you is going to sign for the delivery?'

She doesn't offer a stylus, so I once again smear my signature with a finger. Joan looks from me to Pete, and then turns on her heel, carrying the three empty crates back to her van. Pete closes the door, and lifts three bags and proceeds towards the stairs. I glance into the two remaining bags, my heart dropping when I see the bottles inside. I lift them and hurry after Pete.

'This isn't what it looks like,' I say breathlessly when I make it back inside the flat. 'I know you're not going to believe me, but I swear I didn't order any of this. It's clearly some mistake.'

'I think the only mistake is that you didn't pick a better timeslot for your delivery. But maybe you figured I wouldn't come over in the middle of the day and you'd be able to hide the evidence before I got here.'

'That's not what happened.'

'Oh, Eve, please just stop lying,' he says in a raised voice. 'Stop lying to me. Stop lying to Dr Winslow. And stop lying to yourself.'

'I'm not lying. I swear to you I didn't order anything last night.'

He snatches the two carriers from my hands and lifts them onto the kitchen counter, before extracting the contents one by one.

'Three bottles of white wine, one bottle of vodka, a bottle of gin, and a bottle of tropical-flavoured rum. You haven't told me you're having a party, so why else order this amount of alcohol?'

'You're not listening to me, Pete: I didn't order this.' An idea shoots to the front of my mind. 'I can prove it to you.'

I collect my laptop from the desk and bring it over so he can watch me. I open the Tesco website and see that I'm already logged in. I open my account page and then order history, and my mouth drops open when I see the date and time of the last order.

His look is a mixture of concern and pity.

'Eve, it's time to accept that you have a problem.'

'No, you don't understand. I was asleep at this time. Somebody broke into my flat last night and it must have been them who placed the order.'

'Can you hear yourself? Do you know how ridiculous that sounds? Wait, are you drunk now?' He leans closer and sniffs my breath. 'Hmm, I can only smell mouthwash, but then that was the same trick Mum used to pull to cover her own issues with alcohol.'

'I am *not* like Mum.'

'Maybe I should look inside your airing cupboard and see whether you're hiding a stash there as well.'

I don't want him going anywhere near the airing cupboard in case my intruder has been back up when I've been out and left the hatch open.

'Mum thought she was so good at hiding it, but Dad knew. He didn't know how to help her, and ultimately it cost her her life. I don't want you to develop cirrhosis of the liver like she did.'

'I swear to you, Pete, someone broke into my flat last night.'

'Who?'

'I don't know who.'

'And how do you know anybody was here?'

'Because when I woke this morning, George was locked outside of the flat, and my keys were moved.'

'Were you drinking last night?'

'No.'

'Oh, really? So you didn't go down to Bill's flat last night and ask him all manner of questions about whether Dad knew murderer John Cooper?'

There's only one way he could know that.

'Bill phoned me this morning,' Pete continues. 'Said he was worried about you. He said you came calling late and he gave you some Scotch because you looked so haunted. He told me you were asking him questions about Cooper but then seemed to get hung up on the possibility that Dad knew one of the victims.'

'Okay, yes, I had a drink at Bill's but just the one. I wasn't drunk last night.'

I hate lying to my brother, but I don't know any other way to convince him that I'm not making this up.

'They say the first step on the road to recovery is admitting you have a problem, Eve.' He checks his watch. 'I need to go, but please think about what I've said. Locking yourself away like this and drowning your sorrows every night is only going to shorten your life. Is that what you want? Are you depressed?'

I shake my head.

'Will you do me a favour and make an appointment with Dr Winslow?'

'I don't—'

'Please? I don't know what else to do to help you.'

I sigh.

'I'll think about it.'

He raises an eyebrow, and then kisses my cheek before heading away. I wait until the door closes before I allow my emotion to rise to the surface, and then I fall to my knees and sob.

## 28

### WEDNESDAY, 12.30 P.M.

It takes all my willpower to drag myself from my bed, having spent the last hour chastising myself for being such a failure and terrible sister. At first I was angry that Pete didn't believe me when I told him I didn't order all the alcohol that was delivered by that unsympathetic woman. His first loyalty should be to me. Then, the more I thought about it, in his mind that's exactly what he's trying to do.

Pretending to have received a birthday card from me when he probably suspects I forgot to send one is more kindness than I deserve. If I was a half-decent sister I would have come clean and admitted to forgetting it was his birthday, but like always, he came to my rescue. And as much as I dislike his insistence on me seeing a therapist, it's because he doesn't know how else to help me.

Despite the evidence suggesting otherwise, I am certain I didn't place that Tesco order when I returned from Bill's last night. I couldn't admit it to Pete, but I was in no fit state to do anything when I got back here. Bill told Pete he'd given me Scotch, but neither knows I'd been drinking before I got down there, nor how unsteady I felt before knocking on Bill's door. I might have been able to load up my laptop, and at a push I might have been able to open my account, but I don't think I would have been in any state to add new items to my repeat order. And nothing would have compelled me to add vodka, gin and rum to my basket. I don't enjoy spirits. It is so out of character that deep down I *know* it can't have been me that placed the order.

So, the question is who did and why?

It's a bit of a chicken and egg situation though. If I knew who was responsible, I might be able to figure out why they've done it. Similarly, if I could figure out why someone would want to make me look like an out-of-control drunk, I might be able to determine who's behind it. Right now, I have no leads to go on.

Sitting down at my desk I open a tube of the Pringles that arrived today, and in spite of myself I pour a large glass of the new wine. I think better after a glass of wine. I know how dependent that makes me sound, but it's the truth. And I need my creative juices flowing right now.

Taking a deep breath, I stare at the laptop screen and allow my mind to look at the problem from as many angles as I can see.

I could tell Detective Atwal what happened and ask whether one of her colleagues could dust the laptop for fingerprints, but she'd probably be as difficult to convince as Pete, and I've used the laptop since so have probably smeared any other prints, and that's assuming the intruder wasn't wearing gloves to begin with. That won't help, so I dismiss the idea.

I take a second sip of wine, wincing at the bitter aftertaste; definitely not a variety I would have chosen.

If I hadn't seen the hatch raised and George locked out of the flat, I'd have had no idea anyone had been inside, and even when Joan arrived to deliver the food, I wouldn't necessarily have suspected that somebody else had placed the order. Supposing for a moment that *I* left the hatch raised – not beyond the realms of possibility – and that in my drunken state I missed that George had managed to sneak out, then the only other way someone could have placed the order is if I'd been hacked.

I open the internet security app on the laptop and run a scan for viruses. I can't think how I would have downloaded anything malicious as I don't visit dodgy websites and don't recall clicking on any links in an email, but I allow the scan to complete anyway. I can't say I'm surprised it finds no malicious software installed.

I reach for the wine and wince again.

Whoever it is wouldn't necessarily need access to my laptop to order groceries, all they'd need is my username and password. My username is my email address which is displayed on the Vector Designs website and on every email I've ever sent, so it would be easy to find it. And I'm embarrassed to admit that my account password is the same one I use for most of my online activity, so if it was found elsewhere, this person may have got lucky and put two and two together and hit the jackpot.

A flash of inspiration strikes as I swallow a handful of crisps. I should have received an email confirming the order and delivery slot, but I didn't see any such message this morning. I open the app and check, but there's nothing unread and no confirmation email. I check my trash folder and it isn't in there either. Does that mean whoever placed the order also has access to my email and was able to cover their tracks by permanently deleting the message? It feels like a stretch, but I have no other explanation.

I update the passwords for both accounts, which brings a certain peace of mind, but it isn't enough. I lean over and stare at the airing cupboard door. Behind it, the dumbbells remain on top of the hatch, so even if someone managed to lift it, I'd likely hear them falling off, but only if I'm home. It isn't enough. *If* someone has been in here already, there's no guarantee they won't return. And as much as I'd love to channel Kevin McCallister and booby trap my home like he does in *Home Alone*, it isn't safe or practical with George roaming. I need another way.

The thought of Jenny's voice stirs something in my mind: *There's no way you could always know what's going on unless you've hidden microphones and cameras in all of our flats.*

Of course! I don't know why I didn't think of it sooner. What I need is a home security system; some strategically placed cameras to capture any uninvited guests. That way, if someone does return, I'll be able to identify who they are, how they gained access, and prove to Pete once and for all that I'm not losing my mind.

I open a new window and search for home surveillance. There are several local companies listed, and I click on a couple of the sites, but they seem to be targeting businesses rather than personal security. There are also a number of links for private investigators. If I can't figure out who's targeting me, then that may be an option, but I can't afford to take that step yet.

I don't know the first thing about setting up a home security system, and in an ideal world it's the sort of task I would ask Pete about; however, given our last exchange I don't want to add fuel to the fire. In a day and age when people have video cameras built into doorbells, it can't be that difficult to figure it out. And so I read a couple of articles and watch several online videos and it really is more straightforward than I initially assumed. I'm about to order four mains-charged cameras when I stop myself. It's all very well me knowing that my home is secured, but I don't want to make it obvious to any intruders, and these cameras are all pretty obvious. Even trying to hide them out of sight would be a challenge in this flat. What I need is something more discreet; less obvious that can be hidden in plain sight. I eventually find a shop that sells such items and guarantees next-day delivery. Ideally, I'd have preferred to have them in place today, but I'll just have to monitor the hatch myself tonight.

I select one shaped like an air freshener that can stand on the kitchen countertop and monitor any activity in the living room, and especially on my laptop. I find one built into a digital alarm clock that can sit on the bedside table, then one which resembles a smoke alarm that can go in the hallway and monitor activity by the front door. And finally I choose one that looks like a thermostat that I can attach to the wall opposite the airing cupboard door and should show me any attempts to get through the hatch.

Once all four are in my basket, I look at the cost and my mouth drops. Nearly seven hundred pounds including delivery, but guaranteed to arrive tomorrow. It is more than I'd anticipated spending, but I'm not sure I have any other choice. At the moment it isn't just Pete I need to convince that I'm not going crazy. I could wait and see if I observe any other strange goings-on around the flat, but I shiver every time I think about some stranger moving about in here, touching my stuff while I'm fast asleep. And what if last night's visit was just to test the water, and they're planning to return and do something worse tonight? I'd feel so stupid if I was attacked in my bed and hadn't tried to mitigate it. That said, all these cameras would do is capture any attack, hiding the pepper spray and taser within easy reach may be all I have to prevent an attack.

I add my credit card details and confirm the purchase. If I'm wrong and I don't catch an intruder, then I'm going to have to accept that Pete might be right about my fractured mental health. I can see it from his perspective. He feels guilty that he wasn't there for me when I was previously attacked and he can see I'm barely a shadow of the woman I was before and ultimately I do sound like I'm spouting conspiracy; but that doesn't mean I'm wrong.

I just wish I could figure out who broke in here and ordered groceries. I want to laugh out loud at how ridiculous it sounds. Jenny downstairs has made no secret of her dislike and mistrust of me, and she claims to have heard me moving about back there, but it could just as easily be my intruder she heard. I can't see how Jenny would access the passageway, but then I can't think how anybody else would either. I've checked the walls around every flat and there are no hidden doors or portals, so there's no logical way for anyone to get in there. India has also questioned my methods, yet I can't see either of them devising a plan to make me paranoid. In fact, I can't imagine any of my residents planning something like this. No, if I had to guess at this point, I'd say there's something else at play here and I just can't see it yet.

I drain the glass for further inspiration. One thing's for sure, I'm not going to sit back and let them get away with it. It's time I took back control of my life and that's exactly what I plan to do.

# 29

## WEDNESDAY, 4.30 P.M.

If they came through the hatch into my flat, then there must be a passage to one of the other flats too; nothing else makes sense.

I descend the ladder, with the torch gripped tightly, ready to swat out at anyone I encounter down here. When I first located these passageways I did search for hatches into the other flats; there were no obvious doorways or portals, but that doesn't mean one hasn't been added since my provisional check.

But as I reach the platform on the first floor, I'm uncertain where to begin. I've heard Jenny and India plotting against me, but I can't see what they'd gain by trying to freak me out. If they think hiding my cat and ordering groceries online will drive me out, then they've underestimated who they're dealing with.

I check Jenny's and Chad's flat first, and can hear the pair of them arguing inside. I'm actually beginning to feel sorry for Chad. Jenny's insecurity about their age gap is driving a wedge between them, and I don't know how to fix that. She's a trained medical professional who I'd argue is prettier than me despite her age, so there is no sound reason for her self-doubt. I run my fingers over every piece of brickwork I can reach, but find no obvious signs of a door or portal.

I perform the same check on Fi's, India's and Mike's flats, but find nothing to suggest an entrance into their homes. I head down the next ladder to the ground floor, and move to Bill's flat. I can't quite get around to the far side of Bill's flat due to low beams, but a cursory glance confirms he's not the one who's been harassing me.

I'm scanning the wall by Danielle's flat when I hear voices nearby. I quickly move along until I'm as close to the corridor as I can physically be. India's voice is unmistakeable, but I freeze when I hear what she's saying.

'And Jenny said she caught Eve sneaking out of Fi's flat this morning.'

'Maybe Fi was home and had let her in,' I hear Caz say.

'No, because Eve told Jenny that Fi wasn't there, which means she must have let herself in.'

'Yeah, but you know how overly dramatic Jenny can be.'

'Why would she lie? Have you seen Fi recently?'

'Well, no, not for a while.'

'I haven't seen her in over a week. My mum always used to say when it feels like it, smells like it, and sounds like it, then it's definitely bullshit.'

'But Fi could just be away on holiday.'

'The police are treating her disappearance as suspicious, which means they can't get hold of her either. And given what happened to James...'

'What are you saying exactly?'

'What if Eve killed Fi, and then James confronted her about it and she killed him too?'

'Oh, that's ridiculous.'

'Is it? Nobody thought Dennis Nilsen was chopping up his

victims and flushing them down the toilet, but we know how that turned out, don't we? For all we know, there are parts of Fi still floating about in our pipes.'

I want to hammer my fists against the wall and shout that I had nothing to do with Fi's disappearance and James's death.

'Do you really think Eve could do something like that?'

'She had the means and opportunity, and she was seen using spare keys to enter both James's and Fi's flats. Who's to say which other flats she frequents when we're out or asleep?'

I can't believe what I'm hearing. It's one thing to revel in a bit of idle gossip, but this feels more like a campaign to turn my tenants against me. I expected more of India, but then maybe I've been underestimating her.

'Doesn't it bother you that Eve always seems to just know what we're thinking? It's like she has a sixth sense or something.'

'I like that she's so conscientious. She seems to go out of her way to make sure we're all okay.'

'Jenny reckons she has hidden cameras in all of our flats, and spends all day up there just watching us. Creepy as hell if you ask me. And the fact that she never goes outside is also a massive red flag. If I could afford to live somewhere else, I definitely would.'

This is getting beyond a joke! I desperately want to march out to India and warn her to stop spreading lies about me.

'I think the safest thing we can all do is barricade our doors from inside so we don't receive any unwelcome visitors. Listen, I need to head back up to my room, but just stay safe. We don't want anyone else turning up dead.'

I hear Caz's door close, and make my way back up the ladders, now seeing the possibility that there might be more to India's campaign than turning others against me. If she's the one who's been using these passageways, I know exactly how to catch her.

## 30

WEDNESDAY, 6.45 P.M.

I'd never appreciated how many creaks and groans this place emits when the flat is otherwise silent until now. Sitting here in the dim light, with the curtains blocking interference from the outside world, I've been stirred by so many insignificant sounds that I feel strung out. Armed with the taser, I have been sitting beside the open hatch for several hours, waiting for *him* to return. The pepper spray can is hiding in plain sight on the basin just inside the bathroom should I need to get at it.

It seems so obvious now. It has to be *him*; the bastard who preyed on me when I was at my most vulnerable all those years ago. I was right that the wine would boost my creative thinking.

Clearly obsessed with me, he's been waiting for me to emerge so he can finish the job, but he didn't anticipate I'd not step foot outside again, securing myself behind these walls. And in his desperation, he's managed to burrow his way inside somehow, and now he intends to toy with me until I break and am unable to fend him off any longer.

I tip the dregs from the bottle into my glass and down them in one.

I want him to think that I'm either asleep or not home, so he feels safe enough to venture back up the ladder and through the trapdoor. And that's when I'll strike. I'll spray his eyes first, so he can't see me coming for him. He'll scurry back down the ladder, but he won't be able to see his way back to his lair, so I'll hurry after him and use the taser to stop him where he is, and then I'll phone Atwal and tell her I've incapacitated him.

I've figured out what to say while I've been waiting for him. I'll tell her I became aware that someone had been in my flat – I'll tell her about George and the Tesco order – and so I searched my flat for other evidence. I'll tell her I happened to stumble upon the trapdoor in the airing cupboard – which I'd never seen before – and when I headed down I caught him. There's no reason she won't believe me, and then it will be over and I'll be free.

My stomach grumbles at the lack of proper sustenance today. I should take a break from my vigil and fix some dinner, but I'd hate for him to hear me and realise it's a trap. That said, if I don't get some food soon, my grumbling gut will give the game away.

I start at sudden banging, until I realise it's somebody knocking urgently at my door. I grip the taser tightly, and then I slowly stand. Maybe I was naïve to think he'd come for me through the hatch again. If he's realised I'm onto him then there's no point in him sneaking secretly up here.

Standing, I move slowly towards the door, partly because my joints feel tired from sitting in that chair for so long, but mainly because this is the moment I've been dreading since I conceived this plan.

I gasp at three further bangs against the door, and my nerves are shot.

'W-who is it?' I stammer when I'm a couple of metres from the door.

'Detective Atwal. Can I come in?'

I freeze, my mind unable to process the response.

'Say again,' I reply meekly.

'It's Detective Sergeant Atwal, Eve. I've got an update I need to share.'

I'm sure she must be able to hear my hammering heart, but I can't let her in to see what I've been doing. I quickly thrust the taser into my pocket.

'Can it wait until later?' I try. 'I've... just got out the shower.'

'No, it can't wait. Can you throw on some clothes and let me in?'

*Shit!*

She's not going to go away, so I need to get things straightened in here. I flick on the hallway light, and then turn to look at the rest of the flat. I race to the airing cupboard and lower the hatch, covering it with the strip of carpet and quickly close the door. Then I collect the chair and return it to my desk. I put my used wine glass back in the cupboard and stuff the bottle beneath rubbish in the bin. I hide the pepper spray in the bathroom cabinet and take a swill from the bottle of mouthwash and then spit.

My reflection looks almost dead, the skin so pale and hanging from my face. I plaster on a fake smile but what stares back at me is like something out of a horror movie. I hurry to the door and open it, inviting Atwal in.

Her eyes dart around as she enters, as if she assesses scenes for criminal activity as a default setting.

'I'm sorry to call round so late,' she begins, once she's made it into the living room.

'That's fine,' I say, trying to keep her on side so she doesn't immediately demand a search of the premises.

She's about to speak, but catches herself and tilts her head slightly.

'I thought you were showering? Your hair's dry.'

*Shit!*

I knew I'd missed something in my blind panic.

'I... um... meant I was about to shower. I'd literally just stripped off when you knocked.'

I can't tell from her expression whether she believes me or not and can't help yawning. I suddenly feel overcome with fatigue, but I've only had one bottle and this feeling doesn't usually strike until the end of the second.

'You said you had an update?' I say, stifling another yawn.

I can practically feel her reading my thoughts as she continues to stare at me.

'We managed to track down Fiona Erskine's firm and they've not seen her since she finished work on Friday lunchtime. So, I want you to confirm the last time you saw her as you weren't certain when we last spoke.'

I still can't be certain when I last saw Fi, because I didn't consciously record it as the last time I saw her.

'It was towards the end of last week, I think, but can't be certain.'

'Did you see her at the weekend?'

'Definitely not.'

'How can you be so sure of that?'

'Because I distinctly remember that she was dressed in her formal work clothes when I saw her.'

'Can you be more specific about what she was wearing?'

'Yeah, sorry, what I mean is when she goes to work she usually wears a skirt or trouser suit. Very professional. But at weekends she's usually in jeans or trackie bottoms. You know?

She relaxes more at the weekends, and the last time I saw her she was definitely dressed professionally.'

Atwal writes this in her notebook, and then considers me for a moment.

'Would it surprise you if I said we are now treating Fiona Erskine as a missing person?'

A shadow of dread creeps across my shoulders.

'You think something bad has happened to her?'

'Not necessarily, but her phone hasn't connected to a network since 5 p.m. on Friday evening, and none of her debit or credit cards have been used since then. We've not managed to pick her up on facial recognition since Friday afternoon. It's as if she's disappeared off the face of the planet.'

Poor Fi. I knew Atwal was wrong to assume that she could have had anything to do with James's passing. But what if the person who was involved in James's death is also the cause of Fi's disappearance?

'Could they be connected?' I blurt out before I can stop myself.

'In what way?'

'Well, we know James and Fi were supposed to meet for dinner on Friday night because of the message he left on her answerphone. When we were in her flat, that message hadn't been listened to, which means she didn't know he was running late. It also might suggest that she didn't come back here after finishing work on Friday.'

My mind is working quicker than my voice.

'What if the person behind all of this was waiting for Fi at the restaurant and did something to her? What if James witnessed it and that person came back here and strung him up so he didn't report the crime?'

Atwal opens her mouth to interrupt, but I raise my voice.

'What if there is a copycat killer at play here? John Cooper used to target people that stayed here when it was a hotel, right? What if this new killer is targeting the people who live here?'

Her eyes widen and she takes a nervous step backwards.

'Whoa, that's some conclusion to leap to without a safety net.'

'Is it? How long did Cooper prey on victims before he was finally caught? Given it's the fiftieth anniversary of his spree this year, maybe someone is attempting to pay homage in some way.'

'Pay homage? So you think John Cooper's crimes are worthy of celebration?'

'What? No, I don't but someone might.'

'Someone? Who?'

'Well, I don't know. You're the detective, maybe it's something you could look into.'

'What else do you know about John Cooper's crimes?'

'I know that he was found guilty of killing five women connected to this building when it was a hotel, and that he was the manager of the place.'

'A bit like you're the landlady now?'

I can see how her mind is connecting the wrong dots.

'No, listen, I have nothing to do with Fi's disappearance and James's death.'

'Are you sure about that? What were you doing in Fiona Erskine's flat this morning?'

'This morning? I was with you. You wanted to look inside her flat.'

'No, I mean after that. We received a tipoff that you returned to her flat midmorning.'

I instantly picture Jenny arguing with me on the first floor when I was leaving Flat 5. No prizes for guessing who she phoned as soon as Pete and I headed back up here.

'I heard noises inside the flat and I thought it might have been Fi, so I used my skeleton key to let myself inside.'

'And was she there?'

'No, the place was empty, but I found the bedroom window was open and two footprints on the side of the bed. I reckon someone broke in and escaped through the window when they heard me knocking at the door.'

'Let me get this straight: you thought you heard Fiona Erskine inside her flat, so you knocked on the door, and when she didn't answer, you used your keys to enter.'

'Yes, exactly that!'

'And when you found nobody inside, you noticed the bedroom window was open and think somebody climbed on the bed to get out of the window?'

I'm so pleased she's more willing to believe my account than Jenny.

'Yes, that's right.'

'And even though you knew we were actively looking for Miss Erskine, you didn't think you should phone the police and report the intrusion?'

'Well, yes, obviously. I meant to phone and report it, but then... with one thing and another, I forgot.'

My head is spinning with this interrogation, and I really don't feel right. I should sit before I collapse.

'It all sounds very convenient, Eve, if I'm honest.'

My legs feel so weak that I have to reach for the counter to steady myself.

'Convenient how?'

'Let's say, hypothetically, that you are involved in Fiona Erskine's disappearance and what happened with James DeVere. You take me to her flat this morning so I can listen to the answerphone message and connect them. Maybe you were hoping I'd assume that he killed her and couldn't live with the guilt and decided to take his own life. Case closed and we move on without suspecting that you had anything to do with it. But that wasn't the connection I made and so you had to sneak back to check there was no evidence of your involvement. But you were caught by one of your tenants and then had to invent this story about hearing an intruder.'

I lean in to the counter as the room begins to spin.

'That isn't what happened,' I say but my voice sounds weak.

'It's just a hypothetical situation at the moment, but I'll tell you what's going to happen next, Eve. Firstly, a team of Crime Scene Investigators is going to inspect every inch of Flat 5 tonight looking for forensic evidence of a crime. And the second thing is that you're going to hand me your set of skeleton keys.'

'My keys?'

'Yes, because I don't think it's right for you to be letting yourself in to your tenants' flats without their permission. And if you *are* involved, I need to stop you from targeting anyone else. Give me the keys now, please.'

If I move away from the counter I know I'm going to collapse.

'They're hanging on the hook by the front door,' I say, and she moves across to collect them. I grip the counter until I've manoeuvred myself to the sofa and then I drop into it.

She returns a moment later holding the keys.

'Are you okay? You don't look very well.'

'I'm fine,' I lie, willing her just to go so I can figure out what's wrong.

'Okay. Don't get up, I can let myself out. If you want to tell me anything else about Mr DeVere and Miss Erskine, please call me. You'd be surprised how many people I've met who've felt so much better when they've unburdened themselves.'

The walls of my vision are closing in, and I hear the door open and close, and then everything fades to black.

## 31

### THURSDAY, 9.55 A.M.

I wake abruptly, instantly knowing something isn't right. My heart is racing as glimpses of the last nightmare remain in my mind's eye. I was back at boarding school, once more being accused of something I didn't do, but again nobody believed me.

I try to lift my head and in doing so realise what feels so wrong. My face is pressed against something hard, rather than my pillow, and my entire body aches. My eyes flicker open and I see now I am lying on the floor outside my bedroom.

*How did I get here?*

I have no recollection of last night, but the fog in my head also feels different, and there's an unfamiliar aftertaste in my mouth. I push myself up, wincing as my muscles complain at the strain. Getting my bearings, I realise now I have slept on top of the hatch in the airing cupboard. My mind claws at any trace of memory and I see Detective Atwal telling me about Fi's disappearance and then demanding my set of skeleton keys.

*She thinks I've killed Fi and James.*

I have no idea what time it is, but a hot shower should definitely help shift some of the fog. I start at urgent buzzing at the intercom.

*Was that what woke me?*

I stand and stretch out the remaining aches, and lift the handset, blinking at the tiny video image. Lauren's red-streaked, cropped hair is the last thing I expect to see.

'Morning, Eve,' she says. 'Sorry, we're a couple of minutes early. Is that okay? Or do you want us to come back at ten?'

Tim appears behind her, and shakes his head, glancing at his watch.

'Early for what exactly?' I ask, stifling a yawn.

Lauren glances nervously at her brother and then looks back at the camera.

'For the presentation.'

'What presentation?'

She glances at Tim again, and her brow creases.

'Your email,' she says, pulling out her phone and thumbing the screen. 'You said you'd made good progress and wanted to show us a first draft of the campaign pitch.' She pauses and reads her screen. 'Yes, you definitely said for us to come round at ten on Thursday.'

She turns the screen towards the camera but the image is too small for me to see what it says. Despite sitting at my laptop for hours yesterday, the presentation is in no state to be looked at yet. I was planning on pulling all the pieces together this afternoon. I wouldn't have invited them over...

I freeze when I realise who must have sent the email.

'When did you receive the email?' I ask.

Lauren studies the screen.

'Just before midnight on Tuesday.'

When I checked my email yesterday for confirmation of the Tesco order, it never occurred to me to check if any emails had also been sent without my knowledge. So, not only did my intruder order groceries, he also set up this appointment. But how on earth could he have known that Lauren had approached me about this project?

I should tell them there's been a mix-up, and that I didn't send the email, but given my own brother didn't believe me, I don't want to tell them about the intruder messing with me.

I can see Tim growing more frustrated and my confusion this morning is probably just confirming the doubts he already had about using me for the launch of their second business. If I let them go without an explanation, they'll probably email later and cancel the contract.

'Sorry,' I say, 'I meant to say Friday morning in my email, not Thursday.'

'Oh, I see,' Lauren says, and I can see the disappointment cross her face. 'So, you want us to come back tomorrow instead?'

'No, no, listen, um, it's my fault, not yours. Come on up.'

I return the handset to the cradle and rush to the bedroom, searching for anything I can change into, but they're knocking at the door within seconds, and I have to open it in my creased clothes.

Tim makes no effort to hide his disapproval when he sees my outfit.

'The marketing campaign isn't yet in a state where I can show you the visuals,' I say as I open the door, 'but why don't you both come in and I can talk you through what it will look like to give you a flavour. You've made the effort to come here today and I don't want your journey to have been a waste.'

I step backwards and invite them inside.

'Can I make either of you a cup of tea or coffee?'

'No, can we just get on with it?' Tim says, frowning at the

empty wine glass on my desk and the crumpled blanket on the sofa.

I collect both and ask them to sit.

'I'd like a tea if it's not too much trouble,' Lauren says, smiling sympathetically.

I put the glass in the sink and fill the kettle.

'Whilst that's boiling, I'm just going to quickly change and then I'll be right with you. And once again, apologies for the mix-up. I promise that I'm not usually this disorganised.'

I disappear into my bedroom and close the door before Tim can criticise any further, and slowly slide down the door until I'm sitting on the floor. This is an awful start to the day, and worse still I have no idea what I'm going to tell them. I had so many ideas when we first discussed the opportunity on Zoom on Monday, but there have been so many distractions that I just haven't processed them properly. Every time I've tried to focus on the campaign, my mind has quickly wandered to what my tenants really think of me, the prospect of my dad being involved in Patricia Robinson's disappearance and murder, and trying to figure out who broke into my flat on Tuesday night.

It probably would have been easier just to apologise to them both, explain that I've got a lot going on at the moment and that we go our separate ways, but having forked out nearly a grand on surveillance cameras yesterday, I could do with the money. I also don't like reneging on commitments.

All I need to do is remember what we discussed on Monday, and how that can translate into an eye-catching campaign. This is where I excel.

*I can do this!*

With renewed energy, I stand and strip out of yesterday's clothes. Rummaging through the wardrobe I locate a fresh pair of trousers and a blouse and lay them on the bed. I'm about to close the doors when something catches my eye. It's on a hanger all the way to the side, so I didn't notice it at first, but when I slide the other clothes out of the way, I stare at it with growing confusion.

*I don't own a dress suit.*

The hanger doesn't look like one of mine either.

*How did that get there?*

I lift it out, holding it up to the light streaming through the bedroom curtains. It's emerald in colour, which definitely doesn't suit my complexion, and isn't something I would choose to buy. And then when I hold it up to my body, it's clearly a size too large for my emaciated frame. And then I catch a whiff of perfume and I realise what I'm holding. I instantly release it and it crumples to the floor. I stagger backwards in blind panic.

*How the hell did one of Fi's dress suits end up in my wardrobe?*

The question might as well be rhetorical, because deep down there's only one way it could have got there. My skin crawls as I picture a faceless figure entering my room on Tuesday night whilst I was asleep, and placing the suit in my wardrobe.

*He's trying to set me up for Fi's disappearance.*

If Atwal turns up right now with a search warrant and she discovers the suit, it will only confirm her worst suspicions about me. I need to get rid of it as quickly as possible.

Dressing in the trousers and blouse, I bundle the green suit into an old sports bag and exit my bedroom, opening the airing cupboard door so that I'm hidden from view of Lauren and Tim. I quickly lift the hatch and shove the bag into the darkness, making a mental note to dispose of it properly later. Lowering the hatch, I return to the living room, and see that Lauren has made tea for us both and her bright blue eyes are eagerly awaiting my pitch.

I step in front of them and clasp my hands together, willing my mind to recall what we agreed on Monday.

'When we spoke earlier in the week, you said you wanted a glossy two-page spread to be published in a number of corporate journals, and I said I thought you were targeting the wrong people with that concept.'

My conversation with Lauren is starting to come back to me and I remember her telling me not to worry about bruising Tim's ego. He may have a marketing degree, but that doesn't mean he's right.

'In my experience, the people responsible for coordinating the type of corporate events you want to be part of aren't the senior executives; it's the people who work beneath them on the ground level; executive assistants and the like. And whilst it's wrong to assume they don't all read the big corporate magazines, you're far more likely to succeed if you can hook *them*. And to do that, the key is to have your website at the top of every search engine they use.'

I'm blagging right now, and desperately hoping he doesn't see through me.

'Rather than wasting your budget on magazines, you need to focus on online advertising.'

'Can you be more specific?' Tim says.

'Social media.'

Tim rolls his eyes and sighs.

'I don't do social media.'

'Neither do I really,' I admit, 'but those executive assistants more than likely do. We need to build your new brand online. What I'm proposing to develop for you is an on-brand campaign that targets all the major social media sites. These sites have algorithms that are able to track eye movement, the amount of time spent watching the ad, and cookies that mean when they search for their next event, they'll see your website first. And if they remember the ad they've seen, there's a 75 per cent chance they'll click through to the website. And if the website is well-presented, with competitive package pricing, they're more likely to order.'

Lauren smiles encouragingly at me, and I'm actually pleasantly surprised by the idea. Without realising it, I actually think the proposal could be successful. A lot of work, but successful nonetheless.

'Can you show us the sort of imagery you intend to use?' Tim asks.

'Not today, but I should have something I can send to you on Monday.'

'That sounds reasonable,' Lauren quickly chimes in before Tim can speak. 'Given everything that's been going on here with the police, I think a couple of extra days is a reasonable accommodation we can make.'

'There was one other thought I had,' I continue as I embrace the moment of inspiration. 'I think you should offer a significant first-use customer discount. If we get them as far as looking at your site, you need an incentive to make them pick you over competitors they may have used before. Offering a one-time 50 per cent discount for new customers will drive them to book you. And if you then wow them on the day, they're more likely to return and book you for other events.'

'Don't be ridiculous,' Tim bellows. 'You want to turn us into a loss-making business.'

'No, but a loss-leader strategy is a sure-fire way to attract new customers and then it's up to you to keep them loyal with the quality of your service and products. And if you really believe you can deliver that, then it's a price worth paying.'

He doesn't look convinced, but I'm not surprised.

'We should go away and talk through it,' Lauren says, pressing a hand to his knee. 'We don't need to make a decision today. Eve will send us her draft visuals on Monday and then we can chat through next week.'

'Our financial strategy wasn't built around accruing onerous contracts. Such a strategy could set us back a further six months, and stop you building the fourth shop. I think we should cut our losses here, and see what else is available to us.' His eyes flit around the room. 'Particularly when you consider the history of this place.'

'What are you talking about?' Lauren asks.

'This place. The Freemantle Hotel of Death. Didn't you know? This used to be a hotel and the man who ran it was a serial killer.'

Lauren looks to me, maybe hoping I'll correct him, but I don't know what to say.

'That was a long time ago,' I try, but there's a look of enjoyment in Tim's eyes as he makes me squirm.

'The hotel had to close not long after his arrest, by all accounts. Nobody wanted to stay here because of what had happened. There were rumours it was haunted by demons and it was them that made Cooper kill his victims.'

Even I shiver at this claim.

'Maybe those demons still reside here,' he says, staring directly at me. 'It would certainly explain the police presence downstairs.'

I'd forgotten Atwal said she would be sending a forensics team to Fi's flat.

'I assure you that's all in the past,' I counter, but immediately picture Fi's dress in that sports bag. 'I should let you both go so I can finish pulling together the campaign. Let me show you out.'

I lock the door once they're gone but don't feel any safer. I can't explain why but something about Tim's knowledge of John Cooper's crimes has left me on edge.

## 32

### THURSDAY, 4.15 P.M.

I really should fix myself some lunch, and it's only when I spot the clock in the bottom corner of the screen that I realise how late it is. The warm sunshine is still pouring through the window and I had no idea it was nearly evening. I've been so focused on Lauren's campaign that I didn't realise how hungry I am. I push myself away from my desk and scour the cupboards for sustenance. I should cook myself something nutritious but that will take time, so I grab a packet of chocolate-covered digestives and tuck in.

I carry the packet back to the desk and take a final look at what my efforts have produced. I'm not one for bragging, but actually I'm proud of the outcome. Eye-catching visuals with a clear message and call to action. I'm certain that if I was in a position to be arranging a large social event this would certainly have me clicking to open their website. I could email it over to them now, but I don't want them to think I rushed it, and in my experience it's always better to double-check for typos with a fresh set of eyes. I've been staring at these glossy images for so long that I can still see them when I close my eyes.

Saving the file, I close down the laptop and stand, stretching out the aching muscles in my shoulders and back where I've been huddled over my desk. Even though it terrifies me that someone arranged this morning's surprise meeting with Lauren and Tim, actually had I not had to pitch to them I don't think I would have come up with half the ideas that I've pulled together, so it's all worked out for the best.

This time.

I can't ignore the fact that someone emailed Lauren from my laptop, though there's no sign of the email in my sent box, but I saw it on her phone so the perpetrator must have sent it and then deleted all trace so I wouldn't realise. Add in the Tesco order that I didn't place and all the alcohol that arrived and clearly someone wants me to look like I'm losing control of my faculties.

I jump when someone knocks at the door, before composing myself.

'Who's there?' I call out just in case.

'It's Bill, Eve. I have a package for you.'

I smile when I hear his croaky voice and unlock the door. He's in his usual moth-eaten green cardigan and chinos. His grey hair is squashed at one side, making me think it's not long since he's woken from one of those power naps he told me about the other day. I can't help but smile at the memory.

'Your package, mademoiselle,' he says holding out a large brown box as long and wide as my laptop, and just as deep.

'What is it?' I ask, uncertain why Bill would feel the need to buy me a present.

'Beats me. I told the delivery driver I'd bring it up to you.'

I accept the box and carry it through, leaving the door ajar as Bill follows me inside. I fetch a knife from the kitchen and cut through the brown parcel tape and then raise the flaps, smiling again when I see what's inside.

'Something exciting?' Bill asks, as I lift out the first of four boxes.

The picture of the digital clock on the box makes it look like any run-of-the-mill bedside alarm clock. There is nothing on the box to suggest it contains a discreet video camera.

'Just a few bits and bobs I found in a sale,' I lie.

Whilst I trust Bill with my life and am in no doubt that he is not my intruder, I don't want to worry him unnecessarily by telling him I'm kitting out my flat with surveillance equipment. He'll only want to know why and I don't want to cause him alarm. I also don't want him to inadvertently tell anyone else that I'm laying a trap up here, just in case my antagonist is closer to home than I realised. And I don't want word of this getting back to Pete either.

I remove the remaining boxes and stand them on the coffee table, before flattening the box, but stop when I see my name and address on the label.

'Why did the delivery driver call on you instead of me?'

'He said he was buzzing you for ages but got no response so tried me next. I said you must be in a meeting or something and that I would bring it up to you.'

I frown. I've been here all afternoon and my intercom hasn't sounded once.

'When was this?'

'A few minutes ago. Just before I came up here.'

'Nobody buzzed for me though.'

'Oh, well, that's what he said. Maybe you were in the bathroom when it happened.'

I shake my head.

'No, I've only just finished work and haven't left the room.'

I put the flattened box on the floor and cross back to the front door where my intercom handset hangs in its cradle. I lift it out and press the receiver to my ear, and that's when the cable drops free.

'Ah, there you go: loose cable,' Bill declares, pinching the cable hanging from the cradle on the wall. He takes the handset from me and reinserts the end, pressing it to his ear before returning it to the cradle. 'There we go, all fixed now. What would you do without me, eh?'

He chortles at this, but I'm not so easily swayed. Although the intercom is now very much dated, I've never had an issue with the cable loosening and falling out. I lift the handset again and pull on the cable, but it's secured tight enough and doesn't come loose.

'Maybe you caught it accidentally,' Bill offers, seeing the confusion on my face.

I think back to Lauren and Tim arriving this morning. The intercom was working when they got here, and I certainly didn't do anything to the cord to make it come loose. And nobody else has been in my flat since I showed them out.

It doesn't make sense. There's no reason Lauren or Tim would unplug the cable. Could the intruder have waited for me to show them down and then snuck in, disconnected the intercom and then hidden again? It sounds too unbelievable, but I have no other explanation. And given we didn't pass anyone on the stairs in either direction, that would have to mean they were already in the building somewhere. I shiver at the thought.

'Perhaps George knocked it,' Bill says, and my eyes widen.

'How do you know—'

He smiles.

'Ah, you forget, I was in the police once upon a time. I've been here enough times to notice the cat fur on the upholstery and I've heard you talking to him before. I figured you either have a cat or an incredibly hairy lover you keep locked away.' He chortles again. 'Don't worry, kiddo, your secret is safe with me.'

It gets me thinking about who else in the building might know about George. The tenancy agreements they've all signed say they're not allowed pets, but I think several of them wouldn't hesitate to complain if they knew I was breaking my own rule. But could something so insignificant be the cause of why someone is sneaking in here and messing with my life?

There's only one way to know for sure, and I pick up the box containing the fake air freshener, open it and begin to read the setup instructions. Bill hovers nearby, when I'd expected him to show himself out by now.

'Is there something else I can help you with, Bill?'

He puffs out his cheeks, as if weighing some moral dilemma.

'The thing is...' he begins, 'there's something you should probably know. I don't want to cause any trouble, but I feel you deserve to know.'

I stare at him, waiting for him to elaborate.

'The thing is...' he says again, 'I don't know how to say this.'

The way he's twisting his fingers awkwardly instantly tells me whatever it is isn't good news. I think back to our last conversation about John Cooper and immediately leap to the conclusion that there's something he left out about my dad and Cooper's final victim, Patricia Robinson.

I take a deep breath.

'Just spit it out, Bill.'

'India has called all the other tenants to a secret meeting.'

I double-take at the statement.

'W-what?'

'I wasn't invited either.'

'Well, then how do you—'

'I overheard Chad and Caz talking in the corridor. The

meeting has something to do with you, which is why I assume I wasn't asked to attend, in case I told you.'

I think back to how outspoken India was about Danielle's potential involvement in James's passing and the fact that Fi wasn't at the tenants' meeting. I thought she was just overreacting to the shock of James's death, but what if I underestimated her, and she was just covering her own tracks? For all I know, she could be the person who's messing with me, and it would make sense for her to involve the others in her conspiracy in case I figure she's responsible.

'Sorry, I shouldn't have said anything,' Bill says, scowling with regret.

'No, I'm glad you did. If the residents aren't happy about something then they should inform me so I can try to resolve the matter. I'm just going to freshen up and then I'll go and find out what they're discussing.'

'Are you okay if I don't come with you? I don't want to alienate anyone, but you know you've got my full support.'

'That's fine, Bill, and I won't let on that you were the one who told me.'

He turns to leave.

'Thanks, Bill. I really appreciate your support.'

I swill mouthwash and squirt perfume on my neck, and then I head out, making sure the door is locked behind me.

## 33

THURSDAY, 4.32 P.M.

I'm about to knock on India's door when a fresh thought strikes and almost knocks me off my feet. If India is the one who's been messing with me, the only reason I can think of for her to gather the other tenants – whilst excluding Bill and me – is that she plans to convince them that *I'm* the one responsible for James's death and Fi's disappearance. I can picture Jenny telling them all how she caught me leaving Fi's flat and that will just help corroborate India's theory.

Bill heads downstairs and I wait until I hear him close his door before I rap my knuckles against hers. I hear the sound of movement inside and hushed voices, before the door opens a fraction and India stares back at me, her face a mix of horror and panic.

'Eve, what are you doing here?'

'I heard you were having a gathering and didn't want to miss what you have to say.'

'A gathering? I don't know what you mean.'

'I know you've called the other tenants together for a meeting, India, and whilst I have no problem with that, if the meeting relates to any issues in the building or to *me* in particular, then I think I have a right to be there.'

She pulls a face of disbelief.

'Are you feeling all right? You look a bit... peaky.'

'I'm fine,' I say, shooting out a hand to grip the edge of the doorframe as a wave of nausea sweeps through me. 'Please just let me in.'

'India, are there any more crisps?' I hear Mike's voice call from somewhere inside. He appears behind her a moment later with his hand in a large bag of Kettle Chips. He looks from the bag to me, then to India and back to me, his mouth dropping and his eyes widening so much that his glasses slip down his nose. He looks as though he would give up his darkest secrets for the mental torture to end.

I fix India with a hard stare, and she eventually puffs out her cheeks and opens the door wider.

'Okay, you can come in,' she sighs.

Gangly Mike waddles through the small hallway and into the open-plan living room, crossing the room until he reaches the window, standing outside the circle of familiar faces. I spot Caz, Chad, and Jenny. The only tenants not here are Bill, Danielle, and Fi.

'Why do I feel like I've entered one of the infamous Salem witch trials?' I say, breaking the awkward silence engulfing the room. 'Is there a reason you haven't invited all the building's occupants? If you're having a meeting to discuss concerns, then it's only fair to include me, Bill and Danielle, no?'

India steps out from behind me and sits in the vacant space on the sofa beside Jenny and Chad.

'Okay, if you must know, I invited the others here to ask their views on building security.'

'If you have concerns or complaint, you should address them directly to me, rather than conspiring.'

'We're not *conspiring*,' India huffs. 'Don't be so melodramatic. Given the question marks still surrounding James's passing and the fact that there's all manner of unusual people coming and going, it's my view that we need to heighten security. And for starters, *everyone* needs to remember to properly close the main door downstairs.' She pauses and looks at each of us. 'The number of times I've returned from work or been hurrying out and found it swinging in the breeze.'

I have to admit I've found the door open a couple of times in the last month and have pushed it closed so the lock engages properly. It's a fair challenge, and the laminated reminder on the window clearly isn't working.

She focuses her attention on me.

'And I also think our landlord should agree to installing security cameras in each of the hallways so we can see who's coming and going from our flats when we're not at home.'

Is that a dig at me because Jenny's told her about catching me leaving Fi's flat, or is she laughing at me because I haven't been able to catch her letting herself into my home?

'I think it's a brilliant idea,' Jenny pipes up, and it wouldn't surprise me if she and India had already rehearsed their parts in this little play.

'It's not right that any Tom, Dick or Harry can get into the building and then maybe break into our homes without us knowing,' India continues, again looking straight at me.

I wish the ground would open and swallow me up right now, and not just because I feel like I'm in the dock being prosecuted. I really don't feel well. There's a cold sweat clawing at my back and hairline.

'Are you sure you're okay?' India now asks, but I don't have time to respond as I race towards the bathroom, barely making it to the toilet before I retch.

What is wrong with me today? I know I haven't eaten anything proper – snacking on crisps and Maltesers while working on the marketing pitch – but this feels like something more. I've had hungover mornings when I've woken feeling the same way, but I've not consumed any alcohol today.

I wipe my mouth with tissue and swill water from the basin tap before spitting it out and looking up at my reflection. My skin is pasty white and my eyes look dull and grey. I don't want to think about what India will now be saying on the other side of this door. I can't believe I threw up in her bathroom. I don't think I could have made a worse impression, having insisted on joining the meeting.

The conversation stops the moment I open the bathroom door and all eyes turn on me, which tells me everything I need to know about the subject matter.

'Don't stop on my behalf,' I say, wiping my mouth with a fresh tissue. 'Would you mind getting me a drink of water, please?'

India heads into the kitchen area and fills a glass from the tap, encouraging me to take her place on the sofa, which I do.

'Mike and Jenny agree that cameras in the corridors is a reasonable request,' India says, glaring at them to speak up and concur.

'Absolutely,' Jenny says. 'You must admit, Eve, it probably would have helped identify the intruder you said you heard in Fi's flat yesterday.'

She's got me there, and to be honest I'm not against the idea of added security around the property; it's the fact they felt the need to collude before raising the request with me, and the cost, of course.

'Chad agrees it's the right action, don't you, Chad?' Jenny says, nudging him with her arm.

I'm sure I see him glance at Caz in my periphery before looking at me and nodding. Caz looks so timid, as if she's frightened to speak out against the others.

'And how do you feel about cameras being installed for security, Caz?' I ask her.

She seems to fold in on herself, before clearing her throat meekly.

'Aren't they an invasion of our privacy? I'd hate to feel like I'm being watched all the time.'

'It would only be Eve watching,' India challenges, but that seems to irk Jenny.

'Why should Eve be the only one who sees who's coming or going? It would make more sense if we all had access to the footage.'

'That's what I mean,' Caz replies. 'With all due respect, I don't want to see what happens outside your doors on floor one.'

'Well, maybe we just have access to the cameras immediately outside our rooms,' India interjects.

'No, we need to be able to see who comes and goes from the front door as well,' Jenny says.

'That's exactly what I mean,' Caz says. 'A camera on the front door would then allow you to see into mine and Bill's flats.'

'Well, it's not like you've got anything to hide, is there?' Jenny snaps.

Someone needs to take control of the conversation as otherwise it's going to turn into a full-blown argument.

'I'm not saying we shouldn't improve security measures in the building,' I say, speaking over the murmuring conversations, 'but we would need the consensus of the whole building. That includes Bill and Danielle—'

'What about Fi?' Jenny interrupts.

'And Fi, of course, when she returns,' I say, avoiding confronting the elephant in the room. 'I think it's right that we debate the idea of security cameras, but everyone's views need to be considered. My suggestion would be that we reconvene in a day or so and then we can talk about it with clear heads and with everybody present.'

'Given the police now seem to be treating Fi's disappearance as suspicious, I'm not sure we should wait for her return,' India says, blissfully unaware of how blunt she sounds, or maybe not caring.

'We shouldn't be jumping to conclusions,' I say, now wishing Bill was here to be the sage voice of reason he usually is. 'She could just be away for a few days visiting friends.'

'Tell that to the team in white coveralls who were scouring her flat for evidence overnight.'

I suddenly picture the emerald dress suit I found in my closet. I'd totally forgotten I'd shoved it in a bag and thrown it down the hatch. I need to get rid of it before Jenny and India start spreading their suspicions to Detective Atwal and her colleagues. I dread to think what Atwal would think if she found Fi's clothes in my possession.

I stand so suddenly that I almost keel over, but push my hands out to the side to regain my balance.

'I'll speak to Bill and Danielle, and then I'll arrange a tenants' meeting for early next week when I've had chance to consider all security measures and not just transform our home into *Animal Farm*.'

Nobody else makes any effort to leave, so I imagine the debate will rage on once I'm gone. As much as I hate the idea of them talking behind my back, I've made my point, and I'm in no state to remain in social company. I need to get back upstairs and lie down until this nausea passes.

I stagger to India's door and open it, pulling it closed behind me, welcoming the gentle breeze that catches my cheeks. I lurch towards the staircase and grab hold of the handrail, using it to guide me back up the stairs to my flat, but it takes all of my energy. Slipping my key into the door, I push it open, and physically jump when I see the masked figure staring back at me from inside.

## 34

THURSDAY, 4.58 P.M.

Suddenly it's like I've been transported back in time to that night when I was naively walking home from the shop, blissfully unaware that I was about to become someone else's prey. I feel his arms grab hold of my waist and physically lift me off the ground, before pushing me into the small forest of darkened, leafless trees. Internally I was bellowing for him to release me, but not a single syllable escaped my throat. Overwhelmed by terror, I remember thinking, 'This is the end,' and fragments of my life – mainly my regrets and failings – flashed through my mind. Despite the sense that it was so unfair, my body accepted the sentence and I waited for death.

Thankfully, my brain managed to repress most of what followed, and so my next memory is of coming to on a bed of broken twigs and brown leaves. I could just about make out the moon through the branches overhead, seeing my breath escape in silver plumes. At first, I assumed I'd died and this was some kind of purgatory for the part I played in what happened to Simone in boarding school; karma had come for me and this was the result. I don't remember how long I lay there, waiting to see a ghostly figure bearing a scythe, but eventually I managed to stand and stumble back through the clearing and onto the street.

It was like an out-of-body experience or as if I was a puppet and someone was pulling my strings to make me continue the walk home. I recognised my surroundings and yet there was something different about them now, and I still can't place my finger on what that was; almost as if I was now operating on a different frequency to the rest of the world.

I snap back to the masked figure in black standing just inside my flat.

*Is this it? Has he returned to finish the job?*

My fight or flight has failed me again. I know I should do something, but my usually racing mind is silent. I'm frozen to the spot, and unable to scream.

The figure lunges forwards, and grabs my arms, dragging me inside and throwing me against the wall across from the door. I gasp as my shoulder catches on the edge of the plastic light switch, and it's enough to trigger a memory.

*A few squirts of this in a person's eyes, and they'll be temporarily blinded – incapacitated – whilst you beat a hasty retreat.*

Of course! The pepper spray that Pete gave me. If I can get to that, there might just be a chance... but where the hell did I leave it?

His dark eyes are staring at me through the balaclava, but I don't have time to think. I rush forward, catching him by surprise and push him with all my might. He staggers back out into the hallway, blocking any chance of escape, so I hightail it further into my flat. It's dim where the curtains are closed, the sun trapped behind a blanket of dark cloud beyond the windows. I turn into the kitchen area, my eyes scanning every nook and cranny for the small can of spray. The tower of unwashed crockery stares back at me from the side of the sink, but my eyes dart over the rest of the counter as I hear footsteps approaching from behind.

I spot the taser beside the microwave and as I'm about to reach for it, there are suddenly hands around my waist once again, lifting me into the air and then we crash into the counter that separates the kitchen area from the open-plan living room. The edge of the counter digs into my waist as he continues to force me into it. I try to resist, thrusting my right foot back and manage to connect with his shin. The respite is temporary, but it allows me to press my hands into the rim of the counter and lift myself a fraction off the floor. When he crashes back into me, the momentum is enough to take me over the edge of the counter and suddenly I'm freefalling, headfirst towards the living room carpet. I manage to adjust my torso slightly and my right shoulder is the first thing to hit the floor, sending a shooting pain through my whole body. The rest of me crumples on top, but there is now a barrier between us.

As I roll onto my back, I see the figure peeling around the edge of the counter and coming for me again. I continue rolling to try and get in a better position to stand, but he flies through the air, and lands on top of me.

*No, not again!*

I don't know whether I say the words out loud or it's just my mind shouting at me, but I feel renewed strength and purpose flash through my body, and I manage to drive a knee into his groin and push him to the side, but rather than fleeing and escaping through the front door, something else takes over, and I kick out again, catching his knees, and then I'm up on one elbow and pummelling his chest with my balled-up fist.

*How do you like that?* the voice in my head yells.

But I've overestimated my position, and I don't see him reaching for the used mug of coffee on the table until it's too late and he cracks it against my temple. I'm so shocked that I don't immediately feel any pain, but then the throbbing cuts through the adrenaline like a locomotive and I crumple back onto my back. He is crouched on hands and knees now, and my head is so foggy that the room is starting to blur.

In the distance I hear someone calling my name.

*Dad? Am I dying? Have you come to help me pass over?*

'Hey, get the hell away from her,' a man's voice shouts nearby, and then I hear a loud crash, and then there is someone taking hold of my hand. 'Eve? Eve? Can you hear me? Eve?'

I blink several times and then Ethan's blurred face appears in front of me. I don't know whether I passed out and he's found me, or what, but then I hear the front door crashing against the wall, and immediately sense my attacker is still in the flat. I grab hold of Ethan to use him as a lever to sit up, almost knocking him over in the process.

'Did you see the masked man?' I demand.

'Yeah, I think he's gone.'

I can't allow him to escape. I need to know who he is and why he's doing this to me. I'm unsteady as I clamber to my feet, but I ignore the warnings of my inner monologue and stagger towards the door, gripping the handrail for dear life as I try to descend the staircase without tumbling.

I can hear his footsteps on the next staircase and need to hurry if I'm going to stop him. I leap the last four stairs, and wince as my ankle buckles on landing, but I use the pain as a much-needed shot of adrenaline and plough on. I reach the ground floor and can just about see the shadow of the figure in black sprinting towards the main door.

'Stop!' I yell out, as a shooting pain erupts from my left ankle again.

I bite down and stumble forwards, willing the retreating

figure to stop and trip over so I can gain ground, but they're out of the door in a flash and my momentum keeps me racing head-first towards the breeze.

You can't go out there, my mind tells me.

But I have to. He's haunted me for too long, I can't let him get away.

*But think about all the disease and pollution out there. Remember how vulnerable you are without these walls to protect you.*

I crash into the frame of the door, but don't progress any further. Staring out, I can hear the figure's racing footsteps hurrying down the driveway and out onto the street. I can still catch him.

But my body won't move. I try to lift my foot and push it through the open doorway, but it won't budge. I'm panting so much that I'm feeling lightheaded. My knees buckle and crash into the straw fibres of the rust-coloured doormat.

He's getting away and my body is fighting against me. I'm so close but there's an invisible forcefield that I can't break through. Tears sting the edges of my eyes as he slips through my fingers.

## 35

THURSDAY, 5.03 P.M.

I feel the warmth of someone beside my shoulder.

'Eve, are you okay?' Ethan asks. 'Did he hit you again?'

I want to tell him everything – Dad's links to John Cooper, my own role in Simone's death – but instead my face balls into a sob and the tears stream down my cheeks as I lean into his chest.

'Hey, it's okay, I'm here now,' he says, putting a gentle arm around my shoulders. 'I won't let anything bad happen to you.'

I can't remember the last time anyone held me so tenderly.

'I think we should get you upstairs and get that cut cleaned up,' he says now, whistling through his teeth while staring at my forehead. 'I'm no Florence Nightingale, but I'm a dab hand when it comes to attaching plasters to wounds.'

I find myself snickering despite the embarrassment of crying in front of a virtual stranger. He stands and pulls me up, but immediately notices me wince when I try and put weight on my throbbing ankle. He doesn't say anything but places my arm around his shoulders and helps me to the stairs.

'Are you going to be able to walk up?'

I nod, but he keeps my arm in place and I put my weight on

him and the handrail and we take it a step at a time. When we finally reach the top, I'm genuinely starting to worry that I may have seriously injured my ankle. The thought of having to go to a hospital for an X-ray and treatment fills me with instant panic.

Ethan helps me in through my still open door and onto the sofa in the living room. I hear him close and lock the front door before he returns and helps me lift my legs on to the sofa, building a tower of cushions and placing my left leg on it.

'Do you mind if I take a look?' he asks, gingerly lifting the cuff of my tracksuit bottoms.

I shake my head, but I see the look of fear in his eyes when he looks at the huge swelling.

'Do you have any ice?'

I nod.

'There should be some peas in the freezer in the kitchen.'

I watch as he turns into the kitchen area, locates the freezer and returns carrying the unopened green bag. He rests it over my skin and the sudden cold makes me tense up.

'Sorry,' he says. 'Do you think we should phone for an ambulance?'

I instantly shake my head.

'I'll be fine.'

'I'm not sure I agree. It could just be a sprain, I suppose, but it would be worth getting it checked out. And that cut and bump to your forehead doesn't look great either. You could be concussed.'

I'd forgotten about the figure hitting me with the coffee mug, and press my fingers to where I can now feel additional throbbing. My fingers touch something sticky and I see red when I pull them away.

'Have you got a first-aid kit somewhere?' Ethan asks.

'No, but there should be plasters in the medicine cabinet above the sink in the bathroom.'

He clicks his fingers and goes in search of the bathroom, returning a moment later armed with cotton wool balls, antiseptic and a box of plasters.

'I can do it,' I tell him when he kneels down beside me.

'I have no doubt that you can, but given what you've just been through, please let me do it. It's okay to allow other people to help.'

He unscrews the cap on the bottle of antiseptic and dabs some onto one of the cotton wool balls. I feel like a child being cleaned up by a parent after a spill. I can't remember the last time I allowed someone else to be this close to me.

'Now, this is probably going to sting a bit,' he says, as he presses the ball to my head.

I bite down to hide my reaction to the instant sting, and allow him to wipe up the blood. With the frozen peas helping to calm the pain in my ankle, my head is now starting to pound. There's a large bump either side of the cut I felt and Ethan's remark about concussion might not be as ridiculous as I first thought. The nausea I was feeling at India's flat earlier has passed, but I'm still conscious that it was probably brought on by a lack of decent sustenance today. I'm in no fit state to hobble around the kitchen and cook, but ordering a takeaway would still require me to go down two flights of stairs to collect it at the door. Injuring my ankle really has left me in a precarious position.

'How's the pain?' Ethan asks.

'I'll survive.'

He fastens a plaster to my forehead and moves back to the kitchen. He returns a moment later and passes me a large glass of white wine.

'You look like you could do with something for the shock,' he says.

I stare at the glass for an age, uncomfortable with how desperately I want to snatch it from him.

'I can fix you some sugary tea if you'd prefer?'

I accept the glass and take a large swallow, but it barely touches the sides.

'Can I ask you a personal question?' he says next, sitting down in the armchair across from me.

'Sure.'

'Did you know who the man in the black hoodie was?'

My eyes snap to his as he asks this. I wasn't sure how much of a glimpse he got of the figure, and God knows what he must be thinking about me having such a monster in my flat. I can't tell him that deep down my mind wants the figure to be the same man who assaulted me five years ago, so that I can finally bring him to justice. It's far more likely that whoever was in here today isn't the same person and it's just my overactive imagination finding links where none exist.

'We need to contact the police and report what happened,' Ethan says when I don't respond.

'What's the point? He's long gone and probably dumped the mask and hoodie.'

Ethan tilts his head empathetically and lowers his voice.

'The point is this person attacked you in your own home. Anything could have happened if I didn't turn up when I did. The police need to know that this figure was here in case he returns and attacks someone else. Is anything missing? They weren't carrying anything when they raced out of here, but you should check any cash or jewellery you have lying around. He was probably looking to fund some habit.'

I resist the urge to take another drink from the glass, because I don't want him to see how vulnerable I feel.

'The only valuables in the flat are my television and laptop and they're both here. My passport is expired and I have no use for cash. And he'd be lucky to get his bus fare with the value of the little jewellery I own.'

'He still needs to be reported. A crime has happened here.' He pauses again. 'Sorry, I'm a bit of a stickler when it comes to people paying for their crimes.'

If he knew I think the figure in black has been sneaking into my flat during the night and ordering groceries and making appointments with clients, I think he'd be even more insistent. And for all I know this figure was also terrorising James in a similar way before he couldn't take any more...

I dial Detective Atwal from my mobile but it rings out with the answerphone finally kicking in. I leave a message asking her to call me back as I've had an intruder in my flat. I don't want to think what might have happened had Ethan not burst through when he did.

I take another drink of the wine and look at him.

'What are you actually doing here? I'm grateful that you came along when you did, but we didn't have an appointment to meet, did we?'

His brow furrows for a moment.

'I came to collect the final few mementos from my brother's flat before I head back up to the Midlands. I was going to buzz you on the intercom and ask whether you could let me inside again, but the front door was wide open so I figured I'd ask in person. But then your door was ajar and I heard banging inside, so I wanted to check you were okay, and then...'

India's words echo through my mind: *It's not right that any Tom, Dick or Harry can get into the building and then maybe break into our homes without us knowing.*

If the door was left open by someone again, it's no wonder

the figure in black was able to get up here, although I've no idea how they could have got through my locked door. My brother is the only person with a spare set, and it definitely wasn't him beneath that mask.

'So, would you be able to let me borrow the spare key to James's flat? I promise I'll bring them straight back up when I'm done; I don't expect you to hobble down the stairs.'

I'm about to tell him they're on the hook by the door when I remember Atwal confiscating them last night.

'I'd happily let you in, but the police took the keys yesterday as part of their investigation. I have no access to your brother's flat. I'm sorry. I can give you the number for the detective who has them and she might be able to stop by and let you inside.'

'Is that the same detective you just tried to call and she didn't answer?'

I nod sheepishly.

'I'm sure she's got more important things to do than come down here and open a door for me. It's fine. I'll be back this way in a couple of weeks for the funeral, and I can arrange to collect the remainder then. Is that okay with you? You're not desperate to let it to someone new? If that is the case, I don't mind paying what remains on my brother's tenancy agreement to keep it vacant until I can return.'

'I appreciate the offer, but there's no need. James was always prompt paying his rent, and no money is due for another three weeks. And even if it was, given the circumstances the least I can do is keep it vacant until you've said your goodbyes.'

I lower my leg from the tower of cushions, and attempt to stand, but it isn't the pain in my ankle that makes me topple back into the sofa. I feel so lightheaded that it takes violent rubbing of my eyes to stop the room spinning.

'Whoa, are you okay?' Ethan asks, joining me on the sofa.

'I'll be fine,' I mouth, but I've no idea if any sound escapes.

He presses the back of his hand to my forehead, and gives me a concerned look.

'You don't look great. When did you last eat something?'

I attempt to say I've been snacking all day, but the best I can manage is a shrug.

'Then before I go, I'm going to fix you something to eat. It could just be the shock catching up with you, but also wine on an empty stomach can be lethal.'

He claps his hands together and stands. I don't like the thought of him poking around in the kitchen and silently judging me for the lack of nutritional value of what's in the fridge and cupboards, but I can't even tell him to stop.

*What is wrong with me now?*

I must pass in and out of consciousness, because in no time Ethan is back beside me on the couch, a bowl of steaming tomato soup on a tray and the end crust of a loaf. He keeps the tray on his lap and tells me when to open my mouth and he proceeds to feed me like a child. It's embarrassing, but the soup is sweet and hot and exactly what my body is craving. The bowl is half empty when I start to feel better, but he refuses to let me take the tray from him.

I yield and allow him to keep feeding me and by the time the bowl is empty, I'm better able to communicate.

'You must think I'm such a drama queen,' I say.

'Not at all,' he says, smiling. 'I'm glad I've been more use than I was when I first arrived.'

'What do you mean? You stopped him from throttling me.'

He pulls a disappointed face.

'Yeah, but I wasn't strong enough to stop him getting away. I lunged at him and he brushed me off like I wasn't even there.'

## The Tenants

'You're still a hero in my eyes,' I say and mean every word.

Ethan stands and carries the tray to the kitchen, but I insist he not wash up as well. He's cooked for and fed me, and I've offered him nothing in return.

He reappears, looking at his watch.

'I should really get going.'

'Already? You can stay for a bit if you want. You can fix yourself something to eat as well.'

He sits down beside me.

'You're very sweet, Eve, but I have a three-hour journey ahead of me, and I can stop and grab a bite to eat to break up the journey. Are you going to be okay if I go?'

I can't shake the feeling that the man in black is going to return the moment Ethan leaves, and I grab his arm, and pull him closer, before pressing my lips against his. He responds and it's like the world around us melts away, but then he pulls away.

'Stay,' I say, breathless.

'I can't. Don't get me wrong; I want to, but it wouldn't be right. With everything you've been through today, I wouldn't feel right taking advantage of you.'

'You wouldn't—'

He kisses my forehead.

'I like you, Eve. And if things were different... But they're not. Listen, I'll be back in a couple of weeks, and then maybe we can talk more.'

He kisses my forehead again, and then departs, closing the door. I don't hesitate to stand and hop across to the door, but by the time I open it, I can already hear his footfalls on the floor below. He's making a hasty retreat, and I'm filled with regret for throwing myself at him in that way. The poor guy is grieving his brother and I tried to seduce him. I close the door and make sure to lock it. Despite the pain in my ankle, my night is just beginning. I reach for the first of the boxes and pull out the fake thermostat. If the man in black does return, I'm determined to get proof.

## 36

### FRIDAY, 8.45 A.M.

I'm woken by something brushing the corner of my cheek and my mind creates dozens of terrifying images of what my attacker is about to do to me. My eyes snap open and I tense, ready to reach for the taser beneath the spare pillow, when George plops himself into the gap between my arm and shoulder. I look at him and he offers a little purr by way of greeting. I ruffle the fur between his ears as my heartrate gradually slows.

I don't remember coming to bed, but setting up the surveillance devices took longer than I'd expected. It required me to download an app on my laptop and then connect them via Bluetooth so they could then join the Wi-Fi. It probably would have taken Pete half the time to figure out the instructions, but I actually felt quite proud of myself at the end. And it is with this sense of pride that I push the duvet back and swing my legs over the side of the bed.

A shooting pain in my ankle reminds me to tread carefully. I strapped it up with a tight bandage last night, and this allows me to put minimal weight on the foot and I hobble into the living room, grab my laptop and carry it back to bed with me. George briefly glances up at the disturbance before snuggling back down for his pre-breakfast nap.

I lift the lid and log into the app. The views from all four cameras fill the screen in a grid and I can see the live streams of my flat. There's a couple of seconds' time lapse but I can see myself in bed, the closed front door, the hatch and the space where my laptop used to be in the living room. My heart warms with that feeling of pride again.

With a deep breath, I scroll the clock back to last night. The cameras only record when something crosses the invisible field in front of them. The app tells me it captured movement at 1.20 a.m. and at 3.37 a.m. in the living room and when I check the feed I see George stalking the sofa, looking for a warm spot. But there's no sign of a figure in black. I check each of the feeds individually, zooming in to check for anything out of place, but aside from George, the only thing captured was me collecting the laptop a moment ago.

My ankle is throbbing from the brief walk to the living room. The swelling looks worse than when I went to bed, but the thought of leaving the building to have it examined by a doctor fills me with dread. There's probably nothing they would do if it's sprained; just tell me to rest and ice it. So that is what I will do today, and if there's no sign of improvement in the coming days... well, I'll just have to cross that bridge when I get to it. No point worrying now.

*I like you, Eve. And if things were different...*

Ethan's voice in my head is unexpected but serves as a reminder of the fool I made of myself last night. I curl into a foetal position, thinking about my lame effort to come on to him. What must he think of me? Grieving the loss of his brother and then some hapless, paranoid woman throws herself at him. I'm surprised he didn't run out faster. I'm not in the habit of sleeping with men I've only just met, but last night I was so worried about the man in black returning that I probably would have welcomed anyone else to my bed so I wasn't alone. I'm not sure many men would have been as honest and decent as Ethan. Despite the facial similarity between him and James, the two couldn't be any more different.

He said he'll be back in a couple of weeks and we should talk then. Does that mean he might be interested in pursuing a relationship? It's been so long since I experienced anything romantic that I'm out of touch. He lives in Birmingham and I'm down here, but would he consider moving closer?

I sigh at my overactive imagination. I know so little about him and here's me already fantasising what a life together would be like. I haven't even told him about my agoraphobia, though he must wonder why I broke down by the front door yesterday. Even if he was interested in a potential relationship, he'd soon change his mind when he realises I'm confined here. His mention of talking in a couple of weeks was probably just a line so he could make his escape. There's every chance I'll never hear from him again, though deep down I hope I do.

I can't lie in bed all day – as much as I'd like to. I still need to check over the advertising campaign and send it to Lauren and Tim, and then I should think about what I'm going to cook for Pete when he comes over for his birthday meal at the weekend. It should be something spectacular to make up for the fact that I failed to give him a birthday card and present. If I place my order today there's a chance it will come before he arrives on Sunday. I get out of bed, using the wall to help me hobble to the bathroom. I have nothing I can use as a crutch but I may need to order something if the ankle doesn't improve in the coming days. I make it to the bathroom and wash myself in the basin, and then get dressed in combats and a hoodie and carry the laptop back to my desk.

The stack of dumbbells looks undisturbed over the hatch in the airing cupboard, and so I close the door. The pile of pans I left precariously beside the front door also look as though they haven't moved. I figured if the man in black was to return, some kind of audible warning would be beneficial. I leave them where they are for now, but choose to lie on the sofa with my ankle elevated, rather than sitting by my desk. I try to imagine how Lauren and Tim will react when they see the marketing campaign I've produced. I told them I'd produce a documented strategy to go with it, which is what I intend to do now. I open the folder on my desktop, but my face drops.

*Where's the file?*

All the images I've downloaded are there in the folder but the main file isn't.

*Take a breath. Maybe you accidentally saved it somewhere else.*

I try to think back to when I was working on it yesterday. I know I definitely saved the file, but maybe I accidentally saved it in a different folder. That must be what it is. I open the file explorer and search for the title. The egg timer icon whirs for several minutes before telling me there are no search results.

*No, this is impossible! I definitely created the presentation... didn't I?*

I spent hours at my desk yesterday, so hyper-focused on the task. I remember seeing all the visuals I created on the screen, but then I also remember how queasy I felt when Bill arrived to tell me about India's secret meeting. I couldn't have imagined creating the presentation. This is insane.

I now can't help seeing all the concerned looks Pete and others have been giving me these last few weeks.

*Am I losing my mind?*

From the outside I can see why it would look like that. George being trapped outside, the Tesco delivery I don't remember ordering and the meeting I didn't arrange with Lauren and Tim yesterday morning. And now there being no evidence of the presentation I pulled together. It all points to someone losing their grip on reality. Add in Fi's disappearance, the mystery woman I'm sure I saw enter James's flat on Monday night, and me certain that someone has been using the passageway to enter my flat...

No! I'm not standing for that.

I didn't imagine the man in black in my flat yesterday and I didn't imagine Ethan coming to my rescue. As paranoid as this all sounds, I am certain someone is behind the scenes, pulling the strings. I just don't know why they're targeting me in this way.

I open the programme I created the file in and check the history and see the file path on the screen. My pulse quickens.

*I didn't imagine it!*

But when I click on the file path an error message flashes up on the screen to say it's invalid. I try again and the same error message pops up. That means it *was* there but has somehow been deleted. I check the Recycle Bin on the desktop and there are various deleted files showing, but not the file I'm looking for.

Someone else must have deleted it and then removed it from the Recycle Bin so I couldn't restore it. But who and when?

Jenny and India have made no secret of their dislike for me, but I can't see that either would go to the effort to make me look like I'm losing my mind. The cameras revealed nobody broke in last night, and Bill and Ethan are the only other people who've been up here...

I see the figure in black lunging at me when I returned yesterday afternoon. So that's why he was here! He must have deleted the file and was then planning to escape when I returned unexpectedly and then he attacked me.

I have no evidence to support such a theory, but I have no other logical explanation for why the file is missing. I know he's accessed my laptop before to place the Tesco order, so who's to say he didn't access it again yesterday afternoon? But why would he delete the presentation? At worst it's infuriating for me because I'll have to redo it, but the only other person it impacts is Lauren. And I can't see why anyone would want to hurt her too. In fact, the only person who stands to gain from this is Tim so that he can find another designer to support them, but I don't imagine he'd go to that extreme. And I don't think he'd risk his relationship with Lauren just because he doesn't like me.

It's almost nine o'clock and although Lauren said I didn't need to send the strategy and presentation until Monday, I had wanted to send it over ahead of time to make up for the confusion over yesterday's meeting. I also need to get it rebuilt while it's still fresh in my mind. It's so frustrating as I thought today would be an easier day than yesterday.

I did a lot of pacing yesterday to get the creative juices flowing, but I'm incapable with my swollen ankle. That said, I still need to clear away the pans by the door, so I put the laptop to one side and allow my mind to wander, searching for how I got started yesterday. I stack the lids inside the pans, but as I lift them I spot the sharp corner of something white peeking beneath the door. I place the pans just inside the kitchen and then pull out the sheet of white card that someone must have pushed under the door late last night. I turn the sheet over and my legs give way when I realise what I'm looking at.

# 37

## FRIDAY, 8.58 A.M.

The glossy image is one I haven't seen in more than a decade. Mum and Dad had a version of it hanging on the wall by the staircase of our old family home. Sixty or so girls in green blazers, white blouse and green knee-length skirts, standing in three rows facing the camera. I can still remember how cold it was that October morning when the picture was taken. Our head of year kept calling for us all to face forwards and smile. I couldn't stop shivering, my teeth chattering, but it wasn't just the cold affecting me that morning. It felt as though all eyes were on me instead of the cameraman.

*Why would someone have my old Year 11 school photo?*

The question in my mind is rhetorical. There's only one reason someone would have pushed this image beneath my door. It's a message: whoever is behind this campaign of terror knows what I did all those years ago. But it's only when I scrutinise the image more that I realise just how right I am. Whilst I initially recognised the photograph as one I've seen hundreds of times before, this version has been doctored. There aren't sixty or so girls' faces staring back at me, rather two faces. Mine and one that's been duplicated over every other girl's body. Dozens of Simones are all staring at me now, all demanding to know why.

I flick the photograph away as the true horror of what's been going on slowly seeps through my trembling body. The man in black wants me to know that he knows what I did, and all the sneaking about and interfering has been designed with one motive in mind: he wants revenge.

There is no writing on the piece of card, but then they do say a picture paints a thousand words. But it still doesn't help me identify who is doing this to me. A frustrated sibling of Simone's, maybe? But I don't remember her telling me anything about her family, and I don't know how they would have found me after all this time. It's been sixteen years since I last set foot on those school grounds, so why has he waited this long to come for me?

I practically leap out of my skin when the intercom buzzes. My head snaps round to the door and for the briefest second I see the man in black beside it, but when I blink I realise it's just my heightened state of terror playing tricks on me. The buzzer sounds again, and I gasp, before forcing myself to crawl towards the door, and drag myself up to the handset.

'H-hello?' I stammer, half-expecting to hear Simone's voice on the other end, even though it's impossible.

'Eve, it's Detective Sergeant Kim Atwal. Can I come up?'

Why's Atwal here now, so soon after I found the photograph? We didn't have an appointment arranged. Has the man in black lured her here so she will see the photograph and arrest me for what I did?

'Eve? Can you hear me? I said it's Detective Atwal.'

'W-what do you want?'

'You phoned and left me a voicemail last night. Something about an intruder in your flat. Are you okay? Is the intruder still there?'

'No. H-he's gone.'

'Are you okay, Eve? You sound scared. Cough if he's still there and you need me to call for back-up.'

I remain silent.

'Are you going to let me up? There's something else I need to discuss with you.'

I need to gather my racing thoughts, and I'm in no coherent state to speak to Atwal, but I press the door release button and leave my door ajar while I hobble back to the sofa and stuff the taser into the side pocket of my combats. It feels as though all the blood has drained from my face, and although I can see a locomotive steaming towards me, there's nothing I can do to get out of the way.

Atwal gently taps on the door, before pushing it open and entering.

'Eve? Can I come in?'

She doesn't wait for me to respond before I hear her Dr Marten boots stomping across the carpet.

'Oh, there you are. Is everything okay? You look like a ghost.'

'I just had some shocking news,' I say, hugging a cushion tight to my chest.

She sits down in the armchair across from me, her gaze burning a hole.

'Do you want to tell me about last night? The intruder?'

It feels like an age since the man in black was trying to throttle me, but if she's able to help find him before he returns, I can't pass up the opportunity.

'He...' I begin, but catch myself.

*How do I explain all of this? At first I assumed the man in black was the same man who assaulted me five years ago, but I'm now certain the man who was here last night is somehow linked to Simone.*

'Take your time, Eve. I can see you're still in shock. You're pale as a sheet. Why don't you start with when this happened?'

I take a deep breath in, remembering I have the spy cameras in place and that when I checked them this morning, there was no evidence that he'd returned. And I don't think he'd be stupid enough to come for me while there is a police presence here.

'I returned to my flat yesterday evening, around five o'clock, I think. My door was open and when I stepped inside there was... a man here. He was wearing dark clothes and a black balaclava.'

I pause as Atwal removes a notepad and begins to scribble.

'He pulled me inside and proceeded to hit me and knocked me to the floor. He tried to strangle me, but then Ethan appeared and knocked him off. The intruder ran down the stairs and outside. We gave chase, but he was too quick and escaped.'

Atwal's eyes widen.

'I'm sorry to hear that, Eve. Is that what happened to your ankle?'

I look down at my foot atop the tower of cushions.

'No, I injured that when I was chasing after him.'

'I see. And who's Ethan, sorry?'

*What kind of detective doesn't remember the name of the victim's brother?*

'Um, he's...'

I picture the kiss and then him gently letting me down.

'He's James DeVere's brother. He was here to collect some personal belongings from Flat 4.'

'Ah, of course, I briefly spoke to him on the phone. It sounds like you were lucky he arrived when he did. Do you have any idea who this man in the balaclava was?'

I reluctantly shake my head.

'Did he steal anything?' Her eyes wander around the living room. 'Is there anything missing?'

'My business pitch. He deleted it from my laptop.'

She frowns at this statement.

'Tell me more.'

It would be easy to keep all the context to myself, but right now I need all the help I can get. If I come clean about what happened all those years ago, and reveal what he's been doing this past week, then maybe there's a way that Atwal can find him before he returns. If this was a television crime drama, they'd find that tiny, apparently insignificant clue that will ultimately lead to my antagonist being unmasked.

So, I proceed to tell her about George being locked out, about the unplanned grocery delivery, the email to Lauren and Tim, and then about the deleted file from my laptop. I even show her the folder and evidence that there was a file at one point, but how it's now gone. Atwal listens without interrupting, jotting notes throughout my explanation.

'I think the man in black did all of those things, and that he'll return to finish me off sooner rather than later.'

She ruminates before responding.

'Who do you think this man is, Eve?'

'I don't know,' I say, sighing. 'I think he is trying to get some kind of twisted revenge for something that happened to a girl I went to secondary school with.'

She stares at me, like I've suddenly started speaking in tongues.

'He left an old school photograph under my door this morning,' I continue, pointing down at the upturned piece of white card discarded on the floor.

Atwal removes a latex glove from the pocket of her overcoat and uses it to lift the picture.

'Do you see how the image has been doctored so that Simone's face is on every girl except for me?'

Her brow furrows as her eyes dart from one face to the next, before looking back at me.

'Tell me why you think this person is seeking some kind of revenge?'

I choose my words carefully, conscious of saying too much.

'The girl in the picture – Simone – died when she fell from her bedroom on the third floor of a dormitory. I think the man in black thinks I was involved somehow.'

'Why do you say that?'

I try to keep the memories from flooding back to the front of my mind, but it's difficult to restrain them.

'Because we shared a bedroom. I wasn't there when it happened, but rumours started that I pushed her out of the window. There was a thorough investigation – the police interviewed everyone – and it was concluded that she died by suicide.'

'And so now you think the man in black is what? A disgruntled family member out to get you?'

I don't like the sardonic tone she's using.

'Yes, I do,' I snap.

Atwal closes her notepad and returns it to the inside pocket of her overcoat.

'Can I be blunt, Eve?'

I nod, but the way she's sitting, arms crossed and a dour expression on her face, makes me uncomfortable.

'Everything you've described sounds scary, I grant you, but also not something that can be corroborated.'

'What? You don't believe me?'

'It's not a question of belief, Eve, but credibility. These stories of someone breaking in and causing small inconveniences to your life sound exactly like the sort of thing someone would say if they were trying to shift the spotlight from them for some greater crime. I looked at your door jamb when I entered, and there's no evidence of tampering, so unless your intruder had a key, how else could they have entered the flat?'

It takes all my effort not to instantly stare at the airing cupboard door and the trapdoor beyond. I can't tell her about that without making myself look guiltier. She already thinks I'm involved in Fi's disappearance, and I can't make matters worse.

'But Ethan will corroborate that I was attacked yesterday, and you've seen the file has disappeared on my laptop.'

'A smart person could ask a friend to lie for them, and for all I know you deleted that file yourself.'

'I'm not making this up.'

She tilts her head empathetically.

'Tell me, Eve, when was the last time you left this building?'

'What does that have to do with anything?'

'I understand from some of your tenants that you suffer with agoraphobia. Is that right?'

I instantly picture India and Jenny gossiping about me.

'That has nothing to do with this.'

'And your brother told me you're currently under the care of a psychiatrist.'

*Pete's been talking about me too?*

'I was hoping when I came up here you might want to tell me the truth about what really happened with James DeVere and Fiona Erskine? It will be easier for you in the long run if you just admit what you've done.'

'I had nothing to do with either of them.'

'I received another phone call last night, Eve. An anonymous tip was called in to the station, stating that not only had you killed Fiona Erskine, but that I'd find evidence in your flat to support such an accusation.' She reaches into her overcoat once more and pulls out a folded sheet of paper and passes it over to me. 'This is a warrant that authorises me and my team to search your premises for forensic evidence to either prove or disprove that you are lying about your involvement with James DeVere's murder and Fiona Erskine's disappearance.'

I unfold the piece of paper, but the typed words blur and seem to dance on the page.

*This can't be happening!*

Before I know it, my flat is filled with faceless people in white coveralls, inspecting everything I own, whilst Atwal sits with me on the sofa. They're turning my whole life upside down, because someone – India? Jenny? The man in black? – has lied to the police. And in that moment I see myself opening the wardrobe door in my bedroom and discovering Fi's emerald dress suit.

*Did the man in black leave the dress suit there, so the police would find it when they came here to search my flat?*

Thankfully I put it in that sports bag and shoved it down the hatch, but if they discover the trapdoor and head down there, I'll have no way of explaining what it's doing there. My heart is racing so fast that Atwal must be able to hear it. I just have to pray they don't find the trapdoor.

## 38

### FRIDAY, 9.45 A.M.

Watching other people tear through your life is a disheartening experience. This flat has been my sanctuary for so many years, and it feels like a violation to have all these faceless men and women in coveralls lifting every ornament, checking inside sofa cushions, and dismissing each item I consider precious. For the briefest moment I picture John Cooper on the sofa beside me and wonder whether he felt the same way when he became the prime suspect in the murder of Patricia Robinson.

*I am not John Cooper. I did not kill Fi, and had nothing to do with James's murder.*

I can feel the bulge of the taser in my pocket and am glad they haven't asked to search my person. Detective Atwal hasn't taken her eyes off me the whole time we've been sitting here, and I can't tell if that's to look for any minute changes in my temperament as I see the team move from one section of the flat to the next, or whether it's just to make sure I don't try to make a run for it. Given the state of my ankle and my agoraphobia, running is the one thing I can't do.

One of the women in white comes across and bends as she

whispers something into Atwal's ear. The detective whispers something back, and then turns to face me.

'Why don't we get out of here?' she says, but it feels like less of a question and more of a statement.

I wave my hand towards my swollen ankle.

'It's fine, I'll help you hobble downstairs.'

*Downstairs? Why does she want me to go downstairs?*

They haven't discovered the trapdoor yet, but I can't escape the sense that she wants to force me into a police car and drive me away from my home. She knows why I can't leave.

She stands and stares down at me until I eventually try to stand.

'Where are we going?'

'Somewhere we can talk privately.'

I don't know if I can refuse to leave, as I'm not sure what my rights are as a murder suspect. She hasn't arrested me yet, but I don't know if that makes a difference. If I refuse to leave the building, will she accuse me of resisting arrest? I don't want to make a big scene in front of all these strangers.

She lifts my arm around her shoulder and the sea of coveralls seems to part as she leads me through. I deliberately hobble slowly, trying to delay the inevitable for as long as possible. I should demand to speak to my brother. Pete will know what to do, or he'll be able to find me a great solicitor to sort out this mess. But my phone is on the table, and as I stare forlornly back at it, Atwal drives me forwards.

'Where are you taking me?' I ask, when we reach the top of the staircase, Atwal closing my door behind me.

'Let's go downstairs, away from all this noise and activity.'

'Am I under arrest? If so, you need to know I can't leave this building. There are so many toxins out there and if you force me outside you're breaching my human rights.'

I grip the handrail and use it to prevent myself moving any further forward, and shake my head for good measure.

'You're not under arrest, Eve, and I have no intention of taking you outside... not yet, anyway. There's something urgent I need to talk about and it would be easier if we do it somewhere quiet.'

'I didn't kill Fi. I swear to you.'

'We'll talk about all of that in a bit.'

'So, where are we going?'

'Let's go down to Flat 4, there's something I want to show you inside James DeVere's flat.'

I can't tell if this is just a ruse to get me down the two flights of stairs where she has more officers waiting to lift and carry me to a waiting police car, but I have little choice but to trust her at this time. I soften my grip on the handrail and we slowly make our way down the stairs. I see her reach into her overcoat to remove my set of skeleton keys when we make it to James's door, and she then proceeds to unlock it.

I'm instantly transported back to the moment when Danielle and I opened the door on Tuesday morning and discovered James inside. It feels like a lifetime ago, when it's only been a couple of days.

Atwal pushes the door open and we hobble awkwardly inside. There is black dust covering the frame of the living-room door, and more dust on the windowsills inside. The sofa is covered by a transparent plastic sheet, but I don't know if the police left it there or Ethan when he was collecting mementos the other day. Atwal helps me onto the sofa and searches for anything she can use to help me elevate my ankle, but there are no cushions. She eventually drags over a straight-backed chair and I lift my foot onto the seat.

'There's no sign of a kettle any more, but can I fetch you a glass of water instead?'

It feels wrong being in here. It's as much a violation as the team in my flat upstairs. I'm sure if James was alive, he wouldn't be happy knowing we were in his home, poking about and using his things.

'I'm fine,' I say, despite the dryness of my throat.

Atwal fills a glass regardless and places it on a coaster on the table to my right.

'Now that we're on our own,' she says, dragging a second chair over and sitting in front of me, 'I'd like you to confirm your movements on Monday night again.'

'But why? I didn't speak to James after the incident with Danielle's bike in the hallway. When I went to speak to him, I saw the woman with dark hair heading into this flat with him and then I overheard them having sex. Have you even found the woman he was with? You seem so focused on me that you're ignoring the real culprit.'

She stares at me for a long time, before clearing her throat.

'We know the woman you saw had nothing to do with James's death.'

'Wait, how do you know? Have you found her? Who is she?'

'It doesn't matter. What's important is that James was very much alive when she left here and couldn't have been further from wanting to die by suicide.'

'So you have spoken to her? How do you know she isn't lying? And why are you so certain that James didn't take his own life? Just because there were markings on his wrists?'

'The marks on his wrists are consistent with him having been restrained, but that isn't the only evidence that something else occurred after his guest left. The medical examiner found bruising to James's chest and face, suggesting he'd been in a fight shortly before he died.'

'But the woman could have done that.'

Atwal shakes her head.

'She's confirmed that the bruising wasn't there when she left.'

'But why are you so convinced she's telling the truth?'

Atwal slaps her hands down on her knees.

'Because *I* am the woman who was with James on Monday night!'

## 39

FRIDAY, 9.57 A.M.

I blink several times, uncertain whether I really just heard her say that.

'You were—'

'Yes, I'm the woman you saw arriving late on Monday night.' She stands and turns her back on me, letting out a heavy sigh. 'I didn't realise anybody had seen us until one of the uniformed officers mentioned your statement. I decided to come up and speak to you, convinced you'd realise who I was, and then I'd have to admit my involvement to my commanding officer and withdraw from the case. But you never twigged. I kept asking you to describe the woman, and at no point did you connect me and her.' She turns back to face me. 'James and I had consensual sex on Monday night. He asked me to restrain him, and I used my police-issued handcuffs. When I left here around 1 a.m., he was very alive and telling me what a great time he'd had and that we should meet up again. I wasn't against the idea, and told him to message me on the app we both used. Does that sound like someone who was planning to end their life?'

I think back to our first meeting upstairs, and realise now she did keep probing me about what I'd seen, but I assumed it was because she didn't believe my story. This changes everything.

'That's why I'm so convinced that something else must have happened after I left. But I can't tell the team any of this, or I'll be immediately suspended, pending disciplinary action. But, in my eyes, there is nobody better placed to figure out what really happened than me.'

For all I know this could all be some fabrication to try and trick me into admitting something I didn't do, or so she wins me over and I don't question whether she is lying about her interaction with James. Yet my instinct tells me she's telling the truth. From the moment I saw him hanging here on Tuesday, something has felt off about all of this. I can't explain why but I am convinced James didn't voluntarily tie that noose around his neck.

'I need to know what happened between 1 a.m. and the ME's estimated time of death at four,' Atwal continues. 'After I left, James must have had a violent coming together with someone who then presumably strung him up to make it look like suicide.'

'I swear I was passed out in bed by one.'

She sits back down.

'I believe you, Eve. Given the injuries and James's bulk, I don't think you would have been capable of lifting him up to the makeshift noose. But you know more about everyone who lives here than I do, and I need you to think hard about whether any of them could have been responsible.'

It's a relief to hear she believes me, but I've no idea who else would want to hurt James. Danielle was the only person who had any known beef with him, but I don't think she'd have the strength to lift him either. That said, I haven't seen or spoken to Danielle since that morning. I've been assuming she was at work, because I know how sporadic her shifts can be at the hospital, but could there be some other reason I haven't heard from her? Could she also be missing, like Fi? I'm about to ask Atwal whether she or her team have caught up with Danielle since Tuesday, but she doesn't give me the chance.

'When I came to see you on Wednesday evening, you mentioned the former concierge who worked here when this building was the Freemantle Hotel. Why?'

I take a minute, desperately trying to calm the racing thoughts in my head.

'Um, I overheard mention of John Cooper's crimes on a news report. I had no idea this place was a hotel before my dad bought it. The report said it was the fiftieth anniversary of Cooper's crimes and I don't know... It was just my overactive imagination.'

'No, I think there's more to it than you realise. Maybe on some subconscious level you think one of your residents might be a killer, and it's that thinking we need to access, Eve. Think about everyone who lives here. Did any of them have an issue with James? Did you ever witness anyone arguing with him, or saying bad things behind his back?'

'No,' I say, sighing with frustration. 'A week ago, I'd have told you I have a great, close-knit community of tenants living here, and nobody had any issues with anyone else.'

'And now?'

'Now, I don't know. James is dead, Fi is missing, and I haven't heard from Danielle in a few days.'

'Danielle? You mean Danielle Jacobs, the woman who was arguing with James about her bike being in the hallway the night he died?'

I nod. 'Would you be able to check if any of your team have spoken with her? Or can you check she's not missed any shifts at the General Hospital?'

Atwal jots a note in her pad.

'The bike was still in the corridor when I left here at one,' Atwal admits. 'James mentioned its inconvenience when we had to squeeze past it when we arrived here.'

'I can't believe that Danielle could have...'

'And she's the only person who had any disagreements with James?'

'Yes, that I can remember.'

My eyes widen.

'Chad,' I exclaim.

'Who's Chad?'

'He lives in Flat 7 on the first floor. His partner Jenny told me he keeps sneaking out and she had the gall to accuse *me* of having an affair with him.'

She writes his name in her notepad.

'What else can you tell me about him?'

I shrug.

'He's athletic – training for a marathon allegedly...'

I hear Jenny's voice from the other night when I was in the passageway: *Explain where you were on Monday night... I woke up at four and you weren't in bed. I checked the flat and you were nowhere to be seen.*

'I overheard him and Jenny arguing the other night, and she said he wasn't at home at four on Tuesday morning when she woke up. She said she lied to the police that they were both home.'

'Is this the same Jenny Carlisle who reported seeing you leaving Fiona Erskine's flat on Wednesday?'

I nod.

'And you now dropping her and her boyfriend in it with me isn't some kind of revenge?'

I'm shocked by the question.

'No! I'm telling you the truth, Detective Atwal.'

Satisfied, she writes his name in her pad and then looks back up at me.

'Have any of your residents mentioned Cooper's crimes to you, even if only in passing?'

I'd never heard of John Cooper prior to hearing the news report through India's wall late on Tuesday night, so I'm confident nobody has mentioned it in passing. It was me who raised the name with Bill, so does that put him in the clear? Bill is the sweetest man I've ever met and he's always looked after me, so I can't see how he could be involved in any of this.

A thought pops into my head, but I dismiss it almost as quickly. Bill was part of the investigating team when Cooper was arrested and tried for the five murders. He was a younger man back then, living in the city and had access to all the evidential materials being collected against Cooper. He said himself it felt *convenient* that the other four murders were tied back to Cooper following his arrest for Patricia Robinson's murder, but is that because he knew Cooper wasn't guilty? Could Bill have been responsible for one or more of those murders, and is at play again?

I think about how frail Bill is, in his late seventies, and always so calm. No, I can't see that he would want to kill James.

A shiver runs the length of my spine as I hear another man's voice in my mind: *I remember my friends and I would tell each other ghost stories about the building. How it was haunted by demons... Maybe those demons still reside here.*

'What is it? What's wrong?' Atwal asks, staring at me with concerned eyes.

'I... um, no, it's ridiculous.'

'What is? Tell me, Eve. No matter how unlikely you may think it is. You have someone in mind, don't you? Tell me who.'

I sigh, already conscious of how stupid this is going to sound.

'Someone I know – a client – mentioned the Freemantle Hotel and Cooper's crimes to me yesterday morning.'

'Who is this client?'

'He is the Financial Director of a small bakery company who've invited me to pitch a marketing campaign for them. His name is Tim... sorry, I've forgotten his surname, but I can look it up.'

'What was the context of him asking you about Cooper?'

'I think it was just a throwaway comment, you know? He and his sister – she's the Operations Director of the company – were leaving my flat yesterday morning, and he happened to mention living locally at the time of Cooper's crimes, and how he and his friends used to make up stories about the building being haunted.'

'And how long have you known this Tim?'

'I wouldn't say I *know* him, as such, but I've been working with him and his sister for about a week. Um, they contacted me on the back of a recommendation from a friend of theirs, I think.'

'Describe this Tim to me.'

I puff out my cheeks and hold his face in my mind's eye.

'He's about six feet tall, well-built and a little overweight.'

'Hair colour?'

'Brown, but he's very bald. He only has hair directly above his ears.'

'Do you know his date of birth or where he lives?'

'He looks like he's in his early forties, but could be a fraction younger, I suppose. His sister said he's walking distance from this address, but I don't know which road.'

'Is there anything else you can tell me about him?'

I hear Lauren's voice in my head next: *His wife just learned he's been cheating on her. She's taken my niece and has flown to Madrid... She's threatening divorce.*

I shake my head, but I now can't stop picturing him inside my flat whilst I was sleeping. Was it him who arranged the appointment with them from my laptop to make me look stupid? Could it be him who was in the mask last night deleting the marketing pitch?

'What are you holding back, Eve?'

Tim being the man behind all of this doesn't make any sense in my head. He has nothing to do with Simone, and I can't see how he could know I was at school with her, and how he would know how on edge I'd be to see that doctored school photograph.

'Eve?'

'I'm still certain some of this – maybe *all* of this – relates to what I told you about my roommate at boarding school.'

'The girl who fell from the window?'

'Exactly. I wasn't making any of that up. There *was* an intruder in my flat yesterday when I returned home. I'm sure he's the one who's behind all the weird shit that has been going on this week, and that he's targeted me because he thinks I hurt Simone.'

Atwal looks at me for a long time, but I sense the concerned frown is not because I'm in danger. I'm about to continue with my argument, when she raises her finger and answers her phone. She stands and disappears back into the hallway, and whilst I can still hear the gentle rumble of her voice, I can't make out a word of what is being said. She returns a couple of minutes later.

'We can go back upstairs now. The team have finished searching your flat.'

I stare, trying to read her. If they'd found the bag with Fi's emerald dress suit, wouldn't she just arrest me here? I can't see why she'd make me hobble all the way back upstairs, only to force me back down and into a van for transporting to the police station.

*The Tenants*

'I'm not going anywhere until you tell me what you were looking for in my flat.'

It's dangerous to challenge her authority, especially after I feel like I've finally earned her trust.

She watches me for what feels like an age, before finally speaking.

'The tipoff we received said we would find blood-stained clothing belonging to Fiona Erskine inside your flat. That's what we've been searching for.'

I picture myself shoving the emerald dress suit into the sports bag and throwing it down the hatch. I really should have made more of an effort to get rid of it.

'And?'

'We didn't find anything.'

It takes all my willpower not to sigh with relief.

'That's because I have nothing to do with Fi's disappearance. I suffer with agoraphobia, Detective Atwal, so where would I stash a body if I was a killer? It's not like I can find a quiet place to dump or bury a body.'

She narrows her eyes at this statement, and a new fear flows through me. If the man in black has been sneaking into my flat through the trapdoor, then he knows about the passageway. And if he really wanted to frame me for Fi's murder, there's no better place to hide her body.

'The tipoff you received,' I say quickly, 'who was it from?'

'I didn't take the call. They were phoning from a withheld number.'

'It was him. Don't you see? The man in black. He's trying to make me suffer. He's the one you need to find.'

Atwal doesn't respond at first, simply shaking her head.

'It wasn't your intruder who phoned the tip line, Eve. The

information about the blood-stained clothing was provided by a woman.'

And in that moment, it's like the colours of the kaleidoscope have finally aligned as I hear Jenny's voice loud and clear in my head: *I'm on to you, and I will expose you for the wretched and unstable woman you really are.*

## 40

FRIDAY, 10.45 A.M.

I can't stop replaying memories of my interactions with Jenny through my mind. The tenants' meetings she didn't attend without explanation; the way I *sensed* that she was looking at me differently to the other residents; and then more recently the times she's confronted me.

*I'm not someone to be fucked with, Eve. I'm on to you.*

Were the signs always there and I just chose to ignore them? I assumed her cold front towards me was from jealousy because she thought I was after Chad, even though I tried to reassure her that I have no interest in him.

*Are you worried the rest of the building will learn how you've been spying on us?*

That confrontation outside Fi's flat on Wednesday showed her true colours, and I've no doubt now that she was the one who phoned Atwal and reported seeing me leaving Fi's flat. What if she was the person I heard moving about inside, but snuck out whilst I was looking out of the window? There's no way she could know about the passageways, but maybe I'm wrong about that as well.

The one question I can't seem to answer, though, is *why*. I can't connect what Jenny has to do with Simone. In my background checks on Jenny I found no evidence of a sibling, and I met Simone's mother countless times and Jenny isn't her. I must have missed something in my preliminary checks, and maybe that needs to be my next step: I should get back upstairs and research Jenny all over again. Now that I know some kind of connection exists between Jenny and Simone, it might be easier to connect the dots.

Atwal told me to wait inside James's flat for twenty minutes whilst she checked her team have left my flat in a reasonable state, and that time has now passed. She promised to dig into the backgrounds of Tim and Chad, and I'm to wait to hear back from her. I hobble to the door, the throbbing in my ankle more painful than yesterday. I should be resting it, not hunting for answers.

I exit James's flat, and immediately hear voices just around the corner. I recognise Chad's voice instantly, and in that moment it suddenly dawns on me that he could be helping Jenny with her campaign against me. He has no alibi for the time when James died, and is bulky enough to be the masked man who attacked me in my flat last night. I edge closer to the voices, sliding along the wall, using the cool plasterboard to keep me upright.

'It's going to be okay,' Chad says. 'We're going to figure this out. Hey, you know I love you, and I'm not going to let anything bad happen to you.'

I wish I had my phone on me so I could record this exchange. I need to gather evidence to prove to Atwal that the conspiracy against me is real.

'Listen, I'd better head back up before she figures out what's going on. Are you going to be okay?'

'I wish you didn't have to go back to *her*. The thought of the two of you being intimate makes my skin crawl.'

My eyes widen as I realise that isn't Jenny's voice. I creep closer to the corner, and very slowly poke my eyes around it to double-check. Chad has his back to me, but the door to Caz's flat is open and he's speaking to whoever is just inside the door. I snap my head back before either sees me.

*I woke up at four and you weren't in bed. I checked the flat and you were nowhere to be seen.*

My brain can't process all this new information. Jenny has been so convinced that I'm having an affair with Chad, but it's Caz he's actually been seeing. I think back to India's secret tenants' meeting yesterday and how Caz was so adamant that she didn't want security cameras fitted in the communal walkways.

*A camera on the front door would then allow you to see into mine and Bill's flats.*

She doesn't want people to know Chad has been sneaking into her flat on a regular basis, least of all Jenny. And whilst I'm now recalling that secret meeting, both Jenny and Chad were in attendance, so neither of them could have been the figure in black waiting in my flat.

'You know I'm thinking of you when me and her... you know. I insist we have sex in the dark, so she can't see me picturing you instead.'

'But when are you going to tell her the truth? I hate all this sneaking around. It's not like the two of you are married. I know it's going to break her heart, but she'll get over it.'

'I promise I will speak to her when the time is right. She's so paranoid about everything at the moment that I'm worried it will tip her over the edge. She's been self-prescribing antidepressants for herself, and I'm worried she'll take a deliberate overdose. She keeps banging on about hearing noises in the wall, and...' He sighs. 'Let me handle Jenny. It won't be long until you and me can be together and get out of this dump.'

I hear them kiss, and I shuffle back along the corridor towards James's door, desperately praying Chad won't look around the corner as he passes. He doesn't look back as he takes the steps two at a time.

I count to sixty to give both him and Caz time to return to their respective homes, and then slowly make my way up the stairs and back to my own flat. I'm in absolute agony by the time I make it in through the front door, and George gives me a curious look. Poor boy is probably wondering why I haven't fed him yet this morning. I pick him up and give him a squeeze and a kiss, promising I will sort myself out and then proceed to open a pouch of food and squeeze it into his bowl whilst I dress and clean my teeth. I haven't eaten breakfast either, but I have no appetite right now.

I'm about to sit down and take the weight off my ankle when I hear Atwal's voice in my head: *The tipoff we received said we would find blood-stained clothing belonging to Fiona Erskine inside your flat. That's what we've been searching for.*

It's only a matter of time before whoever it is tips them off about the passageway, and if they find Fi's emerald suit down there, I'll have no defence to offer. I need to get rid of it before I do anything else. Securing George in my bedroom, I move the weights from the trapdoor lid, and slowly descend into the darkness. I wait until I reach the platform before switching on the torch, but no matter how much I wave it around, I can't see the sports bag anywhere. I try to think back to the moment I threw it down here. I was in a desperate hurry to get the clothing out of my flat, but I can't see how it could have rolled much from the foot of the ladder.

I lower myself to my hands and knees, keeping my swollen

ankle elevated behind me as my knees grate against the wooden boarding. I make it as far as the end of the board, where the passageway splits towards the separate ends of the corridor, and I still can't find the sports bag. That can only mean that my antagonist has found and moved it. But when, and where have they put it now? Atwal said her team didn't find the suit in my flat so he or she hasn't put it back up there. But it also confirms my worst fear that I'm not the only person who's been using these boards to commute between properties.

I pause, and take shallow breaths, conscious of all the insulation fibres hovering in the air. There must be another hatch or trapdoor into one of the other flats. That's the only way whoever it is can come and go unseen, and if I was a betting woman I'd say whichever flat has an opening belongs to the person who's been messing with me. I head right towards Jenny's flat, standing when I'm beside the cold breezeblocks. I listen in for any sound of conversation between her and Chad, but all I can hear is the sound of the shower. I run my hands over the breezeblocks, using the torch beam to search for anything that resembles a door of some kind, but there's nothing obvious, so I continue on to Mike's flat next door. Again, there's no sound of movement or voices inside, but given the day and time, Mike is probably at the school. He was at India's secret meeting, so he wasn't the figure in black who attacked me either; I think I'd have noticed his above-average height had he been anyway. There's also no obvious sign of a secret doorway into Mike's flat either.

I turn and crawl to the opposite end of the hallway, but I'm starting to feel hot and lightheaded. It could just be the poor-quality air down here, but the last time I felt this way was right before I threw up in India's bathroom.

I can hear music playing inside India's flat, and her singing along, but no secret doors or hatches here either. Unsurprisingly, there's no sound emanating from Fi's flat, and no place for a secret door either. Frustrated, I crawl back to the centre point of the floor and sit, trying to compose myself. If there are no hidden exits from the flats on the first floor, then the figure must be one of the ground-floor residents. With James dead, that leaves Caz, Danielle and Bill. I don't want to think that any of them could have been pulling the wool over my eyes all this time, but there's no other explanation.

I take several breaths, willing the nausea to stay at bay for long enough to let me complete my search and get back up to my flat. Crawling towards the ladder down, I turn and swing my legs over the edge, gripping the sides of the wooden frame as if my life depends on it, and slowly begin to descend. My head is spinning, and my vision is blurring in and out of focus, but then something catches my attention. A glimmer of light beneath the floor between the insulation and ceiling beams of the ground-floor flats. I stop my descent and stare at the glimmer. I shine my torch at it, but I can't quite see what it is or where it's coming from, so I lean closer, the ladder straining under my shift in weight. I stretch my torch arm out and flatten some of the insulation.

*Is that...? Yes, it's a crawl space.*

I've never noticed it before, but there is definitely another wooden platform there between the two flats. I hurl my torch along the wooden beam so that I'm able to use both hands to grab the sides of the platform and pull myself onto it. The space is so narrow that my bottom scrapes against the beams above as I pull myself through and I can feel the taser and my keys digging into my legs. For all I know, it could be a dead end, and coordinating my limbs back onto the ladder will be a challenge, but instinct tells me I've finally found a key piece of the puzzle. There isn't enough space for me to turn my head and explore the narrow tunnel I'm in, but switching off my torch allows me to focus on the shard of light ahead. I continue dragging myself towards it, and when I push at it, a hinged hatch rises above my head and I'm able to crawl through. It's only when I roll out from under the bed that I realise exactly where I am. It's the same flat I found myself in on Wednesday morning when I was convinced I heard someone moving about inside.

Standing, I sit on the edge of Fi's bed and look at the bedroom window. When I was in here the other day, I assumed whoever I'd heard had jumped out of the window, but what if that's what they wanted me to think, when secretly they went under the bed and into the passageway? It would certainly explain why I didn't see anyone outside.

So, whoever has been sneaking into my flat and messing with me has been accessing the passageway from Fi's flat, but that doesn't necessarily mean it's Fi herself. She's been missing since Friday, and maybe that's why the masked man killed her: to make use of this hidden exit. He could have been hidden beneath the hatch the entire time I was in here with Detective Atwal and when her team searched the property.

I shiver at a fresh thought. I know the figure isn't in the passageway now as that's where I've just come from, but that means they could still be in the flat. Scanning the corners of the bedroom, I search for anything I might use as a weapon to defend myself, but there's nothing useful. All I have is my torch, and that will have to do.

I stand, and hobble to the bedroom door, listening at it for any sound of movement the other side, but it is deathly silent. I slowly ease the handle down, and pull it towards me. The door creaks open, so I pull it quicker and practically leap out, but there is nobody in the living room. I check the kitchen area and bathroom too, but the flat is empty. In fact, I see now the flat really is empty. Although there is furniture, there is no food in the cupboards or fridge, and when I check back in the bedroom, I see there is no bedding and the wardrobe is empty. Is that because the police have taken those items for forensic examination, or is the real culprit trying to cover her tracks?

I've spent so long assuming that Fi is as much of a victim as James that I hadn't considered the prospect of her being culpable. And then I recall that message James left on her answerphone.

*I'm so sorry but I'm running late for our dinner. I've got something to sort at work and then I'll head straight to the restaurant. I should make it by eight o'clock at the latest. Any problems, just give me a call. Love you.*

Atwal's instinct was that Fi must be involved, but I dismissed it out of hand. I need to phone her and tell her what I've discovered, but my phone isn't in my pocket, and I now recall leaving it in my flat when Atwal led me downstairs. I head to the front door and am about to open it when I find a black bin liner leaning against the door. I open it and pull out the contents: a black hoodie, black trousers and a black balaclava. There's also a small black shoulder bag that I lift out and open. I desperately hope the purse doesn't belong to Fi, but I find her driving licence inside, but that's not all. There is a small photograph tucked inside, and when I open it I immediately recognise one of the girls in uniform. Simone's awkward face and glasses stare back up at me, but there's something very familiar about the face of the younger girl standing beside her. The photograph must be at least twenty years old, but I'd recognise Fi's pointy nose anywhere.

## 41

### FRIDAY, 11.09 A.M.

My hands shake as I continue to stare at the photograph, unable to make sense of it. The uniform they're wearing is the same dark green blazer and yellow blouse that used to itch at my neck; I remember what a relief it was every night when I'd be able to strip out of it and into pyjamas. I had no idea Fi also attended the school, let alone that she knew Simone. In the photograph they're both smiling at the camera, and Simone has an arm draped around Fi's shoulder; a proximity generally reserved for a close friend... or family member.

I shake my head, trying to flush the idea out. The Simone I knew didn't have any siblings. I close my eyes, trying to recall any splinters of conversation where details of family arose, but my mind is too filled with competing questions. She never mentioned a sister, and never had any photographs of family members hung in our room. I used to have a gold frame with Mum, Dad, and Pete in it on my bedside table, but Simone had nothing like that.

I run a finger over Simone's face, her laughter echoing in my head. I screw my eyes shut, not wanting to remember anything more; I've spent too long burying the past, but I'm struggling to restrain the floodgates.

I look back at the photograph, focusing on the second girl. Her hair is a brilliant blonde, but the Fi who lives in this flat is more of a mousy brown. Maybe I'm mistaken about the younger girl being Fi. I scrutinise the image, but the picture quality isn't great. The nose looks like Fi's, but is my mind just leaping to conclusions?

*If it isn't Fi, then why did you find the photograph in Fi's purse?*

I have no answer to the question repeating itself in my head. I did a thorough background check on Fi when she applied to move in. I found nothing that made me think twice about accepting her application. I'd have to double-check my notes, but I don't recall any mention of siblings. I certainly would have noticed Simone's name had it come up.

I look down at the bag with the black hoodie and balaclava, and then back at the photograph, and I have only two possible explanations for why these items would be in Fi's flat: either someone is trying to make it look like she's the one who's been antagonising me, or... she's the figure in black who attacked me yesterday and has been sneaking into my flat.

As much as I *want* to believe it's the former, deep down I know I'm lying to myself. Either way, I need to share all this new information with Detective Atwal. She's off investigating Tim and Chad, when she should be focusing on Fiona Erskine. I need to get back upstairs to my phone to call her. I glance back at the hatch beneath Fi's bed, but I don't think I can stomach squeezing back along that narrow crawl space.

I open Fi's door, no longer caring if Jenny or anyone else sees me leaving. The hallway is empty, and I pull the door closed, and wince the moment my left foot hits the first stair. I was so convinced that it was a man behind the balaclava that I chased down these very stairs yesterday, but now that I replay the incident in my mind, it really is impossible to know for certain. The black hoodie was thick and oversized, so I didn't notice a bust, but that doesn't mean there wasn't one there. The figure overpowered me so easily, but then I was terrified, having flashbacks to the night I was dragged into those bushes five years ago. Maybe my mind just assumed the figure was male. I'm sure Atwal can have the clothing examined for Fi's DNA to prove it one way or another.

My heart is hammering in my chest when I make it to my door, and the strain of limping up the stairs has left me breathless. I practically fall into my flat, closing and locking the door behind me, and hurry into the living room, but my phone isn't on the table where I'm expecting to see it. I'm certain that's where I left it, but I suppose it's possible one of the search team might have moved it. I turn and look towards the kitchen, in case I actually left it on charge, and freeze when I see Fi staring back at me.

She's in a light grey hoodie and tracksuit bottoms, and there is a light blue surgical cap over her tied hair. In her gloved hand she is clutching a bundle of emerald green.

'W-what are you doing inside my flat?' I stammer, my breaths short and shallow.

She slowly steps out from behind the counter and throws the dress suit towards me. I instinctively catch it, realising her possession of it only confirms she must have taken it from the sports bag in the passageway. I need to find my phone because my fight or flight instinct is failing me once again.

'I see you found my picture,' she says, nodding towards the photograph between my fingers, her tone cold and detached. 'That should help clear up some of the obvious questions I'm sure are peppering your mind right now.'

The woman before me is so different to the Fi I have known

for more than a year. We've shared laughter, wine, and criticised the world around us. We had a kinship.

'I-I've called the police,' I lie, hoping she'll bolt for the door.

'Good. I hope they make it here in time to hear your confession, Eve.'

She's so close I can smell her perfume, but I'm unable to move. If she's armed, there's nothing I can do to stop her from killing me. The fear is eating me from the inside out.

'Why don't you sit down before you fall down,' she says, and gives me a gentle shove, and I tumble to the sofa like a house of cards caught by a gust of wind.

Fi perches on the edge of the armchair across from me, and removes my phone from the pocket of her jogging bottoms. I watch, helpless, as she extracts the SIM card and breaks it in half, dropping it and the phone to the laminate floor and then stamping on the screen.

'In case you thought you might be able to phone for help,' she says, with a sickening smile.

'W-what do you want?'

'I told you: I'm here to hear your confession, Eve. Think of me as you might a priest. Surely you'd like to clear your conscience before you die?'

I will my feet to move but I remain glued to the seat.

'I watched the recording of you telling that detective about my sister falling from the window of your dormitory, but that wasn't the full story, was it, Eve?'

I instinctively look up at the camera in the fake smoke alarm in the hallway. Fi follows my gaze and smiles.

'I've disabled the four cameras you left here, so nobody is going to find out what we talk about. I just want to know what happened with Simone; what *really* happened.'

My laptop isn't on my desk, so I can only assume Fi has

hidden or taken it somewhere. If she's watched my conversation with Atwal then she's more than likely the same person who ordered the groceries and emailed Lauren and Tim.

I take a deep breath, trying to compose my thoughts and figure a way out of this. I could try to make a run for it, but I'm certain Fi would intercept me long before I made it to the front door. Even if I did manage to get out, she'd easily catch me on the stairs with my ankle throbbing more than ever.

'I don't know what you expect me to say. Simone was very unhappy when we were at school together. She was picked on by a lot of the other girls, and I guess it just became too much for her, and that's why—'

'Bullshit!' she shouts, cutting me off instantly. 'I know the story you spun to the teachers and the police, but you left out a huge chunk of the story.'

'I'm not lying, Fi. That *is* what happened.'

'Oh, you expect me to believe that my sister – who wrote the most beautiful letters to our mum and dad every week without fail – chose to take her own life without leaving any kind of note or explanation?'

That was something the police were hung up on as well in the countless interviews they undertook with me.

'Maybe it was a last-minute decision and she didn't have time to—'

Eve suddenly lunges forward and slaps me hard across the cheek.

'I didn't come to listen to your lies,' she says, retaking her seat. 'I was in Year 7 at the school, and I witnessed you taunting her just as much as the other girls.'

I don't know if it's the result of the slap or my personal shame but the blood rushes to my face. I've spent so long manufacturing a truth that my conscience can just about believe that I'm not ready to confront that part of my history.

'We were both picked on by the other girls in our year,' I say, and I'm no longer in control of the words tumbling from my lips. 'We were both intelligent and consistently completed our work on time and to a high standard. The other girls didn't like that we made them look bad. You must know how jealous and bitter girls can be at that age. Simone and I were both victims.'

'You were just as much of a bully.'

I swallow hard.

'You're right, I was at the end, but that wasn't how it started. We were both victims in the beginning. It's why we became friends. Solidarity. We used to lie awake at night, plotting how we could get revenge on them.'

I picture Simone's face now, lying next to me in bed, and how we'd giggle as we concocted new devious schemes.

'But it was just our way of coping with the pressure we both felt. I don't think either of us believed we'd ever act on those impulses.'

I don't want to tell Fi just how close we became and my awful reaction when Simone tried to kiss me. I think she mistook our friendship for something more and as a terrified, immature fifteen-year-old, I not only rejected her advance, but I tried to put as much distance between us as physically possible. I wanted her to know that I wasn't interested in that kind of relationship, but I didn't have the words to explain that dispassionately.

'So, if you were so close, why did you turn your back on her?' she asks, and I catch a glint of light reflecting off the blade in her hand. I need to choose my words carefully, or she might feel compelled to use it on me.

'We drifted apart and I couldn't stand being a victim any longer. I figured if you can't beat them, it's easier to join them. I was a coward and by channelling my own insecurities into attacking Simone, I was able to stay hidden in plain sight.'

I pause, trying to read her face to see if she's buying it.

'I truly wish I could go back and change things, but I can't. I've had to try and put it behind me and move on. I think that's ultimately why I work so hard to keep the community here happy.'

She tilts her head and lunges forwards again. I flinch, anticipating a second slap, but this time she catches my neck with a flick of her wrist, and I feel the heat of blood escaping the wound. My hand immediately shoots up to my neck. Fi reaches into her pocket and hands me a folded handkerchief, which I immediately press to my neck.

'Lie to me again, and I'll go deeper and longer,' she says, perching once more. 'I know you were in the room the night she died, despite the lies you told the police. I want you to tell me exactly what happened, and why you pushed her out of that window.'

When I look down at the handkerchief, there is a large circle of blood, but I don't think the nick is life-threatening. I press the fabric back against my neck.

'Okay, you're right: I *was* in the room when she fell, but I swear to God, and on my own life, that I didn't push Simone.'

She springs forward but I shuffle back.

'I'm telling the truth. Please, just listen to me and I'll explain.'

She hovers over me, but the knife stays by her side.

'We were in the room and I was changing. Some of the girls used to sneak out of their rooms at night and would congregate in the music room, but it was by invitation only. And this night was the first where I'd been invited. Simone wasn't happy and kept threatening to report us to the head of year. I remember telling her to stop being a baby and how we would make her life a living hell if she told on us.' I swallow my desire to lie. 'She begged me not to go, and even used her body to block the door. I had to drag her away, and we ended up fighting, and she was stronger than I'd realised. I thought she was just jealous that I'd finally been accepted by the other girls, and I was angry that she was trying to spoil things. As we wrestled for control, we crashed into the wardrobe, and the desk... and then finally into the window.'

I close my eyes as I hear the sound of the cracking glass play in my head.

'The building was old, the windows single-glazed, and the glass shattered on impact. We broke apart instantly, both realising just how much trouble we would get into for breaking the window. I couldn't deal with the stress, and so I grabbed my bag and headed for the now free door, but Simone called after me. I was about to leave when I turned back and saw her perched on the windowsill. She said that she'd jump if I left because she couldn't go on without me as a friend. I knew she was bluffing, but then she seemed to slip, and one second she was there, and the next she vanished. By the time I got to the windowsill she was already flat out on the cobbled pavement below, a pool of blood enveloping her like a shadow in the moonlight.'

It's the same image I see every night when I close my eyes, as if she's still calling to me from the grave.

'Why didn't you call for help?'

The truth is I froze in panic, unable to believe it wasn't just a horrible nightmare I'd wake from.

'Someone must have heard her scream as she fell, because it was only seconds before three or four people were gathered around her and one of them called for an ambulance.'

I remember ducking back away from the window just before our head of year stared up at our room. I backed away and raced to the music room, hoping none of the other girls would realise I was late. We were caught minutes later, and to my relief the others corroborated that I was with them when Simone fell.

'Why didn't you tell this to the police at the time?'

'Because I was terrified. I thought because we'd argued and fought that night, I'd be accused of murdering her and would have to spend the rest of my life in prison. It took less than forty-eight hours before I was once again the target of the bullies. They started rumours about me and Simone being lovers and how we made a suicide pact that I chickened out of. Between their lies and the police interrogations, I couldn't cope and begged my parents to move me to a different school.' I pause. 'I am so sorry that Simone died. She was a good person who deserved a better friend than me.'

I'm half-expecting her to strike me with the blade again, but she steps backwards instead.

'What do you think?' she calls out over her shoulder. 'Do we believe her?'

I'm not sure who she's talking to at first, but then I see a figure step out from the hallway leading to my bedroom. When I see his face, my heart skips a beat that he's come to save me again, but when he sidles up to Fi, instead of grappling for the blade, my heart sinks.

'I don't know, sis,' Ethan says. 'I reckon she's still holding back.'

## 42

### FRIDAY, 11.21 A.M.

I don't want to believe my eyes. Ethan is supposed to be back in Birmingham right now. That's what he told me last night. I wince as I remember my desperate attempt to seduce him in this very room. I thought he was just being kind when he said he didn't want to take advantage of me in a shocked state. A wave of nausea sweeps over me at the thought of how I'd be feeling at this point if he had stayed over.

Now that the two of them are standing side by side, I can see a familial resemblance between them. Something about how sunken their eyes are. I don't know how I didn't pick up on it earlier. And then it hits me slap between the eyes: if Ethan is Fi's older brother then she's also James's younger sister.

*Hey, Fi, I'm so sorry but I'm running late for our dinner. I've got something to sort at work and then I'll head straight to the restaurant. I should make it by eight o'clock at the latest. Any problems, just give me a call. Love you.*

When I first heard that message on Fi's answerphone I wrongly assumed it meant the two of them were in a relationship. And even though that didn't fit with the narrative that he'd slept with Atwal the night he died, I never questioned it. At no point did I think they could be related. Neither ever mentioned it, and now that I'm trying to recall any memories where the two of them were in the same room, I'm certain there were no signs of a sibling relationship I missed. They kept it hidden and there can only be one reason they would.

I'm angry that my due diligence checks never revealed their history. But given I also knew nothing about Ethan before I saw him outside James's flat, and that Simone didn't come up in either of my background searches, it's clear I'm not very good at digging into people's backgrounds; that or they carefully concocted new histories for me to find. The background checks are something I've relied on since taking on ownership of the building, but I didn't even know Bill was in the police. And the less said about Jenny's and India's spiteful attitudes the better. I felt safe living here because I thought I knew everything that was going on from behind the walls, but my observations barely scraped the surface. And it's ironic that I've kept myself locked away in here for five years because of the dangers of the outside world, when it was always more dangerous inside.

'Oh, look, bro, you can almost see the cogs turning inside her head,' Fi sniggers. 'I wish we could capture that look on her face. I hope Simone is watching down now and can see it.'

I bite down on my jaw, angry that they've been pulling the wool over my eyes for so long, but no matter how much I tell my body to get up and get out, I remain rooted to the seat.

'I'm sure she is,' he says, sneering at me, 'and I bet she's screaming out that Eve is still lying about what really happened that night.'

I watch as he extracts the knife from Fi's hand and drops

down on the sofa next to me, the blade only inches from my frame.

'She reckoned she phoned the police,' Fi says, perching on the armchair, 'so we need to get on with this, just in case.'

Ethan shakes his head.

'No, I don't think she's phoned the police. We have her phone and there are no landlines anywhere in the building. We've got time, and I'll wait as long as it takes to hear what I came for.'

I think back to the last time he was sitting where he is now, applying ice to my ankle, so kind and understanding. Despite the ire he's showing now, deep down I'm certain there is more empathy he's trying to block in order to intimidate me.

I turn slightly so I can look him in the eye.

'There's nothing else I can tell you. I swear I didn't push Simone from that window. It happened like I—'

'Liar!'

His yell has me retreating back into the cushion, and there's a venom in his eyes that tells me I've underestimated what he's capable of.

'Your only chance of making it out of this room is if you tell us the truth. I won't let you take your secret to the grave.'

Without warning he grabs my wrist and pulls it towards him, sliding up my sleeve and then drawing the blade across my forearm. The skin breaks and an alarm bell sounds in my head as I watch the blood explode out of my arm. I try to snatch it back, but his grip is strong.

'The average human can lose only about 40 per cent of their blood before they pass out and it becomes critical unless they're treated by a medical professional.' He draws the blade across my skin again, the wound forming a bloody cross. 'X marks the spot,' he says, lifting my arm so Fi can see it.

I watch as a second of doubt seems to cross her face, and now I'm panicking that she's also underestimated Ethan's rage. I can hear the blood dropping to the couch with a plopping sound as it lands.

'Should I continue, or do you want to put an end to the lies?'

I look from his eyes to the blade in his hand and then back again.

'It-it happened like I said.'

I gasp as he moves the blade towards my arm again.

'Okay, okay, I'll tell you,' I say quickly, and his hand freezes in midair.

The version of the story I told Fi is the one I repeated to myself in the hours that followed Simone plunging to her death. I actually thought that if I could convince myself that that's how it happened, then the guilt would be easier to bear. I can see now that if I don't come up with a means of escape, they will kill me. I need to buy myself time, and I'd sooner depart without my soul still haunted.

'We fought in our room like I said. She tried blocking the door and I dragged her away. We crashed into the window and the glass broke, but as I tried to make my escape, she came at me again, this time clutching a shard of glass that had somehow fallen into the room.'

I can picture the memory so clearly now, and my legs prick with goose bumps.

'She raced towards me and I only just managed to get out of the way before she would have stabbed me. She was hysterical, shouting that she would sooner kill me than let me go.' I swallow hard as the guilt scratches at my throat. 'She said she was in love with me and couldn't continue if I rejected her. I panicked and told her I loved her too, and begged her to give me the glass. But she grabbed my hand and said we could both be happy if we were free of this world and she pressed the tip of the shard against my neck. I didn't want to die and grabbed her wrist with my free hand, and tried to make her drop the glass. We struggled again and before I knew what was happening she was charging us towards the broken window. At the last second, I managed to plant my feet and slow my trajectory, but she went headfirst through the window, still holding my hand. I tried pulling her back in, and I could see in that moment how scared she really was. She begged me to pull her back in, but our hands were warm and sweaty, and no matter how hard I tried, she kept slipping and then suddenly she was falling. I can still see it in slow motion in my mind, and I can still hear the noise of her body breaking as she hit the ground.'

A single tear escapes my eye and rolls the length of my cheek, but I make no effort to brush it away. My chest sags as the strain of carrying that secret for so long becomes heavier.

'I knew it!' Ethan roars. 'I knew all this time you were the one who killed her.'

'I tried to pull her back in,' I say, defeated. 'I swear to you, but no matter how hard I tried, it was like something else was pulling against me.'

He releases my wrist, and I instantly pull my arm in towards me, the blood blotting against my top. The cuts are deeper than I realised at first, and I think they're going to need stitches.

'I knew James was wrong about her,' Ethan says to Fi. 'I told you, didn't I? I said she didn't deserve our respect. If only he'd listened. I bet he's turning in his grave right now.'

I stay quiet, but I'd forgotten this all started with Danielle and me finding James in his flat.

I hear Atwal's voice in my head: *After I left, James must have had a violent coming together with someone who then presumably strung him up to make it look like suicide.*

'Y-you killed James,' I say, unable to stop the words spilling out.

Ethan stares me down.

'That was an accident, and it was his own fault for moving down here on that crusade. If he'd left well alone like I warned him, he'd still be alive today.'

He's still clutching the knife, and I know he could use it on me at any moment, but I *need* to know what really happened to James.

'What are you talking about? What crusade?'

Ethan glances at Fi and then back to me, weighing something in his mind. He finally shrugs, and his mouth stretches into a satisfied grin.

'Well, let's just say this isn't the first time you and I have met, Eve. I tracked you down five years ago, and couldn't believe it when I learned how well you'd landed on your feet. Our sister was worm food and you were living the life of riley. I was so angry and I told James we couldn't allow it to continue. And although he initially agreed it wasn't fair, he said he wanted no part of a plan to get revenge. He refused to discuss it and threatened to go to the police if I acted. I agreed I wouldn't do anything, but it gnawed away at me. I came down here for a week and observed you coming and going, laughing, without a care in the world. It grated more and more, until…'

He pauses, grinding his teeth, and before he speaks I already sense what's about to come.

'My last day here, I was following you home, and I just wanted to grab you and demand answers, but I wasn't armed. I heard you speaking to someone on the phone, telling them how you had just booked a weekend away at a spa in the Cotswolds, and I couldn't contain my rage. Suddenly I was right behind you, and I needed answers, so I grabbed you and pushed you through some bushes into a wooded area. You fell and bashed your head. I could see a dark patch where blood was seeping, and you sounded out of it. I knew you wouldn't be able to give me the answers I wanted, but that didn't mean I couldn't avenge Simone.'

I hear the panting of the man in the balaclava like it happened yesterday. The smell of his tobacco breath assailing my nostrils from behind me.

'I didn't know James was also keeping an eye on you and when I returned home, he knew what had happened. He said he was going to report me to the police, and refused to see how it avenged Simone. At the time I couldn't understand what he meant, but as the years have gone by, I can see how right he was. It wasn't enough. But by then he'd moved in, stating if I came anywhere near you again he wouldn't hesitate to report me to the police. He made up some story about work difficulties and a reckless affair and to everyone's amazement you fell for it. Probably helped that he cried when you first met, didn't he? I couldn't stand that he was protecting you after what you did to Simone. He chose you over family.'

It's like I'm back in that clearing all over again. I must have lain on the leafy ground for hours after the attack, trying to determine whether it had actually happened or whether it had just been a nightmare after I bumped my head. *He* is the reason I've cocooned myself away for this long, and as angry as I feel, I'm too petrified to take action.

'Come on, we should get out of here,' Fi says now, breaking the silence. 'We've got what we came for, so let's finish this before someone interrupts us. The police were back here this morning, and there's no telling whether that irritating detective will be back.'

I see Ethan nodding in my periphery.

'You're right. You head below and make sure everything is in place and I'll finish up here.'

She stands and moves towards the airing cupboard.

'Oh, and sis, don't forget to secure the trapdoor once you're through. We don't want her using the passageway to get out.'

**43**
---

FRIDAY, 11.46 A.M.

I have to watch as Fi disappears through the hatch in my airing cupboard and the lid shuts. I can see Ethan is also watching her go, and instinct finally kicks in, and I leap out of the chair, ducking as he swings his arm around to stop me getting away, but I barely make it a couple of metres before I feel his arm on my shoulder, dragging me back into the room, and I collapse back onto the sofa. My ankle is screaming at me, and I feel hopelessness bubble behind my eyes.

'Y-you said you wouldn't kill me if I told you about Simone.'

He seems to consider the statement for a moment before shrugging.

'I lied. I can't have you blabbing to that detective, and besides, it's not like you've much of a life to leave behind, is it? Trapped in this old building, jumping at every shadow. What makes it sadder is the fact that you seem to think the people who live here are actually grateful for your efforts to improve their lives. Tiptoeing behind the walls, listening in on their private conversations. Do you realise how twisted that actually is? You think you're helping, but your actions are so manipulative. I'm curious, Eve, have you always been this Machiavellian?'

'I'm not the one holding the knife,' I spit back.

He snickers at this.

'But at least I admit what I'm doing and there's a purpose to it. We've been watching you for months, Eve. We even tested you at times. Fi would deliberately say things to the walls, just to observe how you would react. The funniest time was when she pretended to break up with a boyfriend on the phone. Suddenly you were at her door with a bottle of wine and a tub of ice cream, cosying up like it was the two of you versus the world. She told me you couldn't do enough for her that week. And you were oblivious to the fact that she fitted cameras in the areas behind the walls so we could watch you.'

I've not seen any cameras down there, but I haven't been looking, and it's so dark without a torch that I probably wouldn't notice unless I knew where to look for them.

'You have what you wanted, let me go, and I promise I won't say anything to anyone. You and Fi can disappear and everything else can return to normal.'

He shakes his head.

'Even if I believed you, it isn't enough. Why should you be allowed to live when you didn't give Simone that same opportunity?'

'I didn't kill Simone!' I screech. 'I tried to save her, but she slipped from my grasp. There was nothing more I could have done.'

'You still don't get it, do you? It was the way you collaborated with the other bullies that was the last straw for her. You betrayed her in the worst way. She deserved so much better, and if it wasn't for your betrayal, she would still be here today.'

I told myself as much in the days immediately after her

death, and I came so close to telling the police everything that had happened, but I didn't want everyone to judge me.

'Unlike James, Fi knew what had to happen, and that's why she moved in here. She told James it was so they could be closer, but she was my Trojan horse. She even managed to convince James to keep her real identity a secret from you and the other tenants. At the time we weren't sure how to get at you, but the day she moved in, she ripped up the carpet in her bedroom and found the secret door. It was like Simone was guiding us. The first time she went through, she heard you moving about apparently. She lay in the crawl space watching you and you had no idea she was there. She watched you climb the ladder back up to your flat, and that's when she knew what we needed to do.'

I can't believe I was so wrong about Fi. I thought we were friends, and what he's describing feels so out of character for her. And it sickens me that she would still support the brother who assaulted me in those woods.

And then it hits me.

'Fi doesn't know you raped me, does she?'

He sits down in the armchair and smirks.

'She knows I was following you for a long time and that I roughed you up a bit.'

'Is that how you justify it to yourself? What you did. You sick son of a bitch.'

The smirk instantly vanishes.

'I didn't... I mean, it wasn't like that. I just meant to scare you, but you were so powerless... and... I wanted you to feel as helpless as Simone was when you pushed her out of that window.'

'I didn't...' I begin to say, but he whips out a hand and slaps me hard across the face.

'You brought all of this on yourself. The time for blaming

others is over. Admit what you did, so at least you'll die with a clear conscience.'

My cheek is throbbing, but I continue to watch him, my mind racing with thoughts on how I can get out of here.

'Have you figured it out yet?' he asks, sitting back and grinning menacingly at me.

'What?' I ask, not understanding the question.

'How your story is going to end.'

I look at the knife in his hand and that's the moment a fleeting spark of inspiration brightens the gloom.

*A few squirts of this in a person's eyes, and they'll be temporarily blinded – incapacitated – whilst you make your retreat.*

I remember the feeling of power as I held the taser, but I can't feel it in my pocket any more. It must have fallen out somewhere between the crawl space and here. It could literally be anywhere.

'How's your head right now, Eve? Feeling a bit woozy maybe? Have you been suffering with any waves of unexplained nausea?'

He's grinning at some private joke, but all I can think about is throwing up in India's bathroom.

'After she first dosed your mouthwash with ketamine, Fi was certain you'd figure out what we were up to. But you passing out every night after your bedtime routine gave us the freedom to come and go whenever we wanted. And then it was simply pulling a thread here or a tuft there and watch as you unravelled. How quickly Jenny turned on you when Fi casually mentioned she'd seen you flirting with Chad. And where you were so quiet when you stalked the passageway, Fi made sure India knew someone was there.

'We even managed to make your brother – your own flesh and blood – think you were losing your mind. Fi would come up here at night and call him from your phone, leaving quiet messages. And then when he'd ask you about them you had no idea what he was talking about. He even made you start seeing a psychiatrist!'

He roars with laughter at this.

'At least I haven't killed my brother,' I say, watching for his reaction.

The laughter halts instantly and he leans forwards, his glare ice cold.

'What happened to James wasn't my fault.'

'He didn't kill himself though, did he? The woman who was with him that night said he was alive and well when she left at 1 a.m., but the police know he was attacked by someone afterwards.'

He stands, starting to pace backwards and forwards across the carpet, and it feels as though the balance of power has shifted fractionally.

'The police have launched a murder investigation,' I lie. 'Detective Atwal told me this morning. They found bruising on his chest, and they've managed to extract a thumbprint from the rope he was hanging from. It won't be long until they connect it back to you.'

His pacing increases.

'Fi let slip what we'd been doing when they met for dinner that night, and he said he was going to tell you everything. She phoned me in a panic and I drove down, and when I arrived the woman had just left. I went in to speak to him, to reason with him. I couldn't understand how he would still choose you over Simone, and he said he was going to come up here and tell you everything.' Ethan's pacing slows. 'I couldn't let him go. But as I tried to restrain him, he fought back, and fell, cracking his skull against the counter in his kitchen. I couldn't find a pulse and panicked. Fi said our only option was to make it look as though he'd died by suicide, and so that's what we did. But then the story broke on the news, and we knew we had to accelerate our plan with you.'

Poor James. I had no idea he was here keeping me safe all this time. But I also feel sorry for Ethan and Fi. Their hatred of me must be so mutated that losing another sibling only drove them on.

'The police know someone's been stalking my flat,' I say, clinging to the prospect I can convince him his plan will fail. 'If you kill me, they won't stop searching for you. Your only chance is to go now before they arrive.'

He stops and grins down at me.

'Who said anything about me killing you? Do you really not understand what's happening here, Eve? The majority of your tenants will tell the police how paranoid you've become. Your brother and psychiatrist will corroborate. Hell, even the woman who delivers your groceries will testify you weren't of sound mind. Nobody will be surprised to learn you were so disturbed that you took the only way out you thought was left. There's something poetic about people believing you died by suicide in the same way you made everyone think Simone passed.'

'But that isn't something I would do. My brother won't buy that story.'

He scoffs.

'It doesn't matter. As soon as Detective Atwal reads the email you've sent her – confessing to killing James and Fi and that you can no longer live with the guilt – it won't really matter.'

He crosses to the curtains, and uses a cigarette lighter to set them on fire.

Now is my chance, and I stumble forwards, trying to get to the front door before he realises. My hope rises as I make it to the door and hear him tripping over behind me. But no sooner is the door open than I see his gloved hand slamming it shut, and then he grabs my hair and drags me backwards into the living room.

The fire has already spread to the sofa, and it won't be long until the whole place is ablaze. I throw out my elbow and connect with his face, but he pulls me down as he falls, and I land with my back on top of him. I use both elbows to alternatively pummel his sides in a desperate attempt to get him to release my hair, and then I catch a glimpse of orange as the knife suddenly rises above me, and it's all I can do to stretch both hands up and keep it away from me. I can feel him wriggling about beneath me, and he's starting to slide out, but all my focus is on the knife. My head hits the carpet as he frees himself, twisting his hand from mine and kicking me hard in the face. My head snaps to the side as my eyes close with the pain, but he isn't done yet, and this time kicks me in the back as I roll into a foetal position.

'How do you like that?' he calls out as smoke hovers above our heads.

But I'm not listening. My eyes are drawn to the object just beneath the edge of the sofa. It must have fallen out when Ethan threw me backwards earlier. The flames are licking the carpet, and I can't quite reach it, but as I hear Ethan stomping away I shove my hand into the flame and pull out the taser. My skin is blistering, but I ignore it as I push myself up and throw myself through the air, planting the tongs into the back of Ethan's calf, and squeeze the trigger. He screams out, but I've misjudged the situation, and suddenly he's falling back on me, and before I can roll out of the way, my face smashes into the floor.

## 44

FRIDAY, 12.03 P.M.

I don't know how long I'm out for, but when I come to, the place is so filled with smoke that I can't make out my own hand in front of my face. Fire crackles all around me, and for a fleeting moment I wonder whether I've woken just long enough to realise I'm dying. I don't know how much smoke I've inhaled, but it's all I can taste and when I start coughing, I'm unable to stop. There's no sign of Ethan, but he could be right next to me for all I know and I wouldn't see him.

My head and neck scream out in disagreement as I try to look around me. I know the front door must be to my left, as that's what I was facing when Ethan landed on me. But as I strain to focus on any glimmers through the thick grey fog, all I see is flashes of orange where the doorway is engulfed. Ethan set the curtains alight to start this bonfire, so there's no escape through the window either. If I stay here much longer I'll pass out again through lack of oxygen and then there will be no chance. Pushing my elbows into the carpet, I force my body to swivel to the right, which takes all my effort as I continue to cough and retch. I manage to pull out the neck of my pyjama top, and press it over my mouth and nose, but the filter does little to help my progress.

Ethan told Fi to barricade the trapdoor, so that's not an escape option either. But maybe if I can get to the window in my bedroom, I can wave and signal to someone to tell the fire brigade I'm up here. I crawl into the hallway, and see the door to my bedroom is closed. I drag myself towards it, my lungs straining, and I manage to open it, slide in and close it behind me. Whilst smoke has been seeping beneath the door, the fog here is less, and I drag my duvet from the bed and block the gap to prevent further seepage. A fresh coughing fit leaves me paralysed on the floor until I retch up tar-like phlegm over the floor. George's tail brushes against my cheek and it's only then I realise he's as trapped in here as I am. He's mewing with distress, but I don't have the strength to lie and tell him everything will be okay.

I claw my way towards the window, and use the cold radiator to drag myself up the window ledge. There's no sign of anyone outside, which either means they're not aware of the fire blazing over their heads, or they're all out at work, which given the time is just as likely.

I manage to get the window open, and push my face through, but the breeze is warm and the fresh air only serves to make me cough more. There's definitely nobody downstairs, and as I strain to hear any sound I can't hear sirens approaching. There is nothing but a nest of birds cheeping in a tree at the edge of the car park. And that's when it hits me: I can't hear any smoke alarms sounding either. I regularly check the batteries in the three I have in this flat, and when I look up to the doorway by the ceiling, I see the difference in paint shade where the alarm once hung.

Ethan said he emailed a suicide note and confession to Atwal from my laptop, so if I don't get out of here, she's going to assume it was from me and that I started the fire because I couldn't live with my actions.

I try to scream for help, but I barely get past the 'H' before I'm coughing and spluttering again. George hops up onto the windowsill beside me, his tail curled beneath his body, as terrified as I am. My only choice is to try and climb out of the window. I force my eyes down and the ground must be at least ten metres from me. There is nothing to break my fall, and just a bed of concrete to soften the blow. Could I survive a fall from here? And what about George?

The smoke inside the room is getting thicker, despite the duvet, and if there are no fire engines on the way, I'm a sitting duck up here.

I have no other choice.

Sliding George to the far side of the windowsill, I lift myself onto the wooden ledge, positioning one leg out of the window and one down by the radiator in an effort to keep my balance. I beckon George to come towards me, but where he wouldn't usually hesitate to come in for a stroke and cuddle, he must be able to sense what I'm thinking.

'It'll be okay,' I splutter, but his feet remain planted.

I stretch out and manage to put my left hand beneath his body, but as I'm lifting him my weight shifts and it's all I can do to plant my blistered right hand against the glass to stop myself falling out.

An image of Simone dangling helplessly above the ground flashes through my mind, and the irony that I'm now facing a similar fate isn't lost on me. We were a floor higher, but she stood no chance of surviving, and as I stare down at the grey bed of stone beneath me, instinct tells me it's a fall I may never rise from. George is mewing at me, as I hold him firmly in my lap.

Even if I did somehow manage to survive with injuries, I can't guarantee George's safety as well as my own.

He breaks free of my grasp and saunters back along the window ledge to safety, licking one of his paws dismissively.

This isn't going to work, and I rack my brain for an alternative. With the front door off limits – as well as the prospect that Ethan could still be out there waiting to get me – the only other means of escape is through the hatch. Fi was supposed to barricade it, but maybe that was just their way of making me think plunging to my death from the window was my only means of escape. In Ethan's eyes it would probably be poetic that I die the same way as Simone. Before I risk certain death, I have to try the hatch.

I hop down from the ledge, but leave the window wide open so I can get back to it in a hurry. And if I'm lucky one of the neighbours across the road might see the smoke and call for help.

I drop to my hands and knees, and George leaps down beside me as if in sync.

'We're going to try and go down the hatch,' I tell him, as much for my own sanity as his. 'You need to stay with me. Okay?'

He doesn't answer, but I make a small hammock out of the bottom of my pyjama top, and place him inside. This time he doesn't argue and I crawl back towards the bedroom door. Grabbing a discarded shirt out of the laundry basket, I tie it around the bottom half of my face, and then open the door, keeping as low as possible. The smoke is somehow even thicker than it was before, but it's only a short distance to the airing cupboard across the hallway. I pull it open, keeping my breaths slow and shallow. I reach out and try to turn the handle of the trapdoor, but it's stuck fast. I pull with all my might, but it doesn't budge. She must have somehow blocked the latch from turning underneath. It isn't going to open, but it's only made of wood. If I could break a hole in it somehow, then it could still be a means of escape. I can't see anything I can use, until my gaze falls on the torch hanging from the hook in the wall. I grab it impulsively, and bash it against the wood. The sound of glass smashing on impact tells me I won't be able to use it if I do somehow manage to get through.

I hammer the torch down again, over and over, willing the wood to splinter and crack, but barely able to see it as the smoke plumes around me. I can't stay here much longer. If there's no progress, I'm going to have to get George and me back to the window.

But then there's a snap. I scramble my fingertips along the hatch, and sure enough there is an indent now. It's all the encouragement I need and I hammer the torch down in the same spot, until eventually the torch breaks through into nothingness. Only, now my hand is stuck as shards of wood dig into my wrist. I have no choice but to release the torch and then manage to pull my hand back through. I swivel round onto my bottom, and this time use my slippered feet to kick at the hole until it they both slip through. I'm coughing so much, I'm breathless and lightheaded, but there's still a chance. Checking George is still secure in my top, I feel around for the ladder with my feet, but there's just empty space. Fi must have moved it, but I'm beyond caring. I just need to hope when I land, I hit the platform below, and don't end up crashing through a ceiling.

Lowering my body through the hole, I hang from the splintered wood, trying to remember where the platform below me in the darkness begins and ends. And then I just let go and pray for salvation. My left ankle explodes in pain as it connects with the platform, and I can't help shrieking in agony. I can feel tears streaming, but I'm out of the flat and alive, and that's all that matters.

If I can make it to the crawl space beneath Fi's flat, then maybe I can get out of her door and downstairs. But then I freeze. I haven't stepped outside in five years, and I don't think I have the strength to do it today. I force the fear from my mind. If I can get down to the ground floor, I can wait there until the fire brigade arrives and it may be that I don't need to go outside. Deep down I know that I'm lying to myself, but it's enough to get my hands and knees functioning again. I never realised just how dark it is down here without a torch. I'm blind and having to carefully place each hand, knowing the end of the platform is approaching and not wanting to underestimate how close it is. My fingertips eventually brush the edge of the platform, but as I scrabble around in search of the end of the ladder, I realise something is very wrong.

Although I can't see anything down here, I can smell the smoke. It can't be coming down the hatch from my flat, because then the smell would be behind me, rather than just off to the right. I lean closer, and I've no doubt now that the smoke is coming from the crawl space beneath Fi's flat. When Ethan sent her down here, she must have set a fire in there as well, maybe anticipating I might manage to get through the hatch despite her efforts to block my exit.

With access to her flat and mine now cut off, I'm trapped down here with no way out. And worse still, nobody knows I'm down here.

I start as I hear something loud crash behind me. Turning, I can't see anything, but it definitely sounded and felt like something heavy landed on the platform, and I can only think of one person that could be. I don't wait to find out if Ethan is pursuing me, wheeling myself to the left, away from Fi's flat. I just need to stay hidden long enough for Ethan to give up his search. If he's down here with me, he must have some way of escaping. If I can stay quiet, then maybe I can follow him.

But the smoke is getting heavier around me, and I can't help coughing and spluttering. I feel along the floor beside the platform, searching for anything that might be used for self-defence, but I can only feel the fibres of the insulation.

I can hear movement on the platform ahead of me, but I'm coughing so much that I can't breathe. Someone is calling my name, but the walls around my vision are closing in, and then I feel my soul slip away.

## 45

MONDAY, 5.45 P.M.

When I open my eyes and see a brilliant white light overhead, my first thought is I must be in some kind of purgatory, awaiting a decision on whether I'm destined to spend eternity in hell. I feel as though I'm suspended on a cloud, and I cannot feel any of my body. Death isn't nearly as frightening as I was led to believe.

But then my head rolls to the left and I see Pete dozing in a chair beside me, and I become aware of a high-pitched bleeping sound somewhere behind me. There is something pressing against my chin, but when I raise my hand to try and relieve the pressure, something pulls against my wrist, and I see a thin plastic tube connected to the cannula in my arm.

'Don't move, I'll get a nurse,' Pete says, suddenly awake and leaping into action.

I watch him move to a door at the far side of the room, but my vision blurs and I lose focus, my head dropping back into the soft pillow. A woman in a lavender tabard is beside me a moment later, but is speaking so quickly that I don't understand a word she is saying. I use my left hand to try and move the mask over my mouth and nose, but she gently extracts my hand from it, wagging a finger of warning. She vanishes a moment later and I see Pete is back in the chair beside me. He is holding my left hand in his, gently rubbing his thumb over my skin.

'I can't believe I nearly lost you,' he says, his voice almost breaking. 'It was touch and go there for a bit, but the doctors have worked miracles. They managed to manually remove much of the mucus and debris from your airway, and they've been pumping you with antibiotics to ward off any infection, and if you're feeling a little lightheaded that'll be the morphine for your foot.'

I manage to lift my head long enough to see my left ankle heavily plastered and suspended in the air.

'You had a compound fracture from all accounts. They'd already fixed and plastered it before I arrived thankfully – you know how squeamish I can be around blood. They've pinned the bone back together for now but will examine it better when your body is more up to it.'

I can't remember how I got here, but as I prod at my memories I remember freefalling out of my flat and landing on the platform. My eyes widen, as a stream of thoughts come flooding back.

The smoke.

The fire.

Ethan calling after me.

'You were lucky Bill found you when he did,' Pete continues. 'He dragged you clear of the building, minutes before the roof structure came crashing down on the first floor. The fire brigade managed to stop the fire spreading to the ground floor, but we're going to need a surveyor to confirm the structural integrity of the building before we decide what to do. Unfortunately, the insurance company is unlikely to fund a rebuild because you started the fire.'

I pull the mask down.

'No... Ethan.'

Pete takes the mask from my hand and puts it back over my face.

'You need to keep that in place. Your lungs were in a bad way, and they need to be flushed out with high-flow oxygen if you don't want to develop emphysema.'

'I... didn't... start... the... fire.'

He frowns empathetically.

'Detective Atwal showed me the email you sent her. Oh, Eve, I wish I'd known things were that bad. I knew you were struggling, which is why I wanted you to open up to Dr Winslow, but if I'd known you were thinking about... then I would have moved in with you for support.'

He's not listening to me. I don't know if it's the morphine preventing me structuring my sentences, or the feeling of Ethan's plan coming to fruition.

'I... need... to... speak... to... Atwal,' I say as clearly as I can make it.

'She wants to speak to you too, but I said she'll have to wait until you're fit enough to do so.'

I shake my head as vehemently as the mask will allow.

'Now. Important.'

He opens his mouth to speak, but I grab his hand and squeeze it with all my might.

'Now!'

\* \* \*

Waiting for Atwal's arrival is torture. I want to tell her everything that has happened, but I'm not sure she'll believe me; Ethan and Fi have done a great job of making me look unhinged and desperate, and with the emailed confession, I don't know how I'm going to convince her without any evidence to support my version of events.

My home – my sanctuary – has been destroyed. Even if a surveyor states the building can be resurrected, I don't think I ever want to step back inside, but I don't know what that means for the future. I spent five years locked away from the evils of the outside world, unaware what was lurking for me inside. It feels like there is nowhere I can now live and feel safe. Maybe Bill should have just let me die in that prison.

When Atwal arrives, she is joined by two uniformed police officers: a man in his forties with a portly belly, and a younger woman who looks like she's not long left college. Atwal informs me that our conversation will be recorded but not under caution.

It's hard to speak with the mask over my mouth, but I am no longer on morphine, so at least my thoughts are more coherent.

Atwal sits where Pete was earlier – he's stepped out to buy a coffee – and tells me to take my time in explaining what happened. And that's exactly what I do. I tell her about finding Fi in my flat on Friday morning, the picture I found of Fi and Simone in her purse, and how Fi was related to both James and Ethan. I recount Ethan's version of what happened to James that night, though I can't be sure how truthful his account was. I tell her he sent the email from my laptop and set my flat alight with the intention of making my death look self-inflicted.

Atwal tells me they are still recovering items from the wreckage but that my laptop is destroyed and no DNA evidence was recovered from it. It's impossible to tell whether she believes me or not.

'You need to find Fiona Erskine, or whatever her real name is. If you look up Simone Cordova and her siblings, you'll find them all.'

'We arrested Fiona Erskine as she was trying to board a ferry from Portsmouth to Caen this morning. The APB hadn't been rescinded, so she was held at the border until I could speak to her. Although we weren't treating her as a suspect at the time, she was unable to account for her whereabouts this past week, and then refused to answer any further questions. She's at the police station now waiting for me to return.'

I picture Fi inside a prison cell. Given her own background in law, I imagine she won't struggle to find a solicitor to defend her and deny my eyewitness testimony.

'One thing that isn't clear at the moment is how and when you discovered the secret passageway behind the walls of the building.'

This is the part I've left out of my story because I'm worried about how it will look. If I want to wipe the slate clean, then I'm going to have to be honest. It may even help support my side of the story. I sense Atwal's question is rhetorical, but she's asked it to better assess my honesty. I open my mouth to address the elephant in the room.

'I imagine you must have seen Fiona or Ethan using the trapdoor hidden beneath your flat,' Atwal says before I can speak.

I meet her stare, uncertain why she's trying to help me.

'Is that what happened, Eve? Did you see Fiona leave through the trapdoor and you used it in an effort to find an escape route?'

'Um, yes,' I say, before reaffirming with more confidence. 'Yes, that's right.'

'We spoke to your neighbour, Bill, and he told us all about the tunnels between the flats, which date back to when the building was the Freemantle Hotel. He said he thought nobody else knew about them, and was amazed when he heard you calling for him.'

Of that I have no doubt, but I can't help wondering what other secrets Bill has been keeping for all of these years.

*We interviewed your dad because he was a friend of the singer from the cruise ships.*

'He used the passageway from his flat and dragged you out. It's lucky for you that he was there.'

She pauses, her lips tight, and I sense she's holding something back.

'Eve, you should know Bill passed shortly after his arrival at the hospital. Whilst your body is young enough to be recuperating from the smoke you inhaled, I'm afraid Bill slipped into a coma, and didn't recover.'

My mouth drops open, not wanting to believe her statement, but knowing she has no reason to lie to me. My vision blurs as tears fill my eyes.

'We believe Fiona Erskine was the woman you saw entering James DeVere's flat late on Monday night,' Atwal says, narrowing her eyes. 'Would you concur with that?'

That's why she's helping me with my knowledge of the passageway, so I don't drop her in it regarding her encounter with James. It's a fair trade-off in my eyes.

'Yes, it very well could have been. I didn't get a good look at her, but given they were brother and sister, it's highly likely that's who I saw.'

Atwal smiles at me with more than a hint of gratitude.

'Ethan said he fought with James over their plans to harm me, and that James cracked his head; that's why he tried to make it look like a suicide. Have you arrested him as well?'

Atwal looks down at her hands.

'What is it? Have you arrested Ethan? He was the one behind all of this. He admitted everything to me; he was the bastard who raped me five years ago.'

'We are still looking for him.'

'What do you mean looking for?'

'He was seen entering the flats by one of your neighbours, but nobody saw him leave, and we are still searching the wreckage, but haven't recovered a body yet.'

I try to think back to when I woke in the flat. I couldn't see Ethan, but the front door was on fire and Fi had barricaded the hatch. There's no way he could have escaped the flat before I came to, and I was sure I heard him in the passageway, but I was in agony and it could just as easily be Bill that I heard moving about. But if Ethan was still in my flat when the roof collapsed, surely they would have recovered his body by now.

'We have put out an APB for him, so if he tries to leave the country, we will find him, assuming we don't recover his corpse in the wreckage.'

Pete opens the door to the room and asks if he can enter. Atwal stands and says she's finished with her questions for today, but will take a formal statement from me in the coming days. She wishes me well and leaves with the two officers in tow.

'The doctors want to keep you in for a few more days,' Pete says, sipping from his coffee, 'until they're satisfied your lung won't collapse again. And then when you're released, you can come and stay with me until you figure out what you want to do next.'

I mouth the word 'Bill', but no sound escapes.

'I know,' Pete says, looking at me with a concerned face. 'If it wasn't for him...'

I close my eyes and the floodgates open. I picture his smiling face, how he always managed to brighten my day with a kind word or gesture. He told me he promised Dad he would keep me safe, and he lived up to that promise.

'It's my fault,' I whisper.

'No, don't be silly. Bill made the ultimate sacrifice, but the blame doesn't lie with you.'

My eyes snap open, and I give a hard stare.

'*I'm* the reason Ethan, James and Fi came to our home, because of what happened to Simone. They wanted to get even with me, so it's my fault that Bill is dead, and the rest of my tenants are now homeless.'

'What are you talking about, Eve? I don't understand.'

I briefly recount my conversations with Ethan and Fi, and the blood drains from his face.

'Bill always knew there was something not right about me. He never said as much, but I think he knew I was hiding from my past. Just like Dad.'

'What do you mean just like Dad?'

I stare at him for a long time, unsure whether I should tell him of my suspicions.

*Fuck it! He already thinks I'm crazy.*

'Bill told me Dad was one of the suspects they interviewed before they found John Cooper.'

'And?'

'And Dad knew one of the victims who stayed at the hotel.'

'Did he? Which one?'

'Patricia Robinson. She was a singer on the cruise ships who was staying at the hotel when she died. Bill told me Cooper claimed she was killed by a mystery man in a sports car. It made me think of that green Jaguar E-type Dad used to drive.'

Pete frowns at me.

'Wait, you're not seriously suggesting...'

'Bill said he wasn't convinced that John Cooper was the serial killer the police claimed. I think... I think deep down Bill knew that Dad was responsible for Patricia Robinson's death.'

He rolls his eyes.

'Oh, that's just ridiculous. Our dad wasn't capable of anything like that.'

'How can you be so sure? I was ready to kill Ethan in my flat when I found out what he was up to. And I think Bill knew the apple hadn't fallen too far from the tree.'

Pete suddenly stands.

'I'm going to go and find the nurse. You're delirious.'

'No,' I snap, slapping both hands against the blanket over my legs. 'I'm not delirious. In fact, I've never felt so lucid.'

He remains rooted to the spot.

'Bill worked for Dad for years, do you really think he would have done so if he secretly thought Dad was a murderer?'

I think back to the night Bill told me about Cooper: *I wasn't totally convinced that he was guilty of all five murders.*

'What if Bill suspected Dad was guilty and spent the rest of his life trying to prove it?'

'Did he tell you that?'

'Not in so many words.'

'I'm going to say it again, Eve, you've been through so much these last few days and I think you're just letting your imagination get the better of you.'

I'm about to tell him how I know Dad was more than capable, but Pete turns and leaves the room.

I picture myself back in the flat with Ethan and Fi demanding I confess to what happened to their sister. I hear my terrified words: *We struggled again and before I knew what was happening she was charging us towards the broken window. At the last second, I managed to plant my feet and slow my trajectory, but she went headfirst through the window, still holding my hand. I tried pulling her back in, and I could see in that moment how scared she really was.*

For years I've been replaying that scene over and over in my head, trying to convince myself that that's what actually happened, but it isn't. Simone was the one the other girls had invited out for the secret gathering. I could see her slipping away from me, and I begged her not to go. She was the only friend I had and I couldn't lose her. I tried to block her exit, but she was stronger than me, and easily pulled me out of the way. I grabbed the shard of glass and pressed it against my neck, telling her how much I loved her, and how I would sooner die than lose her.

I could see her panicking, and when she told me she loved me too, I desperately wanted to believe her, but then she made a move for the glass and I realised she was lying. We struggled, and I knew she would overpower me again, so I charged us towards that window. I kept thinking if I couldn't have her then nobody else should either. She didn't even realise how close we were to the window until her head crashed through it.

I had a firm grip of her hand as she just hung in the air, desperate to get back inside. I could see in that moment how scared she really was. She begged me to pull her back in, and I said I would if she promised not to go out. She said she'd do anything, but I could see she didn't mean it. I'd crossed a line and there was no way she'd forgive me, and so I listened to my heart.

And then I let her go.

I still see it in my dreams every night. Her body falling in slow motion, her arms flailing, and then the squelch as she hit the ground.

I realise now that Bill stayed on after Elsie's passing to keep watch over me. But now that he's gone, there's nobody to keep me safe.

I don't want to move in with Pete, but I certainly don't want to lock myself away for the rest of my life. Smog, disease and illness are rife in this country, and with Ethan still out there, I don't think I'll ever feel safe again; certainly not here. Theoretically, I can run my graphic design business from anywhere in the world, so there's nothing stopping me from finding a tropical paradise; somewhere clean and safe; start over again, away from my history.

One thing I know for certain is that I'm tired of being a victim; if Ethan did manage to escape from that blaze, he'd better keep running, because I won't stop until I find him. He spent years planning his revenge, but now it's my turn, and I won't fail as he did.

\* \* \*

## MORE FROM M. A. HUNTER

The next compelling psychological thriller from M. A. Hunter is available to order now here:
https://mybook.to/MAHunterNewBackAd

# ACKNOWLEDGEMENTS

Thank you so much for reading *The Tenants*, and for sticking around to read this final word from me.

Firstly, an apology to those who picked up the book assuming it was the unauthorised biography of the former Dr Who actor and his family. I hope you're not too disappointed and still enjoyed the story.

Being a writer can be an isolating experience and there have been occasions where I haven't left my home for several days, either because I'm so busy with writing and the day job, or the weather is naff (I am hypersensitive to extreme weather, so struggle to go out when it's raining or simply too hot). My wife actually refers to me as a hermit because I spend so much time indoors, but I always find I end up going a bit stir-crazy and eventually just have to get out even if only for a brief walk.

I'm sure we all remember living through lockdown and the last thing I want is to traumatise you by triggering those memories, but essentially we've all experienced a little of what it can be like to be scared of going outside. It was this reflection that helped formulate the plot for this story. I wanted to explore what extreme agoraphobia could be like, and how their home would become their whole ecosystem.

Eve wants to be sociable, and she sees these tenants as her adopted family, and I genuinely believe she only wants what's best for them; I hope you felt that too. But we writers don't like to give our protagonists an easy time, and so I wanted to create a situation that would test Eve to her limits. Hence placing her in a flat in the same building as her tenants and then having her suspect each of them of murder. The agoraphobia means she is trapped in there with them with no means of escape (I'm sure I'm not the only one who loves an Agatha Christie style locked-room mystery).

It's easy to say that she could have just left the building, but for many who suffer with agoraphobia, that is far easier said than done. Ask anyone who has an extreme phobia about something and they'll tell you how paralysing that fear can genuinely be for them. And take it from me, as someone who is neurodivergent and has struggled to 'fit' in a neurotypical world, you should never judge others until you've walked in their shoes.

I'll hop off my soapbox now to share some gratitude.

Thank you for reading *The Tenants*. Please do post a review to wherever you purchased the book from so that other readers can be enticed to give it a try. It takes less than two minutes to share your opinion, and I ask you do me this small kindness. Please also tell all of your friends and family (and any other person who will listen) how great it is. And please do get in touch with me via the usual social channels to let me know what you thought about it (remember to be kind).

If this was your first read of one of my books (where the hell have you been?) then thank you for taking a chance. If you enjoyed it and want to read more, I have plenty of other, equally-gripping books also available to buy online or from good bookshops.

I am fortunate enough to being taken care of by two powerhouse agents. While Emily Glenister is on maternity leave (and championing me from the sidelines), I'd like to say a huge thank you to Diana Beaumont for taking such great care of me this year. They both work at the DHH Literary Agency, which is one of the best agencies in the land, and I feel honoured to be one of their clients.

Thank you also to my eagle-eyed editor Victoria Britton at Boldwood Books. It is thanks to her that my many wacky ideas, get finely tuned into publishable stories, and she deserves huge credit for identifying where the pace slows, and where I've left big enough plot holes that she could drive a tank through. She also leaves little comments on the side where I've made gasp or laugh out loud and these are hugely encouraging when working through the various stages of editing.

The whole team at Boldwood Books deserve huge credit for the work they do in producing my books in the array of formats available. From line and copy editing, proof-reading, cover design, audiobook creation, and marketing. The fact that you're reading this acknowledgement is testament to the brilliant job they do. But special mention to Niamh Wallace who oversees the pre- and post-publication campaign activities. Thank you for all you do.

Thank you to my wife, Hannah and my children Emily and Ethan who make sure my feet remain firmly planted to the floor. It goes without saying that I wouldn't be the writer I am today without their loving support, even if I do bore the pants off them when I share the latest twist I've conjured and they have no idea who or what I'm talking about.

I remain active as time allows on the usual social media outlets (Facebook, Instagram, and TikTok), so please do stop by with any messages, observations, or questions. Hearing from readers of my books truly brightens my days and encourages me to keep writing, so don't be a stranger. I promise I *will* respond to every message and comment I receive.

Best wishes,
    Stef (a.k.a. M.A. Hunter)

## ABOUT THE AUTHOR

**M. A. Hunter** is the pen name of Stephen Edger, the bestselling author of psychological and crime thrillers, including the Kate Matthews series. Born in the north-east of England, he now lives in Southampton where many of his stories are set.

Sign up to M. A. Hunter's mailing list here for news, competitions and updates on future books.

Visit M. A. Hunter's website: www.stephenedger.com/m-a-hunter

Follow M. A. Hunter on social media:

- facebook.com/anautieauthor
- x.com/anautieauthor
- instagram.com/anautieauthor
- tiktok.com/@anautieauthor
- bookbub.com/authors/stephen-edger
- goodreads.com/stephenedger

# ALSO BY M. A. HUNTER

The Boat Party

One Wrong Turn

Every Step You Take

Sleepwalker

The Reunion

The Woman on Platform 8

The Tenants

# THE *Murder* LIST

**THE MURDER LIST IS A NEWSLETTER DEDICATED TO SPINE-CHILLING FICTION AND GRIPPING PAGE-TURNERS!**

**SIGN UP TO MAKE SURE YOU'RE ON OUR HIT LIST FOR EXCLUSIVE DEALS, AUTHOR CONTENT, AND COMPETITIONS.**

*SIGN UP TO OUR NEWSLETTER*

**BIT.LY/THEMURDERLISTNEWS**

# Boldwood

Boldwood Books is an award-winning fiction publishing company seeking out the best stories from around the world.

**Find out more at www.boldwoodbooks.com**

Join our reader community for brilliant books, competitions and offers!

**Follow us
@BoldwoodBooks
@TheBoldBookClub**

**Sign up to our weekly deals newsletter**

https://bit.ly/BoldwoodBNewsletter

www.ingramcontent.com/pod-product-compliance
Ingram Content Group UK Ltd.
Pitfield, Milton Keynes, MK11 3LW, UK
UKHW021312190825
7472UKWH00036B/662

9 781835 617427